VENOM&
ECSTASY

New York Times Bestselling author Shanora Williams writing as

S. WILLIAMS

Published February 2017
Editing by Librum Artis Editorial Services
Book design by Inkstain Interior Book Designing
Cover Art and Design by Hang Le

NOTE FROM THE AUTHOR

There are a few things you should know before diving into Venom & Ecstasy:

1) It is slightly darker/grittier than book one. There is murder, mild abuse, and violence. Read with caution!

2) Despite the darkness, the romance is a little heavier between the main characters. *Yep, you get to see a gentler side of El Jefe!*

3) If you need to, do a reread of book 1. There are a lot of things revealed in this one that weren't answered in the first book.

3) There is more Spanish in this novel.

I wanted this story to feel real and true to the culture/setting and I couldn't do that without adding in some of these terms. I enjoyed writing this book so much! It's much different, but I love the tug and pull between Draco and Gia. I've created a list of the Spanish terms/slang used most in this book and added the English meanings, just in case you may need clarification while reading.

I hope you enjoy Jefe and Gia!

Niñita—little girl

Reina—queen

Patrona—feminine form of the word boss

Puta (o)—bitch

Hijo—son

Hijo de puta—son of a bitch

Abrela—open it (command)

Gringa—American/white woman

Cajones—balls/testicles

Amor—love

Cariño—sweetie

VENOM & ECSTASY

CHAPTER ONE

RECOVERY

W'*hy am I still here? What am I doing? How the hell do I get out?*
I can't block out the sounds in my head—the noise that
deafens me, the feelings that scald me deep inside.

Panting. Grunting.

Hissing. Sighing.

Heavy sweat. Screams.

Tears blinding me.

I jolt awake, panting raggedly, my spine stacked straight. I stare across the
large bedroom. The door is still shut and locked. None of the lights are on. I'm still
here. In Draco's bedroom.

My heart thunders, and I swallow the dry, gravelly lump in my throat. I realize
I'm clutching the sheets, sticky sweat built up on the back of my neck.

I look toward the alarm clock. 6:02 p.m. He's still not here. It's been hours.
Where in the hell is he? He said he would be right back.

When my panting ceases, visions of the axe tattoo blind me, and I press the palms of my hands into my eye sockets, rubbing roughly in hopes that it will suppress the memories. My breathing becomes ragged, heavy, a chill shooting down my spine.

My body is filled with anxiety; my stomach has been flipped upside down. Even if I wanted to eat, I wouldn't be able to. I was ready for revenge before, but now . . . now I'm just out of it. I blame it on whatever pills Draco had Juanita bring me.

They've made me groggy. Distant.

I push out of the bed and walk to the window. The sun has set now, half a golden disk perched atop the horizon. The sky is filled with splashes of pink and lavender and a slight trace of orange.

The sapphire water shimmers, and I hear seagulls squawking. I lift my hand and unlock the window, pushing it open so I can take in a draft of the warmth. I inhale the salty air, and then exhale through parted lips.

The sound of the large waves running up to the shore relaxes me.

I keep the window open and walk back to bed, sitting on the edge. The breeze is cool enough to chill the heated parts of me. Looking up, I point my line of sight on the wall to my right.

It caught my attention when I first lay down.

It's a weapons wall, swathed in burgundy fabric and bordered in black.

There is the machete Draco used on Axe Man, and it makes me cringe inside, seeing it there. It still has blood on the sharp, silver blade, but not much.

There are his gold brass knuckles, a few pocketknives, a butcher knife, and a *gun*.

The gun is what catches my attention. I push off the bed again and walk to the wall, picking up the heavy silver gun. It has a wide barrel. It could probably leave a wound the size of a golf ball.

I pull the revolver open and check it. There are no bullets. *Damn it.*

I run my fingers over the black handle, but that's when I see the initials carved into it.

CEM.

I don't know what the letters stand for. It's probably another one of his prizes.

Footsteps start up moments later and I stick the gun back in its place, stepping back. The doorknob jiggles, and my eyes stretch wide, sharp fingernails digging into my palms.

It might be Bain . . . or Francesca. He's not here, but they could be.

"Unlock the door, Gianna," Draco orders from the other side. His voice sends a signal to my brain. My mind sparks, my heart drumming. *Relief.*

I rush to the door and unlock it, stepping away just as rapidly as he walks in.

"Where were you?" I snap at him.

"Busy."

"Doing what?" I fold my arms tightly.

"Handling things."

"For ten hours? You said you'd be right back."

"And I am back. I didn't tell you exactly *how* long I'd be."

I sigh, roughly raking my fingers through my hair and then turning. "I want to know what you meant earlier. You said we have stuff to talk about, so tell me. I need to know everything if I'm going to accept you, and this. I don't want to be left out of the loop anymore."

He looks me over, taking note of my shaky hands as they fall at my sides. "You need rest, Gianna. Relax."

"No," I respond rapidly, and my voice is sharp, strained. "No—I've had enough rest. I'm tired of stalling, Draco. I'm a grown woman. Don't treat me like some clueless child."

"You're angry. I get it." His voice is too calm and hearing it pisses me off. "If you sleep, I will tell you in the morning," he says, stepping forward. I know he's lying.

I snatch my gaze away, pointing it at the weapons wall. "I can't sleep. I—I keep waking up. Having these fucking nightmares. I can't get rid of them, even if I try to think of something good before falling asleep."

I don't look his way, but I feel him watching me. After several silent seconds tick by, he walks to the wide dresser against the wall, pulls out a white pill bottle from the top drawer and then comes back in my direction.

When he pops the cap, he takes one out and presses it into my hand. "Take this. It will help."

I raise one eyebrow. "What is it?"

"A prescription I take when I'm too restless to sleep . . . or when I don't want to dream." He walks to the closet in the corner and returns with a small bottle of water. Handing it to me, he says, "In your case, it will block the nightmares."

I study him, and then the pill and bottle of water. "How often do you take these?"

"Only when I kill someone." *So . . . pretty much every night,* I want to say. "It's strong stuff. Takes about ten minutes to kick in. As soon as you take it, lie down."

"You still want me to stay in here?" I probe.

"Yes." He walks around me, slipping out of his pinstripe shirt as he makes his way toward the walk-in closet. I hear shuffling when he disappears. While he's away, I down the pill and then chase it with the water.

I don't know what the pill is, but I'll take anything if it means I can get some temporary peace. I climb back into bed and rest my head on the soft, white pillow. I keep my eyes on the closet—on where he is.

I listen to him move around, and when he comes back out with a black pair of sweats on and no shirt, I sigh. I find it disturbing that I'm kind of glad he's not leaving again.

His chiseled body moves fluidly as he comes toward the bed. It dips on the opposite side, and he pushes the thick comforter down.

He releases a long, weary sigh.

We are quiet for a few seconds.

After letting the question nag at me, I finally roll over to look him. "Where are they?" I whisper.

His eyes immediately focus on mine. "Somewhere they can't get to you."

I swallow hard. "You . . . took them *there*?"

"The shed. Locked in my heaviest chains."

"For how long?" I whisper.

"Until you're ready."

"Me? Ready for what?"

"Payback." He says it so matter of factly that I flinch.

I frown. "What is that supposed to mean?"

Sighing, he pulls his eyes away from mine and focuses on the vaulted ceiling. "I think you'll figure it out. Until then, hush and go to sleep. You need rest."

He starts to turn his back to me, rolling sideways. "Wait—Draco," I call, so faintly it can barely be heard.

He freezes, but doesn't look over. "What?"

I hate that I'm even about to ask, but I might as well. This has to be done. There is no backing down now.

Make him mine.

I accept. I accept. I accept.

"Can you . . . hold me? Just for tonight. Just in case . . ."

When my voice trails off, he says, "No one will come in here to harm you, Gianna," he assures me. "Not ever again."

"I know but . . . please?" I beg, and he turns over, looking me right in the eyes. He stares for a while, his brown irises shimmering from the moonlight, but when he sees the tears building up at the rim of mine, he sighs, shakes his head, and then extends his arm.

He invites me in without words and I slide over, curling into his warm, sculpted body. He still smells like his spiced cologne. The scent fits him. Warm and outdoorsy. Like ocean spray and palm trees, and a spritz of citrus.

He exhales, and I can tell he isn't comfortable with this—having me so close. Feeling my heart beating near his, my arm wrapped so snug around his waist.

I'm like a child clinging to their parent. Needy. Desperate for attention and affection.

There is no one else I can get this from right now, so I'll take Draco.

"Whatever you want, I will provide it," he says.

"I know." I yawn, and then my eyes seal tight. My body feels like dead weight, my eyelids so heavy that I couldn't open them if I tried. "But you aren't used to this," I murmur. "Affection . . . from your prisoner."

I feel him shift, and I think he's looking down at me.

I can't be sure.

"You were never my prisoner, Gianna," he murmurs.

That's the last thing I hear him say before I fall asleep.

CHAPTER TWO

RECOVERY—DAY 2

I *hear the ocean.*

I feel the breeze.

Groggily, I roll over, arms still heavy, head aching in the center. I look toward the open window, the bright, burning sun blazing its golden rays. The sunlight has swept that entire side of the bedroom. It barely kisses the bed.

I twist over and sit up. The sheets are all over the place, the comforter hanging halfway off the mattress. I rub my eyes, clearing the sleep away.

I still feel drained.

My body feels like it's been pumped with lead.

I blame it on the pill he gave me, but I must admit I feel better. And I didn't dream or have any nightmares. It was the emptiest, darkest sleep I've ever had, but I feel rested enough.

I push out of bed and walk to the bathroom to make use of the toilet.

As I sit, I hear a door creak open and shut from the bedroom. "Draco?" I call, peering around the corner.

No response.

I finish up in a hurry and walk out of the bathroom. As soon as I do, I let out a breath of relief. No wonder no one answers. It's one of the maids. She has headphones on. She's humming as she makes the bed.

I step to the side, and when she sees me, she gasps, clutching the heart of her chest. "Oh—sorry! Sorry! I didn't mean to come in here. I thought you were at breakfast. I'm so sorry." She drops her head, backing away to the door. "Please—please don't fire me. Please don't tell Jefe." She says all of this in Spanish, so rapidly that I almost can't comprehend it.

I hold out a patient hand, shaking my head. "No, it's okay," I coo. "I won't tell him anything. You were doing your job. Don't worry." I give her a comforting smile.

As if she's surprised to hear this, she relaxes her shoulders and her eyes stretch wide. "I should go." Her voice is hurried as she grips the doorknob, rushing out.

I watch the door shut, mildly confused.

I walk over it and pull it open, peeking around the corner before walking down the hallway. I'm still dressed in one of Draco's T-shirts and a pair of his basketball shorts.

My hair, I'm certain, is a matted mess because I didn't brush or blow-dry it after that bath. I can taste the morning breath on my tongue. I need to refresh immediately.

I enter the room I was first sent to when I was brought here and shut the door behind me. I find a decent outfit and dress quickly, and then walk to the bathroom to brush my teeth. I've been patched up, somewhat. Draco sent Juanita up during the middle of the night, while I was a bit loopy and drugged up.

I remember the piercing stab of the needle as she re-stitched my wound, but nothing more. Everything else about last night is hazy. I guess he was tired of looking at the damage that had been done to me.

It was a clear reminder that he'd failed me.

I stare into the mirror longer than intended and realize my face looks much worse than it feels.

The entire right side of it is swollen and blue. A bruise has formed—just barely. I look hideous, and for a split second I want to cry.

My face.

My body.

My *life*.

I'm wondering if I should feel rage or another rush of emotion that I can't control, but I don't feel anything. I feel empty, and the emptiness terrifies me much more than the feelings. It scares me, because I know when I actually do feel something, I won't be able to control it. I won't be able to hold back on my actions. I will most likely regret it.

When I'm all set, I walk out of the bedroom, cautious of my surroundings. I hear vacuuming and sweeping. I hear chatting and voices echoing. I know it's the maids, but I am hyperaware of everything. Paranoid, really, of everyone that isn't Draco.

When I reach the bottom of the staircase, I look to the right, at the dining room. I see Draco standing near the French doors. His back is facing me, his hands behind his back, and someone is in front of him.

He's talking quietly to the person.

I walk forward slowly, trying to peer around him to see the person, but I can't. When I'm closer, I hear him talking.

"You don't feed them. You don't talk to them. If they say *anything* to you at all, you cut their fucking tongues out. Don't be lenient and don't trust a word they say. I'm trusting you, Diego." Draco's smooth, fluent accent trickles out of the dining room.

I step aside, continuing to eavesdrop.

"Francesca says she didn't know about the plan they had," Diego says. "She says Bain promised her that if she had sex with him a few times he'd help her escape and get her across the border."

Draco lets out a bitter chuckle. "Don't believe a word that lying bitch says. Tell her I will be dealing with her soon."

When he says that, I step around the corner and walk in. Diego, one of the guards, spots me and his eyes widen. He doesn't say a word. In fact, he looks away so fast that it almost seems unreal.

Draco studies my attire. "You look better today, niñita."

"You're lying," I mutter. "I looked in the mirror. I look hideous."

He extends his arm, his mouth twitching. "Go. Sit. I'll be right there."

I nod, walking to the chair next to his. Sitting, I pull my chair up to the table and pick up a slice of the bacon. I chew it, but I don't taste a thing.

Damn. Even my taste buds are numb.

By the time I've chewed the first slow bite and forced it down, Draco has dismissed Diego and is walking to his chair. He sits down, pulls his chair in, and then picks up his water.

"He's watching over them?" I ask.

"For now."

"Why are they still alive?" I ask, and I know he hears the agitation on my breath.

He picks up a napkin to wipe above his lips. "They won't be for long."

"Draco, you said you would get rid of them. You said you would make them pay."

"And I will."

"Putting them in those cells means they are still breathing."

He places his napkin down. "Are you ready to cut those breaths short then?"

"W-what?" I stammer.

"You heard me," he murmurs, picking up his fork and knife and cutting into his steak and eggs. "Are you ready to *end* them?"

I blink rapidly. "*You* are the one who's supposed to make them pay."

"And I will, but not before letting you take out your aggressions first."

"I have none," I state, looking away.

"That's bullshit, and you know it. You're still in denial. Still trying to block it out. But when it finally sinks in—when that rage ignites you—you'll know. I will know."

I watch him closely as he takes a bite of the steak. I don't say anything, though. Because I am upset—no, I'm *more* than upset.

I want them gone, yes, but I didn't think I'd have to use my own hands to do it. I thought he'd make me watch again, like he did with Kevin. I would have been okay with that.

"You can take your time," he tells me. "There is no rush." He reaches forward and tips my chin. "But when it happens, niñita, I will be there. I will make you feel like *you* again, only much stronger." He drops his fork and strokes the apple of my cheek. "My beautiful niñita. Look what they've done to you." His nostrils flare, and he points his gaze to my lips. "It is taking everything in me not to draw my gun, go down there, and shoot them until the shed is full of blood and bullets."

I drop my gaze.

He pulls away.

I look elsewhere. "Where's Mrs. Molina?" I inquire, ignoring the sudden spark growing between us.

"She didn't want to see you today."

I whip my head up with a frown. "What? Why not?"

"She heard what happened to you." He pauses, only for a brief second. "My mother has the tendency to allow her guilt to eat her alive. She didn't sleep all night, but I hope she's making up for it right now."

His face changes. It's softer. His eyes dart down, focused on the bowl of sliced fruit. "It's not just you she doesn't want to see. It's me, too. I disappointed her." He eats faster, trying to ignore his remorse.

"How?"

"I told her I wouldn't let anything happen to you after I didn't let you eat those three days. She made me promise, and just like that," he snaps his fingers, "the promise was broken. She's a little more than upset."

His unhappiness is clear, but not too much. He hates revealing any type of emotion. He pushes out of his chair and stands up, straightening his back.

"Eat and be sure to go back to my room. I'll have one of the maids send over some of the clothes and toiletries from the room you were staying in before. You won't be going back to it anymore."

He starts to walk around me, but I catch his hand. My mouth opens, but then clamps shut. I don't know what to say. What should I tell him to try and ease some of that guilt?

"Thank you, Draco," I finally say.

He stares down, confused. "I don't deserve your gratitude right now, Gianna."

"You're trying," I murmur.

"Trying isn't enough."

"What's done is done." I shrug one shoulder, but he yanks his hand away. "From here, we move forward."

"Fuck that. This is *not* over," he growls, and then he stalks out of the dining room. Patanza shows up as he's storming out, and he murmurs something to her before taking off.

10

She looks at me, but her expression is unreadable. She has a rifle in hand, the black strap across her body. She has on gloves and what looks like a bulletproof vest beneath her T-shirt. It's the most I've seen her wear around here.

She watches me for a brief moment, then jerks her gaze away and steps to the side, focusing ahead.

That's three times in a row today.

None of them have looked at me for longer than a few seconds.

Was this an order from Draco? Maybe he's onto all of them. Maybe he doesn't trust any of his men now. I didn't realize it before, but he has the house heavily guarded today.

There's a guard in the kitchen where the butlers are when I peer up. I see him standing there with his arms in front of him, guns in each holder.

I glance at Patanza. She doesn't look at me. Not even a peek.

Sighing, I push out of the chair and walk to the door. I can't stomach much more. I'm afraid I'll throw it all up by the time I make it upstairs.

Before I can walk out, Patanza stops me with a gentle hand to the shoulder. Her pleading eyes search my face, her lips trembling a little. "Just so you know, I never liked Pico or Bain, and would have *never* tolerated it if I'd heard what they were planning to do. I would have told Jefe first thing." Her eyes shift down, lips twisting. "Jefe doesn't trust anyone right now because of what happened. He had a talk with all of us yesterday. I don't want him to fire me, because if he fires *any* of us, that means he'll be killing us too. This place is all I have. If you could . . . well, if you could remind him of that for me, I would appreciate it. I would never betray Jefe. Not after all he has done for me."

I watch her carefully, how her eyes well up and her bottom lip continues to tremble, and I realize there is still a human in there. Unlike the others, she still holds onto her humanity. Her feminism. She is still a woman, not the hardcore thug they think she is. The hardcore thug she pretends to be just helps to keep her place here.

She drops her hand and I nod. "I'll let him know."

I walk past her and down the corridor. I hear her following me, but I don't look back. I assume this is something Draco told her to do. When I'm upstairs and in the bedroom, I shut the door behind me, but I can hear Patanza outside the door. She's clearly there to stay.

I lie back down, looking toward the open window. I hear the gulls. I hear the ocean. I feel the heat of the sun, the warm breeze floating in.

But what I don't feel is myself.

Every little noise startles me, from the maids dropping things, to Patanza uttering a small cough.

I want to believe that Draco will never let this happen to me again, but I can't completely trust him.

It happened once.

Why couldn't it happen again?

CHAPTER THREE

RECOVERY—DAY 3

A *hand runs over* my cheekbone.

I spring up, panting, meeting brown eyes surrounded by thick, black eyelashes.

"Calm down, niñita. It's just me." Draco's voice is much softer today.

I blink up at him for several seconds and then rest my head on the pillow again.

"You slept all day yesterday," he says, standing up straight with his hands on his hips. "You should come down and eat."

"What time is it?" I croak.

"Past eight. You know my rule."

"I'm not hungry, Draco. I can't eat."

"You *need* to eat."

"Well, I don't want to."

I feel him staring down at me. Through the corner of my eye, I see him take a small step back. "Fine. I'll have one of the butler's bring a tray up for you."

"Draco—I said I don't want—"

"I don't care what you don't *want*, Gianna!" I peer up and his eyebrow is cocked, eyes as hard as stone. "I'm not going to let you rot away in here. You'll eat the fucking food."

He looks me over thoroughly and then turns, his shoes clicking across the floorboards. The door is shut behind him before I know it, and I release a tattered breath, rolling back over.

I stare up at the ceiling, and then look at the window. It's closed now. I don't know why that bothers me so much.

I felt better when it was open—soothed, sleeping to ocean sounds and squawking birds. I have the urge to get up and open it, but I don't.

I can't.

I don't want to move or do anything.

I just want to melt away and forget everything.

CHAPTER FOUR

RECOVERY—DAY 4

My mouth is dry, my throat thick, and that is the only reason I'm getting up. I see the tray on the table in the corner. I can smell it from here. My belly doesn't even growl.

But the water does look appealing.

I pick up the bottle and crack it open, guzzling it down rapidly. Each chug clears the dryness away, the crisp taste allowing me to gasp after I've lowered the bottle.

I hear footsteps behind the door and someone knocks.

"Come in," I call, turning to look at it.

When it swings open, it's Patanza with some clothes on hangers. "Draco told me to hang these in the closet for you."

I look at the clothes in her hands. None of it looks familiar. As she walks by with it, I realize they all have price tags on them. I follow her to the closet, watching as she moves some of his clothes aside and hangs them all up at once.

"They're new," she says, as if she's read my mind. "He made me go into town with Mrs. Molina. She has great taste for you."

When she's finished, she walks past me and to the door. "Do you need me to tell him you're awake?"

"Are you keeping watch by the door?"

She nods her head, pressing her lips.

"Then, no. I'm okay, as long as you're there." I don't know what possesses me to say that. Deep down, it's the truth. Of all the guards, Patanza is the one I think I can rely on. Let's hope I'm right.

Her face changes, but barely. Her lips don't press anymore, and her eyes aren't as hard around the edges. She gives one quick nod before turning and walking out of the room and shutting the door behind her.

I sit on the bench at the end of the bed, staring down at my feet. It's been a while since my toenails had a good trim and polish.

Looking in the bathroom, I see the square, pink box that was delivered from the other room. It's full of everything a girl needs, including nail polish and remover.

Making my way to the bathroom, I open the case and dig through it, pulling out bottles of blue, pink, and red polish. I study each one, debating on which to go with.

Pink used to be my favorite, but it seems too fluffy for me now. Too sweet and innocent. Red was my father's. He claimed red was a ruthless, dangerous color. Red made a statement, in both blood and confidence.

Blue was Toni's favorite.

I look up at the mirror. I'm healing, somewhat. The right side of my face isn't as puffy or blue as it was before. I stare for a long time, remembering just how I acquired the bruises. The stitches. The pain.

Heavy breathing.

Grunting.

Panting.

Groaning.

Stretches of pain.

Blood . . . everywhere.

"You can stab me, fight me, and even have Draco beat the fuck out of me, but you knew by the end of this shit I would get what the fuck I wanted."

I wince, and pull my gaze away from the mirror. *Fuck him.*

I will not let what he did to me take over my life. I will not let it rule me.

Be smart. Be brave. Think about what Daddy would do.

I'll tell you what Daddy would do.

He'd choose the color red.

CHAPTER FIVE

RESTORATION

I *riffle through the* new clothes, the glossy red on my fingernails flashing from the small, crystal-like chandelier above.

Patanza was right. Mrs. Molina does have good taste. I pluck out the blue maxi dress. It's lovely, with sleeves, made of a light, soft cotton.

I take a rapid shower, blow-dry the kinks out of my hair, and then get dressed in it.

As I'm sliding my feet into a pair of sandals, the door opens, and Draco walks in. He catches me leaning on the mattress to buckle my sandal, and his head goes into a slight tilt.

"You're up," he murmurs, somewhat surprised, sliding the tips of his fingers into his pocket.

"Yep."

"I wasn't expecting you to be. Thought I was going to have to drag you out of bed today." He walks to the left, looking me over. "How do you feel?"

"Better."

He continues his stare. He's quiet for a minute, then looks at his brown dresser against the wall. "I know you were using the pills. That's how you were sleeping through the day without being disturbed or scared awake."

When he says that, I lift my head up to stare at him. "I needed them." I say it hard enough for him to take my statement seriously.

"You can't take too many, Gianna. They are only for severe situations."

"And you don't think *that* was a severe situation?" I snap, straightening my back.

His face remains even. His expression doesn't change. "No more pills," he orders.

"Fine." I drop my foot and straighten my back. "Then give me something else to drown out the memories. Alcohol, preferably vodka."

"I'm not letting you drown them out. I want you to feel them. You can't sleep on the shit that's happened and think everything will be okay later. It will only make you feel worse. You want to forget about that shit, you make it fucking happen by doing something bigger than what happened. You do whatever you can to make sure it never fucking happens again."

"I'm not killing them," I tell him. "I'm not. It's not who I am. I don't kill people."

He doesn't respond. Instead he turns and walks through the door again. In the hallway, he turns to look at me.

"Breakfast," is all he says and then strides off.

I can feel him watching me as I devour my meal. I eat it properly, but I'm hardly taking breaths between bites. I'm so hungry today. Considering I didn't eat the food he brought up to the room the past two days, I shouldn't be so surprised.

Mrs. Molina is here, and she hasn't said a word since I've shown up. Her eyes scream it all, though. She wants to apologize a thousand times for what's happened, even though it wasn't even her fault.

Patanza stands at the door, along with another guard. He's bulky, but not so bulky that it's intimidating. They both have their eyes on the wall across from them, jaws fixed, stances straight.

After finishing off my pineapple juice, I sit back in my chair, allowing my meal to settle.

"You were hungry," Draco notes.

19

"Yeah," I respond.

"Glad to see you eating." Draco looks at his mother. "Mama, you've barely touched your food."

"I don't have much of an appetite, son," she says in Spanish, avoiding his eyes.

He notices and focuses on his plate, pretending he's not bothered by it, but I know he is. "Gianna, I want to show you something. Are you up for it?"

I sit up a bit. "Show me what?"

"Come." He pushes out of his throne-like chair and walks past mine to get to the door. He stops right before walking out and looks back at me, tilting an eyebrow.

I push out of my chair as well, meeting up to him. When I'm right beside him, he turns right and walks down the corridor that leads to his galería.

Ugh. Not this again. I'm not up for manipulative sex today.

Would he even dare, after knowing what happened to me? I shouldn't be so shocked if he does. I can't forget that he's still a heartless, cruel bastard, just like the rest of them.

We make it down the staircase and to the door. He unlocks it and walks in. I follow after him, and when he steps to the right, I do the same.

"I remember this when I used to visit the U.S." His voice is mellow. I have no idea what he's talking about, and frankly, I don't care right now.

He walks forward and up the stairs. I hear rustling and things moving, but then it stops.

And then I hear a violin start to play.

The song is so damn raw, bittersweet and familiar, that I freeze exactly where I stand. I look toward the sound, eyes stretched wide, mouth halfway open.

Draco comes to the top of the stairs with the violin in his large hands, his chin resting on the chinrest and the body extending out.

His head is at an angle, and he is focused on the instrument, strumming slowly during some notes, quickening at others.

Tears creep to my eyes—unwanted, annoying tears.

That was . . . Mom's lullaby.

Her song.

She hummed it to me when I was a little girl and even as I got older.

She played it for me and even tried to teach me, but I wasn't as gifted as her. I'm still not, but Draco?

He hits every chord and note to near perfection. He plays so well that I feel like Mom is here, playing for me. I feel her spirit dwelling, and her angelic arms wrapping around me, silently telling me things will be okay again.

I feel her—like she's standing right beside me.

When he stops, the silence is deafening. Her warm arms are gone.

I hear my pounding pulse.

I feel hotness rolling down my cheeks.

I see him. Draco. There. Looking down at me.

"She taught you," I breathe out.

"The whole thing. During the summers, Mama would make me go to your mother's music studio for two hours every day just to learn. She was a patient woman. She had to be, dealing with someone like me." He smirks, just barely. I'm still stuck.

I don't even know what to say.

Or how to react.

Mom loved music. She loved her violin. It's still in storage back in the U.S . . . well, I hope it is. Knowing my people, they've probably presumed us dead and sold all of Toni's belongings and mine as well. Mama's violin was mine.

Fire streams through my veins. My tears continue falling, even though I'm fighting hard to make them stop. So many feelings overwhelm me, all at once. Too many to handle.

Mom.

Daddy.

Happiness.

Innocence.

Oh, how I miss them.

I swipe my face, catching a glimpse of the red nail polish.

Daddy. *Damn it, Daddy!*

I turn away and burst through the door, zooming up the steps.

"Gianna!" Draco calls after me. He sounds sad, maybe even a little worried.

But I don't stop.

I rush down the corridor and then I hear boots on the marble. Patanza and the other guard must have heard Draco's voice, because they step around the corner to look in my direction.

They watch me dash by them with my head down, my arms pumping.

They don't dare stop me.

But something else does.

Well, *someone else,* rather.

CHAPTER SIX

As soon as I slam into the heavy, thick body, I hear guns cock behind me. I stumble away and look back at Patanza and the other guard, their guns raised in the air, pointed directly at this stranger.

The stranger looks from them to me, his dark eyes flashing. He's not intimidated at all by them. Not one bit.

"Now . . . who is this one?" he asks in a strong Spanish tongue.

"Don't fucking worry about it. Put your fucking hands in the air," Patanza spits, stepping closer, gun still aimed.

She yanks on my shoulder to drag me back behind her.

The other guard steps to my side, but he's still focused on the man.

The stranger has wide shoulders and really brown skin. His eyes are a shade away from black. They are intense, almost scary. He's much taller than Patanza and me, but he's about the same height as the other guard and about the same build.

"Who let you in?" the other guard growls.

"Gatekeeper. He knows why I'm here. And so does Jefe." The man steals another peek at me. "Where is he, anyway?"

"Right fucking here." Draco's voice rises behind me and I whip my head over to look. His eyebrows are drawn together as he glares at the man. There is a gun in his hand now. An all-black handgun.

"Jefe," the man sings, so nonchalantly, like he doesn't have guns pointed directly at his face.

"Where are my guns, Thiago?" Draco asks, stone-faced. No politeness. No greeting.

"Your guns?" Thiago chuckles, holding his hands out. "I told you where they were. Fucking stolen."

"Stolen." Draco steps around Patanza, eyeing him.

"They were taken, Jefe, and the people that took them let me go. I wouldn't lie to you about that."

"Oh, you've lied to me many, many times before, and because you are my cousin, I have given you many, many chances. I see giving you chances was clearly a mistake. *My* mistake. First my drugs, then the cargo from California, and now my guns?" Draco makes a repeated *tsk-ing* noise as he looks him over. "Too many excuses. Too many mistakes," he hisses. "And I have to tell you, I am growing tired of mistakes around here."

"The guns were taken. That's all I can say. Some shit about territory." Thiago shrugs carelessly. "I wasn't about to get myself killed over one little shipment of guns."

"This whole country is my territory, motherfucker! That's no excuse!" Draco gets closer to his face, brows dipped, and his finger on the trigger. "You think that just because my mother tells me to keep you alive that I *have* to?" He scoffs, waving his gun. "You think you're safe because you carry *my* blood in your veins? I've killed blood members and never had a fucking problem doing so. I've killed them and slept like a baby." Draco lifts the barrel to Thiago's head, pointing it at his temple. "Uncles, remember? The same man that fucked me over because he thought I didn't know anything? And you're foolish enough to follow right in his footsteps."

Thiago says nothing. He only stares back, unafraid. His eyes are like charcoal; his skin a few shades darker than Draco's. He's fearless.

Draco's finger wraps around the trigger, but he doesn't pull. He's close to doing it, and as he does, Patanza and the other guard steady their aim, ready to take him down, too, if need be.

"How long have you had the *puta*?" Thiago asks, in English, so I can fully comprehend.

Draco's upper lip twitches.

He doesn't hesitate on his next action.

He doesn't shoot. But he does whack him across the head with the butt of the gun. *Crack!*

Thiago's large body hits the floor with a heavy thud, and a sharp gasp flies through my lips.

"Take her up to my room," Draco orders without looking back. Patanza makes no room for error. She puts the safety on her gun, tosses it over her shoulder by the strap, and then grabs my wrist, leading the way and trailing up the stairs.

I look back, wondering what Draco is going to do to him. Who the hell is he, anyway?

My heart is pounding so hard.

My palms are sweaty.

I see some of his guards dragging Thiago's body, and I have a feeling he's taking him to the cellar. Draco stands in the same place, finger on the trigger, jaw pulsing.

"Sit. Rest," Patanza orders in her native tongue when I'm in the bedroom.

She looks down, and it's now when I realize my hands are shaking.

"No one will hurt you. Especially under my watch. If you are important to Jefe, you are important to me. It's that simple."

"I thought you didn't like me," I respond with an unsteady voice.

"Didn't, but things are much clearer now. You're not like the other girls. You never were like them. He knows you well. He admires you."

I don't know why I care to ask. "How many girls has he held captive here?"

"Just four, including you. But they don't really count for being captive. Francesca was only bought because he needed to pay off a debt to some Americans and the people that had her no longer wanted her." That explained how she knew English so well. "When she came, we all knew she was desperate. She caught Draco at a difficult time—took advantage of it. And the other girl . . . well, she was just stupid. She came here seeking help. She was lost, and he kept her because he didn't trust her to go back out to the world after seeing his home. She got one punishment from Draco and ran away again. She wasn't tracked. He had some men look for her for about a week, and they found her. She was in an alley. Clothes torn. Throat sliced. She'd been raped and killed."

I shuddered. "American girl?"

"Half. Her father was from here. She was visiting her dad, but was caught by Bain when she came near this property. She was on the compound, trying to steal. She was born there, though. Yes."

"What about the last girl?"

She thinks on it. "She just stopped showing up. Haven't seen her in years."

She's lying. I can tell. She's avoiding my eyes now, which means she knows something and probably isn't supposed to tell me. "Patanza," I murmur when she backs away. "Where are we, exactly?"

She swallows thickly, looking around the room. She snatches the map down from the pin board in the corner and then walks back my way.

She points at a name, but says nothing.

"Lantía?" I read out loud. Never have I heard of it.

She jerks her hand away and hurries for the door, not looking back once.

I stare down at the map again.

Lantía. It's a small city on the Gulf of Mexico. And by small, I mean you could easily miss it if it wasn't pointed out.

The population here can't be too big.

I place the map down on the bed and tiptoe toward the door. I hear someone walking, and I think it's her. But I'm mistaken. She's still there, talking to someone. Whispering.

"What in the hell is he doing here, anyway?" she hisses.

A deep voice speaks. "Jefe said he's going to use him as leverage." I think it's the other guard that was downstairs.

"Leverage for what?"

"Jefe heard Hernandez is building up the cartel and wants the boss completely out of the territory. He thinks Thiago is handing over the 'stolen' goods to Hernandez's cartel."

"But why would Hernandez want that? That cartel is supposed to be working for him!" I can hear in Patanza's voice that she's pissed that this Hernandez person has gone against Draco.

"It's the way of the world, P. We can't control that shit. We just do what the fuck we can to make sure Thiago doesn't get back to them. He acts innocent, but I don't trust him. He always comes back empty-handed, and Jefe always accepts it and never does anything to him about it. I don't trust him . . . don't give a fuck if he's family."

"Draco won't kill Thiago. They grew up together. Despite their differences, he has too much history with Thiago to just kill him like that. They committed some of their first crimes together."

"Maybe before," the other guard sighs, "but I don't know about it this time. We've been hearing Hernandez is trying to make hits on Jefe."

"From who?"

"Talk around the city. We're also trying to get No-Arms to talk. He has to know something after being around them before."

"The guy in the cells?" she asks.

"Yep."

Ronaldo? I gasp, backing away from the door, but I can still hear them talking.

"Once we get him to talk," the guard continues, "he wants to send his fucking head to Hernandez to show we aren't fucking around."

"Well, good. Fucking traitor," Patanza spits.

I continue my retreat, looking all around the room, trying to find another way out.

Of course there is only one way, and that is through that door, where two of Draco's best guards are standing. Waiting.

I hurry for the window and open it. Though all I can see is the ocean, I move myself to the far right to see if I can catch a glimpse of the shed. I can't. I don't see anything.

I promised Ronaldo I would get him out of there. It can't be true, what they're saying. The way Ronaldo made it seem, someone turned on *him*. He got caught because of someone he trusted.

It could have been by someone that works for Hernandez. If that's the case, he doesn't deserve to die. I step away from the window and look at the door.

I need to talk to Draco about this. This can't be right. Ronaldo . . . he helped me. He's a good person. I could see the goodness in him.

It would be unfair for him to die, when all he wants is to be set free and to forget about this mess.

When it's time for dinner, there's a knock on the door. Patanza comes in and looks at me, bobbing her head in the direction of the door. I nod back, following her out and down the hallway.

When we've made it down the staircase, I catch up to her. "Hey, do you think you can take me to the cells tomorrow?"

She glances over. "By yourself? Hell, no." Her head shakes rapidly. "Jefe would chop my head off, too."

"I just . . . I need to see them. For myself. I need to know they're suffering much worse than I did when I was in there. Worse than when Pico . . . did that to me in the cellar."

She looks me over, her mouth twitching before she speaks. "Why can't you go down there with him? He'll be glad to show you what he's done." As she says that last sentence, a smirk plays on her lips.

"He has a lot going on right now with that guy who came here." I fold my arms. "I don't want to bother him."

She side eyes me. "I can't take you down without his permission, Patrona."

I frown a bit. "Patrona?" I look her over. "Boss? Why are you calling me that?"

"It's what we are to call you now. Seeing as you are with Draco, and he wants you safe, you are our boss now too, I guess." Her lips press. "The lady boss."

"Oh." I pull my gaze away, scoffing. "Kinda weird."

She chuckles, and then says, "So, *Patrona*, forgive me, but I cannot take you down there. I listen to you, but I obey the Jefe's orders first."

I look away as we get closer to the dining room. "Okay. I understand."

When I make it inside the dining room, Mrs. Molina is sitting in her chair, knitting. I don't see Draco, but I can hear him talking nearby. Maybe the kitchen.

I take my usual seat while Patanza stands guard at the door.

Mrs. Molina pauses on her knitting, looking up at me. "You look better," she says lightly, her smile forced.

"I feel better." I return the smile.

"Good," she breathes. "A quick recovery is something Lion always had. He never dwelled on things for too long. I see you get that trait from him."

I focus on my red fingernails, doing my best not to smile. "I guess."

She leans over the table a bit, running her eyes all over me. "Has he . . . been good to you since . . . well, you know?"

"He's not punishing me, so that's a start." But if he knew the kind of plan I was hatching right now, I'm sure he'd toss me in a cell and chop my arms off, too.

She sits back, barely nodding. She doesn't say much more, not that she can continue. Draco is coming from the kitchen to take his seat now. The butlers follow after him, setting hot plates down in front of us.

When they are gone, Mrs. Molina picks up her fork. "Where is your cousin?" she inquires with a soft voice.

Draco doesn't look at her as he cuts into his pork. "Don't worry about it, Mamá."

"You know you can't kill him. He saved your life once. You owe him."

"I don't owe him a damn thing after all the shit he's caused." Draco's hand tightens around the handle of his knife. He snatches a bite off his fork and finally looks at her. "He has to go, Mamá. It's that simple. He's causing too much confusion and too many problems. If he doesn't, it makes me look weak, and everyone knows I'm far from it. I don't need anyone thinking I'm going soft. He stole from me, and for all I know he might have come here to kill me first. I won't allow that to happen."

She stares at him until her eyes well up. "You can't kill him, Draco. What kind of man would you be to kill your own blood?"

"I killed my uncle and another cousin of mine for stabbing me in the back and thinking they could get away with it. It's business, and they know it. He knows it, and has ever since I took over, but it didn't stop him from stealing from me. I don't take threats from anyone. I *am* the threat." His tone is clipped. I watch them stare at one another—she with her lips pressed, he as he chews thoroughly.

I decide to break the silent, thick tension. "Draco, I think I'm ready," I murmur in English.

And he instantly looks up at me, those brown eyes sparking. "Ready for what?" But I'm sure he already knows.

"To go to the cells. To see them."

Mrs. Molina's shoulders tense up.

"To do what?" He watches my eyes.

"You know what," I tell him.

"Why now? Why today?"

I shrug. "I'm tired of thinking about it. I need to get it over with." He doesn't seem very convinced, so I continue. "I just want to forget about what he did to me. And I want them gone as soon as possible. It would make me feel safer here."

He looks me over once before focusing on his food. "Fine. Tomorrow morning after breakfast." He cuts into his meat again. "But I hope you're sure."

"I am," I murmur.

But I know I'm not. I don't know how I'll get around Draco while I'm in there, but I'll think of something. I'll make up an excuse. I always find a way.

I enter the prisoner's bedroom I was in before and walk to the bathroom, locking the door behind me, and then stand on the toilet seat before climbing onto the tank.

The ends of my feet hang over the edge, but I grip the windowsill and look out. I see the shed there. There are six men guarding it, all of them strapped with guns and swathed in black and gray camouflage pants.

Shit. There is no way in hell I'm going to sneak in there and break Ronaldo out. Every door of that place is covered, every lock secured.

I step down and then hurry to unlock the door. I grab the bedroom door handle and walk out, but it's as I do that I hear hissing and whispers.

I look toward the room where I caught Francesca and Bain having sex, and my pulse skitters.

"I don't give a damn about any of that, Mamá!" Draco's voice booms from the other side and I flinch. "You think he thought about that when he handed over my shit? He came here, to my home, thinking he had the advantage. He has to die. End of fucking discussion!"

I walk closer to the door but when I see his shadow pass by I pause, eyes growing wide. I see Mrs. Molina's shadow follow after him and then I hear a loud SMACK.

She *slapped* him. I cup my mouth, holding back a gasp.

"You are acting like a damn demon, Draco, and I will not tolerate it! I raised you better than this! We do not kill any more family under this roof. You shed any of his blood and, so help me God, I will leave this home and never, ever come back. You will have no one—not even Gia, because I will take her with me too."

It's quiet for a moment, but I hear him seething, most likely trying to control his temper.

Mrs. Molina continues talking. "She hates you, don't you see that? She wants you dead and has ever since you dragged her here. You punish her and then let your men do *that* to her! Those men, and that disgusting woman, are the ones you should be worried about right now. Not your cousin—*them*!"

"She isn't going anywhere," he growls at her. "She's mine now. She's here to stay."

"Oh, she will go. I will escort her myself." She pauses. "Unless it's come to a point in your mind where you think your own mother should be dead for standing in your way, too." I hear her take a step forward. "Are you going to kill me too, son? For going behind your back? For doing what you *know* is right?"

Draco doesn't say anything at all. I know it's not because he doesn't want to. I'm sure he has plenty of shit to say, but he respects his mother. Too much.

"That poor girl is *suffering*. Day by day I am watching her wither away, and I am tired of it. You need to treat her like she matters to you—like a queen, and nothing below it! When Lion promised her to you, he told you what?"

He doesn't answer. I frown, stepping closer, listening harder.

"What did he tell you, son?" she demands.

"That when I make her mine, I have to protect her. But she isn't fully mine yet, Mamá. She still has her heart set on her dead husband."

"Then it is your job to make her forget him."

"It's not that fucking simple!" he snaps at her. "Why do you think she hates me, huh? I killed her fucking husband, and I would do it over and over again because that's exactly what he deserved. That motherfucker didn't deserve her. He wasn't promised to her! He stole everything from me, Ma! *From us!* He wasn't taking her, too. Fuck that. I don't care if I have to break and bend her into submission. I don't care if she hates me right now. Hatred can always be reversed. I'll tell her the truth. I will show her what I am capable of and why she needs me— why she's *always* needed me. He didn't fucking love her. He was using her, but she was too blinded by his pretty face and his tricky ways to realize it."

"Hijo," Mrs. Molina whines.

"No, Ma. No. Just don't worry about it anymore. Let me handle Gianna. She's not going anywhere. She has nowhere to go and we both know it. Her best bet is to stay here with me."

"Then promise me something," Mrs. Molina pleads.

He sighs. "What?"

"Promise you won't punish her anymore. Don't starve her. Treat her like you want to give her the world. Don't treat her like how you did Francesca."

"Fuck Francesca," he spits. "Gianna may not be coming around now, but she will. She'll understand why I did what I did to her. I wanted her to forget him, and if that meant making her suffer for a little while, then it had to be done. She needed to focus on *me*. She needed to see that, unlike him, I am the real threat. I am the one she needs. She's a smart girl. She's not stupid. She's a lot smarter than we think. She knows a lot of shit, and I don't trust her," he rasps. "I don't sleep with both eyes shut around her. She wants me dead, and I know it, but soon those thoughts will change." He releases a bitter laugh. "Truth is, I'd much rather break her first than have her end up breaking me. I did those things because I wanted her to recognize her strength. My woman has to be strong. There is no doubt about that. I didn't want her getting used to any of that soft shit Trigger Toni used to do with her.

"She was promised to me. And when she's ready, I will tell her everything she doesn't know. But until then, I need you to stay out of it. I need you to *trust* me. I won't hurt her anymore. I won't kill her. And I damn sure won't let her run.

Gianna is mine, and my queen has a lot to learn. I won't let her slip through my fingers. Not again."

I stumble backwards, gaping.

"What the hell are you doing out here?" I spin around rapidly and meet Patanza's eyes. Hers are narrowed, her arched eyebrows pinned together.

"I was in the other room," I state quickly, pointing at the guest bedroom I was in. "There was something I forgot."

She looks me over with her narrowed gaze, but doesn't speak.

I return to Draco's bedroom and push the door open, but not before looking back at Patanza. She walks forward and shoos me in, and then shuts the door behind me.

I slump down on the edge of the bed, staring down at my red toenails. I don't know what the hell I just heard. I was promised to him? Why would Daddy promise me to a man like him?

He knew I loved Toni. Is that why Draco killed him? Because I was in love with another man but was promised to him?

Is he really that fucking insane? Toni couldn't help it, and neither could I. Daddy wasn't a fan of us at first either, but I told him I loved Toni, and he eased up on the idea of us as a couple. He grew to respect it . . . or so I thought.

But now that I think about it, Daddy never really liked being around us. He accepted it, but he didn't like it. Whenever Toni came over, he would pull him to the side or put him on a quick run with one of his people, just to keep him away from me for as long as possible.

And of course Toni had to listen. Daddy was pretty much his boss. Toni ran his own side jobs, but he worked mainly for Daddy. Most of his money came from the almighty Lion.

I hear footsteps outside my door and then I hear Draco speaking.

"Have you checked on her?" he asks.

"No, Jefe," Patanza says, and relief washes over me. I don't know why she's protecting me so much lately. I'm surprised she's not snitching on me like Bain or the maids.

"Go take a break if you need it," he tells her. "Eat. Wash. Do whatever you need to do. I've got her covered for the rest of the night."

"Yes, sir."

I hear Patanza stroll off, and it doesn't take long at all for the door to open and for him to step inside. He looks me right in the eyes while shutting the door behind him, and his lips press together as he walks to the middle of the room, looking me over.

"I'm not taking you to the cells tomorrow," he declares.

I frown, sitting up straight. "What? Why not?"

"Because you're not ready."

"Yes, I am!"

He blinks slowly. "No, you're not, and I won't argue with you about it." He turns and walks to the bathroom, unbuttoning his shirt along the way.

I hop off the bed and follow him inside. "Draco, I'm ready. I swear!"

"You want to speak to your friend. I'm not stupid." He looks at me, eyes hard like steel. "One of my men watches the tapes from the camera we have down there. He informed me not too long ago that you two got along really well in there. Lots of whispering, but never loud enough for them to be able to hear you. I thought nothing of it, until we heard him call you by your full name last night."

I swallow the bile in my throat, backing away.

"For the record, his name is *not* Ronaldo," he informs me.

"Then what is it?"

He gives me a thorough sideways glance before responding. "Henry Ricci."

"Ricci?" I gasp.

"Blood of your ex-husband's. His second cousin, actually."

"Why do you have him?" I ask.

He slides out of his shirt and places it on top of the counter. He then turns and walks to the shower to turn it on. "He was spying on me. I caught him."

"And you cut off his arms for that?"

"Can't hold cameras anymore, can he?"

I shake my head, walking forward. "Did Toni tell him to watch you?"

"No, actually. Your father gave the order a few months before he passed away."

"How do you know this?" I fold my arms, wary of his next answer.

"He told me—Lion did. About a week before he died, when he realized Henry wasn't answering his phone. Claimed he was checking up on me to make sure I wasn't causing too much trouble. Wanted to make sure I wasn't doing anything too stupid down here."

"Why would Daddy care what you were doing? And why would he send Toni's second cousin?"

"Henry needed a job. He was good with cameras. Lion agreed to pay him well, even though he knew there was a chance Henry would get caught."

"That doesn't explain why you have him in there— or why you cut off his arms." I'm mad now. What a stupid, stupid excuse.

"Blood of Toni. And I know he works with an enemy of mine, he's just not talking."

"What enemy? He never said anything about Toni while we were down there."

Draco scoffs. "Of course he didn't. He didn't want you to know. Makes it easier for you to rescue him. But you won't be doing that, because you won't be going to the shed. And Toni isn't the enemy I'm talking about."

Hernandez.

"He knows I loved Toni," I state boldly.

Draco turns around fully, nostrils flared now. "Don't say that shit around me." He storms past me, into the closet.

I turn with him. "Well, I did love him. And you can't change that, Draco."

"No?" He tugs down a white T-shirt from a neatly folded stack, picking up a pair of jeans next, and then walking around me to place the clothes down on the bed. When he's done with that, he looks at me again and steps closer.

His hand wraps around the back of my neck and he reels me in. His mouth runs across mine and a buzz rides through my body. The buzz is hot and thick and hard to ignore, making my skin tingle. He hasn't touched me like this in a long time. Not since what happened in the cellar. "You loved a man that didn't love you, Gianna," he murmurs when his lips come up to my ear.

I snatch my body away from him. "You don't know what we had."

"A hit man like Trigger Toni is incapable of love. If you made him angry enough, he would have probably killed you too."

"Shut up," I snap.

"It's the truth and you know it. You've seen him react. He proved himself quite dangerous, no?"

"Shut up!"

Draco grimaces and jerks me forward again. He grabs my hair and wrenches my head back with a heavy tug. He does it so my mouth is angled up and my eyes are only on him.

"I see you got some of your fire back." He smirks and I want to slap it right off of his beautifully twisted face. "The sooner you get over him, the better, niñita."

"What did he do to you?" I pant, grimacing back.

"He ruined my *fucking life*. That's what he did."

"How?! You're still standing here. You're still alive and he's not. Tell me how!"

"You're not ready to know how just yet." He snatches his hand away and walks to the bathroom again. He unbuttons his khakis and they drop down around his ankles. When he reaches for the hem of his briefs and his eyes meet mine, I jerk my gaze away and walk to my side of the bed.

I hear the shower door open and then close. There is an uncomfortable silence . . . for a while anyway.

"Gianna. Come here," he calls.

I frown, looking toward the bathroom. "Why?"

"Come. Now."

Rolling my eyes, I walk to the bathroom, spotting his opaque silhouette from the doorway.

"Shut the door."

I shut it, but don't come any closer.

"Get undressed and come in the shower with me."

"I already took one this morning," I respond with folded arms.

"Well, come and take another one. I won't say it again."

I can't help the second roll of my eyes. He stands beneath the stream and pushes his wet hair out of his face.

I can't fight. I can't resist. I have to remember that. I need him wrapped around my finger, and that starts with doing whatever he wants me to do. For right now, anyway.

He already has people calling me Patrona. Their boss? That's progress.

I get undressed rather slowly and then make my way to the shower door. He pushes it open, welcoming me in without saying a word. His hard eyes travel up and down my body, locking on my breasts and especially the area between my thighs.

He steps beneath the water so I can get in. I watch it cascade over him and his hard, sculpted muscles, but his eyes are still open. It falls through his hair and down his face, running over his full lips and flared nostrils.

He always looks so serious and hostile, even during the calm moments. I'm starting to think that's just the way his face was made.

I close the shower door and as soon as I do, he steps forward and wraps his hands around my middle. He pulls me back into him, and I feel his hard cock pressing on my ass.

"I hate when you try to hide from me," he rasps in my ear.

"How am I hiding?"

"Under those clothes. Beneath your distress. Beneath layers and layers of conflicted emotions. Stop pretending this isn't real, because it is."

He grabs the back of my thigh and forces my knee on the wall. His cock slides between the crack of my ass, and he lowers himself, wrenching my legs apart so that his tip is pressing on the entrance of my pussy.

"I'm going to fuck you," he grumbles, deep and heavy. "Because you need it." He kisses the top of my ear and I shudder. "I know you do."

He grips my waist tight with one hand and uses the other to press it on the back of my head. He forces my forehead on the wall, and a ragged breath passes through me when I feel him slowly entering me.

Each slow, measured thrust fills me up, and I don't know why his patience bothers me. His hands are aggressive, pinning me to this shower wall, but the fact that he's taking his time to "fuck" me bothers me.

He needs to be hard and rough.

He needs to keep making me hate him.

I don't need delicacy right now.

I need fire and fuel and something deep down is telling me that he knows it. But he won't provide it because he loves having control over my needs.

He strokes slowly, releasing my waist and bringing that hand up to cup one of my breasts. He lets my head go so he can spread my ass and sink his cock in deeper. A deep groan rattles in his throat. I feel the vibration of it on my shoulder.

"Draco," I call, my voice shaky. Not from fear, but from pure euphoria. I don't know why I call him, but he answers.

"Sí, mi reina," he murmurs, picking up speed. Skin slaps and water splashes between us.

"Stop," I moan.

"No." His hand comes up to the back of my neck and he holds it tight. "I won't stop." He growls deep, stroking in faster, drilling me even harder from behind.

"Oh, God," I breathe, eyes squeezing shut.

Pulling his hand away, he turns my head sideways so that my cheek is on the wall now, instead of my forehead. Droplets of water collect on my skin, my lips.

"Look back," he demands, "right at me."

I squeeze my eyes tighter instead, but he pulls my hair, yanking it back and leaving me no choice but to look at him.

When hard brown matches green, he leans in and crushes my lips with his. His hard chest rests on my back, his thick cock still filling me up. In and out he goes, while his tongue works its magic with mine.

His body is glued to me and my leg is hitched up, my knee pressed on the wall to help keep balance. His hips works in circles, giving long, full thrusts now, like a rhythmic pattern, and at first I hate it, that he's touching me like this—claiming my body as if it's his own, but then he pulls his lips away from mine and says, "I will make you forget it all. What happened only days ago. Your ex. *Everything.* I will make it so that all you think about while you're here is *me*, Gianna, and that is my fucking word."

His wet mouth is on my ear, his breath warm as it trickles past. He reaches around and grazes his middle finger across my clit, cupping my pussy in his hands and forcing my hips back to bury himself even deeper.

A whimper escapes me from that action alone. The back of my head drops down on top of his shoulder and he presses those full lips to my neck, sucking away the droplets of warm water and replacing them with burning hot kisses.

His body stiffens behind me and then he sighs loud and deep, thrusting hard into my pussy several times before emptying himself inside me.

"Fuck, you feel so fucking good. I've waited for you for so long, niñita." He brings a hand up and rakes his fingers through my hair. "It feels a hundred times better than I imagined it would feel."

He finally pulls out and spins me around. I stare up at him, watching water coat his thick eyelashes.

"Mine," he says, his lips so close I can feel the heat of them. "Say it. You are mine."

I release a tattered breath as he glides a hand down my hip and cups my ass. He hauls me closer so I can really feel him, the water drifting down, sliding on our skin.

I don't want to say it, but he doesn't look away. And he won't pull away until I do. I know I can't deny it now.

"I am yours," I whisper, and then I grip his face in my hands, leaving him no choice but to pick me up in his arms and hold me in his large hands.

I didn't think it would be possible to steal Draco's breath away, but when I do this—kiss him so deep and tenderly, as if I care—I hear him sigh and groan and shudder beneath the embrace.

I feel him let go and melt, even if the feeling is faint and slight. I feel him, and when my tongue slides between his lips and dances with his, that's when I know I have him.

All of him.

He thinks I am his. Truthfully, he has it backwards.

I am not his.

He is *mine.*

CHAPTER SEVEN

RESTORATION—DAY 6

I *don't know when* we fell asleep last night, but I do know he took me once more on this bed before letting me rest. Figuring I wasn't satisfied, he devoured me with his full lips and warm tongue, taking away all my worries for the time being. Making sure all I could feel was him.

I slept like a baby.

When I wake up, the sun beaming down on my skin, fingers are threading through my hair. I look over and Draco is staring right at me. There is no sign that he's just awakened. If anything, his hair looks like the perfect bed hair, but only like he tossed and turned all night while shoving his fingers through it.

"Did you sleep?" I ask, and my voice is dry and scratchy. I clear my throat.

"Not at all."

"Why not?"

"Wanted to, but couldn't."

I press my lips and look away.

He tilts my chin back up. "I was up all night thinking about what I will do to them."

I sit up a bit. "And what will you do?"

"Kill them, of course."

I cringe a little. "How?"

"That's the thing. I'm not sure if I want it to be quick or for them to suffer a little more. I want them to suffer, but the more I think about it now, I'm tired of knowing they are wasting space around me. The longer they stay in there, the weaker and more vulnerable I seem."

My lips twist. As much as I'd love to see them suffer too, I think quick and easy would make me feel less guilty. Isn't it sad that I still feel remorse for people that only wanted to see me dead, that have caused me immeasurable suffering and pain?

"I thought you said you wanted *me* to get rid of them," I murmur.

"I change my mind."

"Why?"

"Because it's not what Lion would have wanted. He would have wanted *me* to handle it. Plus, it will fuck you up even more to do it. I saw how you reacted to me killing Kevin. You could hardly stomach it. With them, it will be worse. You wanted to trust Francesca. I made it so that you wouldn't trust her for a reason. Now you see why."

"Because she could never be trusted," I whisper.

"No, she couldn't. And that's why I only used her. Never craved her or wanted to make her mine. I didn't care about her. She had to be bought, or it would have been my life on the line. The men that had her couldn't stand her. She's annoying and desperate. She tries so hard, but men like me don't want someone easy. We want someone that will put up a fight. Give us a challenge. Someone that will make us question ourselves. You think she gave you that breakfast out of kindness? No, she gave it to you to call to me—to get my attention. She wanted to have you wrapped around her finger instead of you being wrapped around mine. She wanted me, and she knew she wouldn't get to me unless it was through you."

He looks me up and down with hard eyes. The sun reflects off of them, but even so, his eyes are still dark. I can hardly tell they're brown.

He sits up and pushes out of bed. He only has on a pair of boxers, no shirt. "It will happen today and you will see just what I do to the people that thought they could get away with hurting the woman I adore." He's in the closet in no time and

I push up on my elbows, listening to him shuffle around. He comes back out moments later in a gray button-down shirt, a silky navy blue tie, and navy blue dress pants.

He has on the leather shoes he wore the very first day I met him. Clearly, those shoes mean business.

He enters the bathroom to brush his teeth and then smooth his hair with water and a small dollop of gel. When he comes back, he walks to my side of the bed and tilts my chin. He tangles his fingers in my hair and his full, soft lips press down on mine. I feel heat build up and swirl in my belly. My core clenches tight and I try so hard not to moan from his unexpected embrace.

"No one will *ever* hurt you again," he whispers against my lips. "Not while I'm alive and breathing."

I nod, sinking my teeth into my bottom lip.

"Do you trust what I say?"

At first I hesitate, but I know that's not what he wants. So I nod. "Yes, I trust what you say."

He studies every feature of my face. "Good." Pulling away, he straightens his tie and clears his throat. "It's almost 7:30. Get cleaned up and meet me on the terrace for breakfast. We're eating alone today. Much to discuss."

My eyebrows dip. "The terrace?"

"Patanza knows where it is. She'll be at the door to escort you." He walks to the door and pulls it open.

"Where will you be in the meantime?" I call.

He huffs a breath, flaring his nostrils. "Handling my damn cousin," he mutters, and then he takes off, shutting the door behind him.

CHAPTER EIGHT

REDEMPTION

I've brushed my hair back into a sleek, lower bun. I get dressed in one of the white dresses Mrs. Molina bought for me. It's beautiful. No sleeves, a large V cut between the cleavage. Slim at the waist and snug around my breasts and hips.

It almost reminds me of a wedding dress—a really cheap one, but for someone with only pennies to rub together, it would be perfect.

As I stare at my reflection in the mirror, I feel my eyes burn, remembering my old wedding gown, wondering where it must be. One of the maids must have tossed it after that very first shower I took here. I haven't seen it since.

I quickly blink the tears away and step out of the bathroom. It's the past. I won't dwell. I walk to the door, and when I open it, Patanza is waiting across the hallway with her arms folded.

"He's waiting for you," she murmurs.

I nod. "I know. I couldn't decide what to wear."

She looks me up and down. "I say that dress is a little too *clean* for today."

"What do you mean?"

She puts on a light smile. "I think you already know."

Right. The cells. Bain. Francesca. *Death.*

Instead of walking down the steps, she continues forward and I follow closely behind.

"Patanza, can I ask you a question?"

She glances sideways but doesn't meet my eyes. I notice hers are really light. Hazel. "Depends on what you're asking."

"How did you learn English, if you've been here your whole life?"

I catch up at her side, and she finally looks over at me. She stops in front of a set of French doors, where we can both see Draco standing near the railing with his cellphone glued to his ear. His back is to us, the wind tousling loose strands of his thick, black hair.

She watches him carefully before speaking. "He taught me. I knew Jefe young. If I couldn't be stronger, he wanted me to be smarter than the men. The guys like Bain and Guillermo and . . . Pico, they learned on their own because they took trips to the United States often."

"Have you ever been there before?" I ask.

She shakes her head. "No." And then she smiles. "But it would be nice to go."

I half-shrug. "There are a lot of fun things to do there."

"Jefe says he'll let me go one day. But he said that three years ago. I'm sure he thinks I'm safer here, and honestly, he might be right."

We both look over as Draco turns around and glances at the door. He flicks his fingers, gesturing for us to come out.

"Maybe I can talk him into taking you one day." I grin. "Taking *us*."

She smiles back, but barely. I can tell she wants to grin just as hard as I do, but she's too accustomed to looking and being hard. She has to seem as if her heart has been carved from stone. "Jefe isn't as lenient with his guards as you think. We have to earn rewards like that. Going to the U.S. is pretty much a vacation." She grips the doorknob and opens the door.

"Well, I personally think you've more than earned it."

She doesn't respond to that. I don't expect her to.

As soon as she opens the door, the humid beach air brushes past me, making the loose tendrils of my hair twist with the wind. Draco hears us, and when he peers over his shoulder again, he locks those hard eyes right on me.

He continues talking on the phone, but he doesn't dare pull his gaze away. His eyes travel up and down, his face solid, eyes blazing. I'm not sure what he's thinking.

Maybe it's about the shower last night.

Or perhaps he really likes this dress on me.

Or maybe he simply disapproves of it for what I know is going to happen today.

He says something in Spanish on the phone and then he hangs up. He finally looks away from me and tosses the phone to Patanza.

"Get rid of this one. Bring me another," he orders.

She bobs her head and walks away from the terrace. I watch her go down the hallway until she steps around the corner and disappears.

"Sit, Gianna," he murmurs from where he stands by the railing. I pull my chair out and sit at the two-top table that's made of red and black Mexican tile. As I sit, he takes the chair across from me and then slouches back, studying my face carefully. Every detail of it is absorbed, from my forehead to my nose, and down to my chin. "This is how I expect you to dress around here from now on. Tastefully. *Beautifully.*" He rolls the last word off his tongue.

I fidget in my seat and look toward the ocean. "This is nice," I say with a quiet voice.

He gazes around. There is a boat out there, not too far away. We hear its horn blare from a distance.

"Are you hungry?" he asks.

"A little."

He picks up a black device with buttons on it and presses the green one. Soon, I hear wheels rolling and then the butlers appear. Two butlers come out with rolling carts covered in white linens. On top of them is a load of food—way too much for both of us.

One of the butlers slightly bows his head at Draco as he places white plates down in front of us and then slides the cart closer for us to reach.

"Enjoy, Jefe," he murmurs in Spanish.

The other butler lingers around with a pitcher of orange juice and milk on his cart. Draco goes for the orange juice. I decide to go for the milk.

"Leave us," Draco orders and the butler finally takes off, shutting the doors behind him.

When he grabs his food first, I take what I want—a few grapes, some toast with butter and strawberry jelly, and honey-glazed Canadian bacon.

He picks up a slice of the bacon and I notice his knuckles are raw and red. I can tell he wore the brass knuckles again today. Actually, I know he did. They were missing from that weapon wall in his room this morning when I got dressed.

"Did you hit him again? Your cousin?" I probe.

He peers up, chewing what's left in his mouth before responding. "Got a few punches in. Hoping it will get him to realize how foolish he's been."

"You aren't going to kill him, are you?"

He stacks his spine and then straightens his tie, slightly rolling his neck. "It may seem crazy of me—the stuff that I do to people—but I think I'm a considerably reasonable person."

I cock a brow, giving him a *you're-so-full-of-shit* look. That didn't answer my question one bit.

He clears his throat. "I don't know." He pauses, watching me pop a grape into my mouth. "My cousin has to know that his place is to be backing me up. He needs to know this is serious. Hernandez is dirty and catty. He never should have made a fool of himself by showing up here empty-handed."

I stop eating. "Why are you telling me all of this?"

"Because you are my woman now. *La Patrona.* You get to know everything that is going on, even if you don't like it. I—never had anyone talk me in or out of things. I always made the decisions myself. Besides my father, there was no one to steer me. When I saw you in that cellar and that greasy, fat fuck all over you, I lost it," he bites out. "You were mine and he was stupid enough to take you anyway."

I wince, but barely. I think he notices. He studies me briefly before speaking again.

"When I saw it, it made me livid. My woman and this piece of shit—he knew the rules. He knew how badly I did *not* want you being touched but he touched you anyway. I saw that look in your eye. I was going to drag him out of there and take him back to the cells—torture him for a while and then kill him—but you gave me a look. You might not remember, but it happened, niñita. It was almost like you were telling me to do it. To kill him right there. Right now. You didn't have to say it for me to know. I knew that was exactly what you wanted without having to ask."

"I—no. I mean, yes, I wanted him gone, but I don't remember thinking that."

"You didn't have to think it. With shit like that, after what was done to you, you don't think. You just do. You were in survival mode, and you chose wisely. I wanted you to be the one to end Francesca and Bain. I wanted you to have that glory, but I can't taint you. Lion never would have let you seek revenge. He'd keep you under wraps—probably let you watch, but he wouldn't let you lift a finger. He would owe it to you to kill them, so I will do just that. In less than an hour, you will come down to the shed and you will watch me *kill them.* You won't run. You won't turn away. You will *watch,* and you will know that afterwards, you are safe with me. That what I do to them, I can easily do to the next motherfucker that crosses *us* the wrong way." He tips my chin and our eyes hold. "Do you understand me, Gianna?"

"I don't know if I can, Draco," I murmur.

"You have to. For yourself. For *me.*"

His last statement catches me off guard. "For you?"

"We do this together or not at all. I'm sure you don't want them to keep living. We don't want that burden on our backs. They have to go."

I release a ragged breath. I glance at my food and I'm suddenly no longer hungry. It feels like lead has been placed in my stomach. "I know they do. But I'm not used to watching so many people die all at once." Toni was enough. Even Kevin was enough.

"After them, you won't have to. Unless we are threatened, you won't see another death happen in front of you."

I don't speak. Not for a while. I watch him, how he rubs the pad of his thumb and forefinger together. "Do you get satisfaction in doing this? Killing people?"

He half shrugs, picking up his orange juice. He lifts his leg and places his ankle on top of his knee. "Keeping strong threats alive makes you weak. They know too much, which makes them a bigger and stronger threat. If they escaped and ran to the wrong person, I would be fucked. But getting rid of them myself, and knowing those dangerous threats are gone, helps me sleep a little better at night. You'll learn soon, Gianna. This life doesn't come easy, but if you work with me, well, together we can become unstoppable. You just have to get the rest of your fire back, that's all. And when you do, I want to be a witness." He chuckles. "I've heard the stories from Lion. You play the good girl, but you'll dirty your hands in a heartbeat if it means protecting yourself or someone you care about."

I frowned. "I don't know what you're talking about."

"Really?" he taunted. "Eighth grade, a bully named Sarah Cully. She pushed you off the slide and you came after her, pushed her off a swing, kicked her in the stomach, and then punched her in the face. The teacher didn't see so you were proud. You told your father all about it as soon as he picked you up and he was just as proud. His fierce little cub."

I narrow my eyes. "He told you that story?"

"Wouldn't be the first story he shared with me about you. We were closer than you think."

"I see."

Someone knocks on the door. It's Patanza with his new burn phone.

He sighs and drops his legs. After taking a sip of his juice, he places the glass down and then dusts himself off. "You finish eating. I have a phone call to make but it will be quick."

I bob my head as he stands. "Kay."

He kisses the top of my head. When he leaves, I collect a deep breath and then exhale.

I know he's right. And deep down I want them gone, but I don't want to see it happen. I have nightmares, all of them gory at best.

They deserve this, I know it, but no matter how I look at it, that will be *their* blood on *my* hands.

It's time.

I'm not sure whether to freak the fuck out or run. Perhaps I should have hid somewhere. This walk down to the shed is terrifying.

I thought I would have more time, but as soon as Draco made his phone call, he came back, saw I had finished eating, and then grabbed my hand, murmuring, "Come on, my queen. It's time."

Reina. Patrona. Queen and Boss. I was never going to get used to any of these names.

They just didn't fit me . . . well, they didn't fit the *old* me.

As for the new me, I'm not sure how they will fit. If I want to survive, they *must*. It's just a matter of what I do to claim the titles.

My entire body feels heavy, as if gravity has weighed down most on me. Draco is walking beside me, Patanza in front of us with her gun clutched in hand, and Diego behind us, jaw tight, his tan, bald head shining from the golden rays above.

I had already noticed the silver handgun tucked in Draco's belt. He also had the brass knuckles in his shirt pocket, and what looked like a knife in a leather case on the other side of his belt.

Seeing the long knife in its case made my blood run cold. I have no idea what it looks like, but I'm certain it's sharp and deadly. Draco's weapons are not toys. They are dangerous and just as intimidating as he is.

"Draco . . ." I whisper when we take the bridge across. Only a few more steps. I remember this walk, from the first day I was free, trailing behind Patanza like some lost puppy.

"Sí, Gianna?"

I peer up at him. His face is solid, eyes focused on me. His face is much too smooth for what's about to happen. He's way too relaxed.

Is this the way he came down when it was finally time to meet me? On that first day I ever saw him in the cells—when I so badly wanted to gut him right then and there?

Was he *this* confident? This sure of himself, that he would kill me too, if it came down to it?

"Never mind. It's nothing," I murmur with a swift shake of my head.

Before I know it, his men have come to a halt. They all stand aside and Draco finally releases my hand, lifting his head higher and walking forward.

"Ábrela," he commands to one of them.

One of the guards opens the door rapidly. It squeals on its hinges and Draco strolls right in.

"Come, Gianna," he calls over his shoulder. "The rest of you, stay out here," he says to the guards in his native tongue.

I glance sideways at Patanza who has a serious mask on, but her eyes reveal all. She's worried for me too. She's not sure how I will handle it, and she has every right to be concerned.

This isn't me. This isn't me.

I'm not a killer.

That's what I tell myself, but I've wanted to kill Draco ever since I heard his real name. I wanted Axe Man dead way before he ever stole my passion. And Bain—I wanted him gone a long, long time ago.

It's not the same—to want it—as it is doing it. Doing it takes you to a whole new level of evil—an evil that you cannot come back from.

I know for a fact. Daddy used to tell me all the time.

"*Murdering someone can change your entire life,*" *he'd said to me when I threatened to kill a boy who'd stolen my bike. I didn't know what I was saying. All the murder talk I heard from Daddy's mindless adult conversations made my mind a sponge. "Murdering someone is damning your soul to hell for all eternity. Unless you're ready to face the fire and that dirty red devil, be a good girl and let it go. I'll get you a new bike, sweet girl. Don't worry about it.*"

And he did buy me a new bike. That very same night. I also heard the boy was sent to the hospital after being severely beaten.

I'm not prepared to damn my soul to hell. I am a good person. I have a good heart. Right?

There are two cells, I notice.

One is empty. I don't see any trace of Ronaldo.

The other has his captives. His betrayers. Francesca and Bain.

He opens the gate with a key, and when he steps in, I linger outside the gate. I can hardly tell it's them. Francesca has on a blue dress that is now soiled with old blood and ripped at the hem. There is dry blood between her thighs, as if she's been raped brutally or maybe she started her period and couldn't prevent the leakage.

Of course she couldn't. Her wrists are locked in cuffs that are built into the walls, as well as Bain's.

He has no shirt on, wounds all over his chest as if he's been whipped and cut by the sharpest knives around. They're both dirty. Filthy. Bloody. I never thought I would see them so low.

I walk in behind Draco, and Francesca immediately starts to speak.

"Jefe, please!" she begs in Spanish. "This wasn't my idea. None of it was. It was all them. I just wanted to be free! I wanted to go home!"

Draco presses forward, moving slowly toward her with measured steps.

Bain glares at him, but even harder at me.

I don't avoid his eyes. As badly as I want to look away, I don't. I want him to see that I'm the one at Draco's side now. I was once a pawn in this game, but now I'm the one playing it.

"I promise you," she whimpers when he stops in front of her. "I don't love him. I love you, baby. Only you, you know that! I would never betray you. I only wanted out, and I knew you wouldn't let me go because you care for me so much."

Draco scoffs. "Care? Bitch, I don't give a single fuck about you."

She seems shocked to hear that. Her eyes stretch wider, her face going pale. Wow. Does she really think he loves her? Is she in that much denial?

"You're angry now, and I get that. I do! But all I need is another chance. I—I can make this up. I can do better. I won't harm her or you. I will be good. I promise!"

"Just shut up," Draco mutters.

"Please, Jefe, please! I am meant for you! You know it! You bought me out of the kindness of your heart, and you never acted like you regretted it until *she* came along!"

"I said *shut up*, Francesca!"

"She may be prettier, but I can do you better. I can make up for what I've done. I can love you, but she can't! You killed her husband! You ruined her life! Can't you see she's only using you to live, Draco! I would never do that to you because I need you!"

Fed up, he charges for her, snatching out the knife from his holder. It's just as sharp—if not sharper than I expected. Silver and thick. "Hold out your fucking tongue. Now!" he barks. "I'll make sure you don't say another fucking word."

She flinches with thick tears in her eyes, but she doesn't resist. She can't, really. She sticks her tongue out, and he pinches the end of it as tightly as he can while she wails. Clutching the handle of the knife, he slices right through it. Her scream is full of agony as the blood gushes out. It's a shrill scream—one I'm sure I will never forget.

I want to look away, but I can't. I'm frozen.

When he's done, I hear her tongue land with a wet slap on the floor. My blood runs cold as I hear her cries for help, the crimson pouring down like a waterfall.

He wipes the knife off on her stained blue dress and then turns to look at Bain. "Your turn." He looks him over. Bain challenges his stare.

"Look at you," Bain chuckles, his voice thick and croaky, trying to straighten his back and stand taller than Draco. "Pussy whipped by this *cunt*. Never thought I'd see the day The Jefe killed his own men over a worthless *gringa bitch*."

Draco doesn't blink. Doesn't speak. I grimace.

Instead, he walks past Bain, his hand touching the gun in his waistband. He starts to pull it out, but I step forward and hold a hand up, demanding that he waits.

"What the hell are you gonna do, bitch?" Bain scowls at me, his white hair oily, clinging to his forehead.

"I'm not doing anything," I respond. "I'm just here to see you die."

He scoffs. "What? I don't get any last words like your driver did?"

"I think you've had plenty," I say as calmly as possible.

He gives a small smirk. "I don't think you realize just how worthless you really are."

"Fuck you," I spit.

"Enough." Draco's deep voice booms, causing Francesca to flinch. He steps in front of Bain, face-to-face with him, glaring him down. "You face death and you *still* talk like you're a fucking king." He grabs Bain by the roots of his hair and Bain hisses through gritted teeth. "You are *not* the king. You are *not* the boss. You would have tried to steal the position from me the very day I let my guard down around you. I trusted you, Bain. I gave you more than you've ever had in your entire life, and yet you still betrayed me." Draco clicks his tongue. "A shame that such a smart man has to go to waste like this."

He finally lets him go, but shoves the back of his head against the wall before stepping back. I hear the crack from the blow, almost like he's split his skull.

"Anything else you'd like to say to him before he's gone, Gianna?" Draco asks, looking at me through the corner of his eye as he cleans off his gun.

I step forward, mouth twitching. Oh, I have plenty to say. Just the mere sight of him is enough to send me into a black rage.

"I never did anything to you, Bain," I proclaim. "Why would you plan to kill me? To *rape* me?"

"You were getting in the way. Making the boss blind to what you really are—just another piece of pussy. You were unnecessary."

"Hmm. Well, now it seems the roles have reversed, huh?" I smile.

He grimaces. "You're a no good, stupid, insignificant bitch with a dry cunt. Fuck you!"

I rush to him, gripping his disgusting balls in hand and squeezing them tight, until he hollers out in pain, yanking his arms and causing the chains to rattle. "You know, maybe I should cut you to pieces and sell you, instead of having him kill you, yeah?" I seethe in his ear. "Isn't that what you wanted to do to me? Tear me apart? Get rid of me?" I squeeze them even tighter, to the point where they'll probably burst if I hold on long enough. "*These* are what's worthless. Always have been. Maybe we should get rid of them first. Let you live a little longer, so you can really see how it feels to live with no *cojones*. Let you see them hanging around your neck by a thread every day, until they shrivel up and turn to dust. Killing you would be satisfying, but torturing you a little more would be so much better, don't you think?" I flash a smile up at him, still holding on tight, twisting them to make him yell again.

Veins appear on his forehead as he strains for relief, for strength, and words.

"You…" he rasps out, "are so…fucking…stupid." He laughs hoarsely. "I can …still kill you. Still…*fuck* you. You leave me in here…long enough…and I'll…find a fucking way out. And when I do…I'll do much worse than what…Pico did to you in there. Oh, you dumb bitch, I would fuck your little cunt until even your blood can't get it wet anymore. And even when you can't," he grumbles, clearly, as if he can't feel a thing anymore, "I'd still keep going, all while I choke the life right out of you and then break the neck that *he* finds so fucking precious!" He laughs some more.

A cackle that rides under my skin, pricking at every nerve.

But what he does next is the final straw.

He spits in my face, continuing a sneer.

Draco tenses up, fist clenched, but he doesn't move. He stalls, as if he's waiting for something.

My nostrils flare as I yank my hand away from his disgusting balls and swipe the spit off my face with the back of my arm. Heat broils in my veins. I feel my heart rattling, pounding like never before—drowning out all sounds. All of my morals.

That bastard. *That fucking bastard!*

Furious isn't the word.

I've gone beyond that.

All of my fury comes barreling out at once. All I see is red—flashes of so much red.

Flashes of my body being flung around in the cellar.

Flashes of Axe Man, taking what never belonged to him.

Flashes of Toni being killed—shot for dead.

Flashes of being stared at and disrespected.

Tormented and hounded.

Laughed at and abused.

I rush in Draco's direction and swipe his knife out of the holder, hurrying back to Bain and lifting the sharp blade in the air.

"Gianna!" Draco bellows, but I don't look back. I refuse. "Be wise," he commands. "Do this, and it is something that will haunt you for the *rest of your life.*"

"Puta!" Bain spits and then lets out another throaty laugh.

The need for revenge is seeping out of my pores now, throttling at the knife in my hands. All I want to do is wipe that stupid fucking smirk off his face.

Before I can bother thinking it through, I do the one thing I've wanted most since being here.

I fucking retaliate.

I bring the blade forward and deliver a jagged slice across the middle of Bain's throat. Blood gushes out, pouring all over my white dress, seeping down my legs, pooling on my shoes.

I don't even care.

I still see red. So much red. I feel the hotness of it hitting my face, but I don't back away. I want my face to be the last face he ever sees while his heartbeat slowly fades away and everything becomes dark for him.

His blood is mine. His *life* is mine. He thought he'd take me down? He was wrong. So very fucking wrong. I would kill a thousand times before I ever let that happen again.

I guess I'm ready for that dirty red devil to welcome me to Hell with open arms, because he's won. Hell, I'll sit right by his side, queen of his burning hell. It wouldn't be long before I ended up owning *him* too.

That's how great I feel, doing this, getting rid of this sick bastard.

I wanted to do him a solid, and make it easy by having Draco shoot him once in the skull. Quick and easy. But this fucker doesn't deserve quick or easy.

He brought out the sinister side of me, a part of me that I never even knew existed. They did this—he and Axe Man.

Odd. I'm not sure if I should thank them for giving me a sense of such power, or curse their names to hell for causing what was left of my humanity to slip away with the single slice of a knife.

"*Pinche mamon*," I spit out as he lowers to the ground, falling on his knees. *Fucking cocksucker.*

I hear Francesca cry out a muffled scream from her end.

"Gianna," Draco calls again, but I don't look his way. I keep staring at Bain until he's on his knees, gurgling for dear life. He can't grab at his throat to stop the bleeding, can't do anything to block the pain.

Good.

When his eyelids flutter, I lower to a squat, lean forward, and murmur into his ear, "Who are you gonna sell now, *puto*?"

An arm grips mine a second later, and Draco pulls me up. I still don't look at him, not until Bain's eyes are fully sealed, and I know he's dead.

I finally peer up at Draco with a clanging heartbeat and his jaw is ticking, eyes hard like stone. I look over at Francesca and she's panicking, yanking on the chains, begging to be set free, with red running down her chin. She looks like a wild animal.

"Please," I hear her muffle out, tears thick.

I blink rather slowly and start to go to her, but I can't. Draco tugs me back, nostrils flaring as he snatches the knife away from me and wipes it off on his pants. He puts it away and then walks past me, bringing the black gun up and stepping in front of Francesca.

She's still begging for her life, even as he lifts the gun and aims the barrel at the center of her forehead. Jaw still tight, he pulls the trigger without hesitation and the gunshot echoes loudly off the walls. Chains rattle, blood spatters on the wall behind her, clumped and thick, and her body drops instantly like dead weight.

The cell becomes quiet. All is quiet, minus my heavy breathing. He turns to face me, grabbing my hand and studying my eyes. "House. Now," is all he says, and then he drags me out behind him.

I look back at their bodies, how lifeless they are now. Sagging in chains, their arms still up. Bound. Same as I was when I first came here.

Blood. So much blood everywhere, and for some reason it doesn't bring me much satisfaction. Not as much as I'd hoped. No, if anything, it seems they got the easy way out.

Draco takes me out of the cells without a word. He bursts out of the door, still dragging me behind, and as soon as we do, I see all of his men's eyes stretch—not with horror, but with utter disbelief.

They didn't think I would do it.

Well, the proof is here. All over me.

"Clean it up. Make sure there is *nothing* left of them," Draco directs as he passes by with my hand still fastened in his.

They all nod, but as I pass by each set of staring eyes, one pair gives me pause. Patanza's.

Her eyes aren't full of disbelief—they're full of admiration. She's glad that I did it?

I smirk at her before finally pulling away and catching up to Draco's side.

He glares down at me, and there's a flicker in his eyes—one that he'd only give to me.

Pride.

Lust.

Satisfaction.

He bustles through the house, sweeping me up in his arms when we get to the kitchen, and then rushing toward the staircase. I can feel all eyes on us, but he only has his gaze set on one person.

Me.

We're in his bedroom in a matter of seconds. He doesn't waver, taking me to the bathroom and immediately starting the shower.

"Get undressed," he demands when he places me on my feet.

I step sideways as he moves backwards. I take a look into the mirror, spotting my reflection. I look horrific. My dress and even my skin are soaked with blood from the neck down, dark red splatters on my cheek and chin.

"No," I say, voice firm.

He cocks a brow, looking me over. "What?"

"No," I repeat, staring at my reflection again. "Take me," I breathe. "Like this."

His eyes flash, his tongue running over his lips when I face him. "You're filthy with his blood," he responds.

I smirk. "I know. That's the point."

His mouth clamps shut and honestly, I'm not surprised by the look I get. His eyes tell it all—a dead giveaway. Primal and fierce. I've just turned him on. He wants me. Bad. And he's going to take it.

He lifts his arm and his large hand comes around the back of my neck to pull me in, looking at me from head to toe.

"You enjoyed that," he murmurs. It's a statement, not a question.

"Maybe I'll enjoy this"—I tug his shirt open and the buttons scatter all over the marble floor—"a whole lot more." I grin and that grin alone is his undoing.

Gripping my hips, he picks me up and plants my ass on top of the counter. He steps between my thighs, and I make use of my hands, unbuckling his belt, unbuttoning his pants, and shoving them down. When they're gone, I feel the bottom of my heels digging into the backs of his thighs.

He hisses from the pain, frowning at me, but he doesn't let up. He grips my hair and tugs back, angling my mouth so his can hover above. His eyes roam my face. My lips. My bloodstained cleavage.

And then he claims me, mouth dropping down on mine, tongue slipping through my parted lips. I clutch him tight as he uses both hands to rip the dress down, breaking the zipper and exposing my breasts.

"Fuck, you look so good right now," he growls when he snatches his lips away and forces his forehead on mine. "My filthy, filthy niñita."

He clutches my hips, bringing my ass to the edge of the counter.

"I'm not wearing panties. Take me," I whisper. "Now. Please, Draco."

He doesn't hesitate. He spreads my legs wider apart by pushing his hips in closer, his thick tip meeting at my entrance and then pushing in, my ass locked in his hands.

Then he picks me up off the counter and bounces me up and down on his cock.

He's not gentle or remotely easy on me.

He bounces me up and down hard enough so that I can feel every single inch of him as I descend, and the aching absence of him when I rise back up again.

His eyes are like molten amber, focused on mine. My arms are wrapped around his neck, my teeth caging my bottom lip.

There are no words for this moment.

None at all.

Really, what can I say?

This isn't an ordinary fuck. This is a *victory* fuck.

They're gone. I'm still here. He saw what I did. He knew I had it in me. He's been waiting for me to unleash it ever since the day he met me. How twisted, sick, and dirty that is of him.

He fills me up with his cock, squeezing my ass in his hands.

"You feel good about yourself right now, don't you?" he asks, voice feral. "You are *la patrona*. Look how fucking good you look, bouncing up and down on my cock. How fucking sexy you are with me deep inside you." He rushes toward the nearest wall, and when my back slams into it, he sinks deeper. Deeper. Fully inside me now. "I want you to come all over my cock," he demands. "Show me you fucking loved that shit. I know you did, because I fucking loved it too. *Mi reina*," he rasps. "So sexy. So *fucking* perfect." He rams in again, still thrusting, still going.

I clasp his face and notice there's blood on his chest now too. Seeing it makes me reel him in until our bodies are glued. "Take me to the shower," I moan.

He does just so, carrying me to the shower with his full, thick length still inside me, forcing my back to the shower wall with the glass door wide open for anyone to see if they dared walk in. He delivers a harder plunge, breaths growing shaky.

My moans can't be held in anymore. I'm on the brink. The blood is washed away by the steady stream of water and seeping down the drain. We're soaking wet, still grinding. Still going so fucking hard.

He doesn't let up as he drills me like this, holding on tight, sucking on my skin so hard I'm sure it will leave a mark. He brings his mouth up and sinks his teeth into my bottom lip, grazing it, owning it.

"Ah, Draco," I whisper as water collects on our lips. It feels good. Too good.

"You are fucking perfect," he mutters, and the pull of his teeth, his fullness inside me, and his deep, orgasmic voice are enough to make me shatter.

He tenses as I cry out, holding onto him tighter, fingernails sinking into his shoulders, and then I feel him go still, but his cock is throbbing with release—a release I've never felt before.

"Shit, Gianna," he curses. "Why do you have to be so fucking good?"

I rest the back of my head on the shower wall, eyes shut as he finishes off. The hot water coats my eyelashes and my face, but all I see behind my eyelids is red.

Red. Everywhere.

CHAPTER NINE

MERCY

I *t's midnight.*

He fell asleep over an hour ago and I intentionally waited.

That was a nice fuck. A great one. I felt on top of the world while on top of him, but it's still *because* of him that I'm here.

What I did in the shed has made me feel bolder. Fearless. It's because of him that any of this has happened. Now he needs to pay for it. While his guard is down. While he's resting. While he least expects it.

I climb out of bed and examine the weapon wall. There's a pocketknife that I eyed before. It has a black handle with red script. The initials *DM* are on it. Draco Molina.

I take it down carefully, making sure not to make a sound. He's resting on his back, eyes sealed, breathing evenly enough to let me know he's sound asleep. I narrow my gaze at him as I climb back in the bed, the knife gripped in hand. I sling it open to check the blade. Of course it's sharp. All of his knives are.

I watch him.

Study him.

How he can be so peaceful around me astounds me. Perhaps he thinks he's off the hook. Or maybe he really doesn't care whether he lives or dies.

The blade is still out. I hover beside him, bringing the edge close to his throat. All it would take is one slice. One single movement, forward and backwards, just to end him, to leave him bleeding out all over this bed.

I've thought about it. As soon it's done, I'd pack a few things and walk out, making sure to lock the door behind me. I'd leave and let all the guards know that he said I could go for a walk on the beach. Alone.

I would run to the nearest location—but not before freeing Ronaldo first. I would be free—free of him. Free of the lies and the blood and the nightmare I endured.

Draco shifts a bit, putting my focus back on him.

"If you're going to kill me, then kill me. Otherwise get that fucking knife away from my goddamn throat."

My eyes stretch wide and I jerk away with a sharp gasp. I rest on my elbow as he turns his head to look at me. His face is unbothered—way too relaxed for what he knew I was about to do.

"What the fuck is your problem?" he grounds out.

"You owe me explanations," I hiss at him. "You haven't told me anything that you know about my dad or Toni, which probably means you're lying just to keep me in your clutches."

His lips barely press. He turns his head, staring up at the ceiling again.

"Lay down," he mumbles.

"I'm not sleepy."

"I don't care if you are or not. You just tried to kill me. You're lucky I haven't already killed you with that knife for pulling such a stupid move. Now lay down before I change my mind, Gianna." I scowl at him a few seconds longer. Finally, when he doesn't say anything else, I huff and slouch back, but I keep the knife, gripping the handle in hand.

He's quiet for a long time. Almost too long. To the point that I think he's fallen asleep again, or was he ever asleep to begin with?

He's a sneaky one. I'll give him that.

When he finally speaks up, I am shocked by what he says.

"I had Toni killed because I saw him murder my father."

CHAPTER TEN

I *gasp aloud, whipping* my head over to look at him. "What?" I ask, but my throat is so dry and thick that I can barely understand myself.

"I was seventeen," he continues, like I didn't just say anything. "We were in the United States, just me and my father. It happened two nights before we were supposed to fly home . . . here, to Mexico. He told me that night that he had one more important stop to make. It was late so I honestly didn't care. He had other meetings held at later times than this. Normally, I would have joined him, but this time I sat it out and waited in the car for him because I was tired.

"He pulled up to some old restaurant in the heart of New Jersey. It wasn't too far from our hotel. I could tell it was family owned—probably by Toni's sorry ass or someone he knew that would never snitch on him." I hear the anger in his voice when he says Toni's name.

"My father told me he would be back in no time. Before he got out, he told me that I'd been good and that he could tell I was learning a lot. I *was* learning a lot about the business aspect of it. He told me he was proud of me—glad that I was taking this seriously. He finally went into the restaurant and I turned up the music to try and wake myself up. It didn't work, so after ten minutes passed, I got out of the car to walk around. It was starting to drizzle, but I didn't mind it. I needed something to happen to keep me awake. My father was relying on me for a lot during that trip, and I couldn't let him down by falling asleep. I didn't want to disappoint him.

"I paced the sidewalk, but more and more time passed and I became impatient. So I got nosy and walked over to the window to take a look inside." He swallows painfully, as if he has a rock lodged in his throat. "I saw my father sitting down at a single table with his hands in his pockets, his gun on the table, and a smirk on his lips. At the counter was some other man I had never seen before. He looked like an amateur, without a doubt, and couldn't have been much older than me. My dad was talking to him—I don't know what he was telling him—but with each sentence I could see the other man's shoulders hiking up and getting tense. He was getting angrier and angrier by the second, like my father was rubbing something in his face that he didn't want to hear. The man spun around and I could finally see his face. I could see all of him from that dim light. I will never forget his face or what he was wearing—a black leather jacket, a white T-shirt, and black jeans. I will never forget the crazy look in his eyes. That smug look he wore, as he stepped closer and then, out of nowhere, yanked out his gun and stormed to my father. My father wasn't quick enough to grab his, and I assumed he either underestimated this man or he didn't think he had a gun on him to shoot with. My father always told me to be smart and to think ahead, but in that moment, he wasn't thinking. He was too slow. And because of it, he was shot right through the forehead."

Draco flinches, and I realize his eyes are squeezed tight, as if he's reliving the nightmare all over again.

"He shot him through the skull. Twice. There was a silencer on the gun so it couldn't be heard but it fuck sure could be felt. Each bullet through his head was one through my heart. I panicked. I was young so the first thing that came to mind was to run. So I ran. I ran for my life. I ran away from my father instead of going in and helping him. The wind burned my cheeks and the rain was coming down harder on me, but I didn't care. By the time I got to the pay phone I could hardly breathe. I had two options: call the cops, or call the only other number I knew by heart while I was there. I went with my gut. I called the other number."

His nostrils flare, and he clenches his fists together. It's quiet again, and I want to speak, but what the hell do I say?

Toni did this to him? But why would he? He had to have had a reason. Maybe Draco's father was after him, and he got to him first . . .

"Lion came in twenty minutes, picked me up, and then stopped by the place my father was killed. He went inside to check on things but came right back out. Toni wasn't there. The place was empty, minus my father's dead body. When we heard police sirens, we knew it was time to go. We left, and I started shouting at Lion to do something—to help him—but he simply ignored me. He didn't speak much other than to say calm down or to tell me to relax. We pulled up to some house that wasn't their real one and he helped me get out of the car. I think they were on anniversary or on a date. I didn't know, but Mrs. Nicotera was waiting at the door and he told her to get me washed up and in bed. I couldn't sleep and I knew Lion knew that because he came up to the room after I took a shower and talked to me. I hated what he had to say. I thought he was going to tell me that he was going to find the man. Or maybe he would help me find him. I had already been ranting about how I would hunt that man down and kill him myself, but Lion was too patient. He just nodded his head and kept his lips sealed.

"He told me, 'Draco, there are things you should and shouldn't see. And what you saw tonight, you should not have seen. I know you're angry, but Carlos is gone. Okay? And he's not coming back, kid.' I couldn't handle his words so I did the only thing I could.

"It finally hit me and I broke down. I let it all out that night, but the following morning I completely shut down. I didn't eat. I didn't speak. Lion kept trying to get me to interact, but I wouldn't. He kept asking me if I saw the man that did it, or could give a description of him, but I wouldn't."

"Why?" I whisper. "Daddy could have helped you."

"Because the next morning I found out the man that killed my father worked with Lion too. It's obviously how they met. Through Lion. There was a picture of them all on his wall in the den. I took the picture. Did my research. I wanted to handle it myself."

"So what are you saying? That you blame Daddy?" I tense up and grip the knife again.

"No, I don't blame him. I never would."

I ease up a bit.

"But I couldn't tell Lion, because I knew if I did, he would have handled it himself, in his own way. So I kept quiet for a very long time about it. I'm certain Lion figured out later that it was Trigger Toni. He kept sending people over to watch me, way before Henry Ricci showed up. The others were smart enough to run. Henry was dumb enough to get too close and get caught. Lion even reached out to me and told me that I could no longer have you because he couldn't tolerate my behavior. He said I was becoming too unstable."

"What?" I gasp.

"Yeah. Your father told me when I was sixteen that you were promised to me. When I came to the U.S. for the so-called "training" with my father and him, he was preparing me for you. I thought you would always be mine, but then I turned twenty-one and finally got some wits. I think he only said the part about me being unstable to protect that motherfucker Toni. Your father was torn because once a promise is made, it can't be broken. If you were promised to me, then it's simple. You are mine, whether you like it or not.

"So here you were, in love with my father's murderer, and he knew it, but he never told me because he wanted to protect you. He knew I knew, though. But what kind of father would he have been to forbid you from falling in love? He knew you would have hated him if he sent you to me, or if anything happened to Toni on his watch, so he let you stay with him, but he failed to realize that you were only making a fucking fool out of yourself and he was going to regret it." He shakes his head. "If only your father had listened to me, he would still be alive today."

I sit up rapidly, glaring hard at him. "What is that supposed to mean? That *you* are the one who killed my father?"

Draco simply shakes his head. "No, Gianna. I had too much respect for Lion to kill him. Despite him breaking his promises, I could never forget that night he took me in and even made sure I got home safely—or even the times before, when he helped my family when we had absolutely nothing. We owed him more than we gave." He swallows thickly. "Lion loved you more than words could explain. He wanted you happy, and he saw you were happy with that motherfucker. So he told me to lay off, but I kept telling him to watch out for Toni. Finally he'd had enough of me making threats at Trigger Toni, so he had some men sabotage my ability to get into the U.S. for two years, around the time you were planning your wedding—the wedding I didn't know you were a part of. We knew the same people, had the same connections, but they respected him much more than they did me. He was older. Smarter. He had more leverage. It pissed me off, but it didn't change anything. Toni traveled a lot. I knew I would get him one day. And I did." He pauses, pushing up on one elbow to face me.

"When I heard the news about Lion being murdered in his own bar, I instantly knew who it was. Without a doubt, I knew. But I didn't know *why* it was done until afterwards. I had no clue why Lion was making my life a living hell about it. I had no clue why he was cutting me off at the knees and telling me to leave Trigger Toni alone. I didn't get it, but when I saw it was *you* in the cells—when I saw that you were the Ricci wife . . . well, it all made sense. He wanted me to stay away because he didn't want you to get hurt. Lion didn't keep me in the loop about Toni or you. I knew nothing about the wedding back then or even the relationship. After he told me you were no longer promised to me, he never spoke of you again." He scoffs. "Big mistake on his part. It would have spared you the mess and me the drama."

I blink rapidly, batting the tears away.

"Did . . . Toni kill Daddy?" I ask feebly and Draco's eyes grow wide. He says nothing but his silence shouts it all.

"Why didn't you just tell me that from the beginning?" I demand.

"Because you didn't trust me, and you wouldn't have believed me, and I didn't trust you, which is why I did what I did to you. The punishments and the cruel things, it was to get you to forget about him. To make you see that by loving someone like him, you get treated like shit. To forget him, means you get treated like royalty."

"I would have stopped loving him the very day you told me he killed my father, and you know it!" I hop out of bed, glaring at him. "Why? Why would he kill Daddy? Toni loved him! I know he did!"

"That's what he wanted you to believe, Gianna."

"No—he did! He said my dad was like a father to him!"

Draco sighs and looks away. "He was a liar. He was psychotic. He would say and do anything just to make you feel safe. It was a part of his plan. Take down Lion, marry his daughter, become the man in charge with a woman at his side that carries the Nicotera name—to gain more respect. He may have been crazy, but he was no fool. He had to win your heart in order to get what he wanted, and he had to worm his way in with Lion. All he wanted was power. Lion's power. Way too many people respected Lion. He wanted that. He *envied* it. He figured that by being close and marrying you, it would give him the throne. It almost did, but I ended that before it could even begin."

My bottom lip trembles. Draco pushes out of bed and walks around to grip my shoulders.

"I told you, you weren't ready to hear it, niñita."

He brings me back to the bed to lie down. I'm stiff as I climb under the sheets, but I do so, all with the knife in hand.

Draco returns to his side and rests his hands behind his head.

"How do I know you're telling the truth?" I ask after a brief silence.

He doesn't respond right away.

"Just let it sink in, Gianna. Let it marinate. Try and remember the stuff he used to tell you. His goals and dreams. Once you think about it, you'll know deep down it was him."

Draco shuts his eyes. We're both so quiet. There's not much more he can say. Several minutes pass and his breathing evens out. He's resting, but how can he after telling me this?

How does he expect me to fall asleep now? I stare up and blink my tears away. My throat is thick and my body is heavy. The funny thing is, I could assume Draco is lying and believe what I want, but he fell asleep knowing I still have this knife in my hands. He knows I could slice his throat evenly as he sleeps, but that I won't. I can't.

He's given me control. He's putting his life in my hands. The man that kills your father wouldn't give you this much power. He wouldn't let it rest in your dangerous, unhinged hands.

I could blame him, but deep down, I know I can't. Draco isn't the one who killed Daddy. I have to face facts.

Toni wasn't a good man. He was horrible sometimes, but I loved him despite it all. By loving someone like Toni—a man with so many secrets—I may as well have been the one who killed my father.

The knife rolls out of my hand and hits the floor. The pain hits me hard. I cry until I can't anymore, and I don't know when I fall asleep.

But when I wake up, my head is on Draco's chest, and I can hear his heartbeat. His arms are wrapped tight around me, and his lips are in my hair, almost as if he'd been kissing the top of my head as I slept.

I don't move or flinch. I don't push him off or speak.

I just stay, because right now staying feels right.

CHAPTER ELEVEN

ACCEPTANCE

We're quiet when we wake up, though I still lie in his arms. I don't say a word. I really don't have much to say. Well, actually I take that back. I have *a lot* I wish to discuss, but now isn't the time.

He explained mostly everything, as promised. If it isn't the truth, he worked damn hard on that story. I don't see why he would lie. What's the point in keeping me? He can't want me that badly.

Still, I'll have to ask for proof—the truth somehow. I want to believe he was close to Daddy . . . to Mom. But I still have to remember that he is dangerous and ruthless and cruel. He can and will lie to get what he wants, and it's clear he's always wanted me.

He is still Draco Molina, the most wanted, most vicious man on earth. I must never, ever forget that.

"Maybe we can something a little different this morning?" I suggest when Draco sits up on the edge of the bed. The sun is bold and bright today, heat blazing through the window and on my skin.

"Like what?" he asks.

"Like hang out at the pool, drink mimosas. I'd actually like to start treating this place like more of a vacation if I'm going to stay here, and not some prison."

He glances over his shoulder. "Breakfast is important to me. We can do the pool afterwards." He pushes off the bed and enters the bathroom with a massive bulge in his briefs.

I climb out of the bed as well, tiptoeing to the bathroom. Lingering by the door, I think of where to start, like whether I should bring him back to bed and ride him until he says yes to the pool idea, or whether I should actually be decent and ask why he doesn't like to skip breakfast.

To be polite, I go with the latter. I can convince him later.

"Why don't you like missing breakfast anyway? I still don't understand why it's such a big deal to you," I call when I hear the trickle end. The toilet flushes and he lets out a deep, slightly agitated sigh.

"Does it matter?" He comes my way, shoulders broad, eyes surprisingly mellow.

"Yes, it does. I want to know."

He maneuvers past me, walking toward the window to open the sheer curtains. "Personal," is all he says.

"Draco. You told me no more secrets."

"It's not a secret," he says, tone clipped. "Many know the reason why. I just don't wish to share it right now."

He keeps his back to me but I walk forward, grabbing his wrist to spin him around. He huffs when he's facing me, glaring hard like he'll cut my hand off for touching him.

I don't care. He doesn't scare me. He can't because I know now that he won't harm me. After knowing the truth—about Toni, his father, and mine—he won't do a thing to jeopardize this again.

"Tell me," I insist, bringing my hand up to stroke his chiseled jaw. "I am *tu reina*, after all." *Your queen.*

I'm surprised to see him smile at that. Just barely. I grin, but it fades when he speaks. "The story will make me seem weak."

I scoff. "I think I, of all people, know you are far from weak."

He inhales and then releases a drawn-out breath, grabbing my hand and bringing me toward the door. We're both still half-naked. All I have on is a T-shirt. All he has on are his briefs. He doesn't seem to give a single damn.

He pulls the door open and walks down the hallway, toward a room that I don't think I've even bothered to go into before. It's right beside the doors that lead to the terrace. Another set of double doors. A red curtain hangs over the windows from the inside so no one can see what the room has inside.

He looks me over once before reaching above the doorframe and pulling down a key. When it's unlocked, he grips one of the door handles and steps right in.

I expect to see something dangerous in here. Something bad, like a vat of acid with body parts in it, more weapons, or even a collection of skulls.

I'm wrong.

It's a normal room, similar to his galería, only smaller, and no canvases to paint on, but there are paintings hanging on the wall. All of them look the same.

Dark. Red. Horrifying.

There are some of men that look like Draco, only older, with colder, dead eyes. Actually, now that I notice, they are all of the same man. He's wearing different clothing in each one. Looking in different directions. Some with a mustache. Some without.

"This is where I keep my . . . *darker* works of art," he announces, voice heavy and deep.

I step past him, scanning each one thoroughly. The dark paintings with the red obviously prove to be blood by the way it's splattered and aggressively enhanced.

But the man—the same man? I just don't get that one . . . that is until I come across one painting that has the man, but his face is demolished. There are red slashes all over his face, red dripping from his empty eye sockets. His mouth is hanging open in disbelief, as if he'd just seen a monster before losing those eyes.

"Who is he?" I whisper without looking back. I can't pull my gaze away. It's such a terrifying portrait. Almost too real. Definitely gruesome enough to cause nightmares.

"Uncle."

"Thiago's dad?" I inquire.

I look back, and he bobs his head slowly. "You pick up on things well."

"Why does he look like this here?" I point at the portrait. "All cut and mutilated?"

"Because the way he looks there is exactly how he looked the last day I laid eyes on him."

My eyebrows bunch together as I finally face him, begging for details without words.

He swallows thickly. "When my father died and I was sent back here, to Mexico, my mother let my uncle, Manuel, stay here with us. I was only seventeen, didn't know much at first—well, not as much as I'd wanted to—but I knew it would come. I was still naïve to it all, thinking things would get better for Mamá and me. They didn't. They only seemed to get worse while he stayed here to 'care' and 'provide' for us."

"How?" I ask.

"Because he was an abusive, dirty, ignorant *hijo de puta* that didn't deserve to live. While he was here, I was young. I was weaker, which made him assume that I was also dumber. I was still hurting from the loss of my father, so I was quiet, and he thought the quiet would be my ruin. Mother sympathized, but she couldn't get through to me back then, but only because I wouldn't let her. I figured she couldn't understand because she wasn't there. I witnessed that murder first hand. I was there, unable to do anything but watch and run." He pushes a rough hand through his messy hair, glaring at the painting of his uncle Manuel now. "He stayed with us for about a year. At first he was quiet. Calm. But I know now that he was only studying us. Our schedules. Calculating our moves. Thiago stayed here as well. His mother had recently passed, so he was quieter then, and slightly reserved. Still a shit talker, but he mostly kept quiet. He was close to me, though. That was back when he actually had some damn sense—when I could trust him to have my back.

"Anyway, around the fifth month or so of Manuel's stay, he started to show his true colors. I didn't grow up around that man. Hardly knew a thing about him. Mamá trusted him to handle what was left of my father's cartel. I know she only did it so we could continue to live in the lifestyle we had, but I really wish she wouldn't have. He only wanted to steal what my father built, take all the money, and leave us with nothing. I noticed it beforehand, his dirty ways, so I scheduled meetings with the men we had left. Some were still loyal to the Molina family, and still getting paid, thanks to my father's accountant, and Lion, too. I remembered how things were run, what he made them do on each day of the week, the runs and pick-ups. I told them moving the drugs wasn't going to stop just because my father was gone, and neither was the money. We needed it.

"Manuel heard what I was doing behind his back and tried to become the alpha of *our* home. He started making rules for us to follow like this was *his* house. Like he had created this—built all of this," he growls, holding his hands out and scanning the room.

"His first rule was for me to butt out of the cartel business. I refused. I still did my part. It was my job now—my role to carry on this family business. Lion told me not to give up or back down—not to let it tank, because he needed us to make things work for himself. I did it for him, because I promised and I owed him. The second rule was to show up for breakfast at the same time every morning. Seven exactly. Every single day. I did that, not because he wanted me to, but because I rather enjoyed having breakfast with my mother. I didn't want her feeling any lonelier than I knew she was. He expected me to slip up with that, but I woke up before the sun had even risen to take care of business, answer to the guards and the men and go to the docks sometimes. I never slipped up. I was punctual and still running the men my father left behind. He envied what I was capable of—hated that I was catching on so quickly at such a young age. He knew that one day we weren't going to need him anymore, and that the Molina cartel would still be ours.

"So one morning he decided to try to make an example out of me. He wanted to make a statement." His breathing grows heavier. Thicker. His jaw ticking. "He had all of the guards in the dining room, posted, waiting, as we ate breakfast. I didn't know what they were doing. At the time, I didn't care. It was my birthday. I had just turned eighteen. August 22nd. I thought they were there to wish me well without actually speaking on it. To show respect." He shrugs. "I remember it being me, Mamá, Thiago, and Manuel at the table. Mamá had the chef make my favorite pecan pancakes with hot syrup. It was supposed to be a good day.

"We ate some. There was a lot of casual talk between me, Mamá, and Thiago. Manuel was quiet, and intentionally being ignored. I'm assuming he became fed up, because after a while he finally cut in, started with some bullshit talk about how he was running things now, and that he didn't need me to do it. I fired back. I told him I knew what I was doing, and it's what my Pa would have wanted. He got pissed then.

"Thiago was worried, cowering. He never spoke back to Manuel and Mamá never spoke up. She knew not to butt in unless necessary, but I wasn't like them. I was livid. How dare he tell me what the fuck to do on *my* birthday? How dare he try and belittle me? How dare he treat me like some worthless child? I remember cursing and cursing at him, spewing my hatred. The vile words didn't fail me. I meant them all. My rebellious tongue made him want to hurt me. And he did. He hurt me by harming the only family I really had left.

"He pulled out a gun, put it to my head, told the butlers to bring out more food, and told me that I had to finish it all. Every last bite. There were loads of pecan pancakes, eggs, bacon, and sausage. It was way too much to eat for just one person, especially me. But the plates kept coming out. The supply seemed endless. I refused at first, told him to kiss my ass and to go fuck his mother. I shouldn't have said that, because he turned right around and said, 'How about I fuck *yours* instead?'"

I gasp, eyes stretching wide. Draco isn't looking at me, but at the painting, eyes hard, fists clenched, seething. "Oh no," I breathe.

"He had paid one of the guards extra to hold their gun to the back of my head while he yanked my mother out of her seat and forced her over the table, right in front of all of us. He ripped her skirt from the back, exposing her while unbuckling his belt. He told me if I tried to move or do anything to stop him, he would make her suck his cock, too. He told me to eat it all, and that he wouldn't stop fucking her until I finished.

"So, with tears in my eyes, I continued eating. All while he continued to fuck my mother—his own goddamn *sister*," he spits, and he's fuming now. Fists clenching and unclenching, glaring hard at the mutilated portrait he'd created.

Oh, my God. I had no words. None. His own sister? To teach a lesson? To demonstrate power and control? How fucking demented.

"I scarfed it all down for Mamá, avoiding her eyes the whole time, and with a gun pointed at the back of my skull. Thiago ate some of it with me to help. Manuel didn't seem to care that he did. He was too busy enjoying the fact that he was fucking his own damn relative," he ground through clenched teeth. "Mamá wouldn't stop crying, and I could tell she wanted to turn and destroy him, but I could also tell she was taking it and not fighting back for my sake. She always endured the worst for me, but I think this was the worst she'd gotten because of my mouth. I was impulsive and could never shut up, and she always paid the price for it.

"I was getting fuller and fuller by the second. I threw up once, right in my own lap, but I started right back up and kept eating, stuffing myself until every plate was clean. And when I was done, he finally stopped, walked over to me, and came on me. He *came* . . . on me. Like I was his whore. Some fell on my cheek, my chest, and my pants. I'll never forget what he said to me. He said, *'Remember that the next time you try to defy me. I'll fuck your mother right in front of you and use the cum her pussy milked out of me just to squirt it all in your ugly fucking face.'*"

The room is dead silent. I can hear my ears ringing from it—a shrill ring of both terror and truth that nearly deafens me.

Draco finally releases his clenched fists and walks to the painting, nostrils flaring, scowling.

"I think he drew out a side of me that I never wanted to conjure up. A side of me that I always knew was there, but didn't think I'd have to use until I was a little older. I'd seen it before, around my father, around Lion, even from some of the guards. It's a darkness that sweeps over, a shadow that you can't get rid of. It claims your soul for life. I wasn't blind to that sort of darkness, but I never thought I would become the man I did. Something inside me broke that day. It snapped—" he snaps his fingers"—just like that. No warning. No signal. Something just went off inside me, like my internal clock on patience and values had finally run out.

"That very same night, I shot the guard he paid to put the gun to my head, for betraying me. I shot him when he took a smoke break out by the beach, with the first pistol my father ever gave to me. I wanted to wait to kill him. I could come back for him. He was alone, so I hid him by that brown shed, left him injured, making him think he'd die slowly by bleeding out. And afterwards, I went up to Manuel's room—this very room right here—and stabbed him in his sleep. Right in the stomach. He thought I was weak, that I was too afraid of repercussions to retaliate. He was a *fucking idiot* to ever let his guard down while I was still around. He didn't scare me. He only fueled the rage I had trapped inside me, giving me more than enough reason to unleash my aggressions." His jaw pulses, face as hard as stone.

"I stabbed him one good time, just so he could bleed out and suffer, but still feel everything else I did to him. I stuffed his mouth with his own dirty, cum-stained underwear. I cuffed him to the bed with the chains I grabbed from the brown shed. I wanted him to see my face as I tortured him—as I sliced his face open, gash by slow gash. I wanted him to feel it when I gouged out his eyeballs and then slit his throat, bit by bit, relishing his agony. I wanted to watch him *bleed* and *suffer*. I wanted him to know that he was paying the price for every moment I sat at that table for breakfast. It wasn't a quick death. Trust me on that. It was slow and painful. I'm certain he felt *everything*, and I took immense satisfaction in that."

That sounds familiar. Too familiar. It's the same thing I wanted for Bain. Slow and painful. Not the easy way out.

"He was my first kill, and I don't regret a damn thing about it," he goes on. "In fact, I recall enjoying it rather immensely. I sometimes wish I could do it over and over again, the same way he plunged in and out of my mother, over and over again, knowing he was hurting her. Knowing he had shamed her and abused her trust and taken advantage of her when she was so vulnerable." He turns to look at me. "So, when he was gone, I really became the king. I made new rules to abide by. I fired the guards I didn't trust, and then had someone go out to exterminate them so they couldn't say a word about who was in charge and running Mexico now. Me. *El Jefe.*

"Everyone under my roof, besides the guard, was to show up for breakfast on time, but they eat their fill, however much they wanted, and they enjoy it. Being late, to me, is unacceptable, because I was always on time, even for one of the worst days of my life."

He finally looks at me. "I may have been harsh to you at first about breakfast, but I swore to myself after that day that I would never let *anyone* disrespect me in my own home like that again. You follow my rules, and life is easy. Go against them, and it's you that makes it hard for yourself."

"Is that why Thiago hates you?" I ask.

"I'd say he hardly hates me," he chuckles. "He was more than relieved to see his father carried out and disposed of. His father was abusive and ignorant. He didn't give a damn about his son. My mother was relieved as well, though she'd never admit to something like that. She was glad, and, I think, even slightly proud of me. Thiago is just confused now. He thinks he's smarter than I am. He has his talents, but running a cartel on his own is not one of them. I'm certain he'll come around and know where he really belongs. He knows what happens to those who betray me."

"Wow, Draco I—I'm sorry. I didn't know—"

"There's not much you can say about it, Gianna. Don't try and speak on it. You wanted to know the truth and you got it, so please, let's eat breakfast, and then we can discuss swimming. I will give you whatever you want, just as long as you can follow the rules I already have set." He steps toward me, tilting my chin. "Okay?"

"Okay," I whisper.

He plants a small kiss on my lips and then leads the way out of the room with my hand in his. But before he shuts the door and locks it, I catch sight of another painting that I missed, one that is above the bookcase in the far corner.

On it is a Caucasian man with a gun pointed at a Hispanic man sitting in a chair. They're in a public place. A restaurant with a bar.

I realize right away who the people are.

It's Toni, killing Draco's father.

An image burned into Draco's memory bank, one that will never, ever go away.

CHAPTER TWELVE

As usual, we ate a large breakfast in the dining room. Mrs. Molina was there, and she seemed more upbeat than usual. I couldn't figure out why, until I saw Thiago walking around the mansion.

He wasn't cuffed or being dragged around. He was roaming at his own free will, with two guards trailing him.

Seeing him was strange. His face was bruised, lip busted, and nose broken, most likely from Draco's wrath. I felt him look into the dining room as we ate. He stared right at Draco for a split second, and Draco glared right back. Of course Thiago pulled his gaze away first.

Their silent battle was interesting.

"I have some business to handle," Draco announces when we're back in his bedroom. "I'm not sure how long I'll be."

"Okay." I sighed, sitting on the bottom edge of the bed. "I'm sure I can find something to do to occupy myself."

"What do you like to do?" he asks, like he's really curious. "Your hobbies?"

"I used to write a lot. Most times just in my journal. I made up my own romance stories here and there. They were all so sappy and cheesy." I shrug, taking off my earrings. "I kind of miss it—writing, I mean."

"There is a library downstairs, across from my galería. There are a lot of books in there, though most of them are in Spanish. My mother loves to read. She used to spend all her time there. She hasn't been in there in a while, and I'm sure she wouldn't mind you using it. There's paper, pens—whatever you might need to write."

"What about a laptop or a computer? I typed a lot, too. I liked seeing the words on screen and then printing it off. Made it feel kind of real." I flash a small smile.

His jaw slightly ticks. "If I give you a laptop, it won't have any sort of connection to the internet." His voice is gruff and firm. "Anyone could hack the system and find out where I am. I've been in and out of this home for years with no problems. Never been caught here because I keep most technology at bay. I don't trust computers."

"I don't need the internet to write," I laugh, even more so because I'm sure that's not the only reason why he doesn't want me to have a connection to the Internet. It would be way too easy for me to just log into some form of social media and post where I am—who I am. To snap photos to show proof and have someone come for me.

I could, but I'm not sure I see the point anymore.

I can't face Toni's family or his men after knowing what he did to my father—to Draco's father. I can't look into his mother's eyes knowing she raised a monster that was much worse than I had ever imagined—than she'd ever imagined.

I would blame her for something she didn't even know about. I would feel like a fool. All of us would. Perhaps she's better off not knowing what he really was.

I should consider myself lucky that Draco took him out, but a part of me still doesn't believe Toni could do that. Maybe it's just my heart speaking, still remembering the times when we were happy. Trying to ignore the times when I really thought I hated him.

Draco presses his lips, observing me when the silence surrounds us. He's been doing a lot of that lately—well, ever since the brown shed. "I will have Patanza bring you something." He finally pulls his gaze away, taking down his pocketknife and the brass knuckles from the weapon wall.

"What are you going to do with that?" I nod at the weapons he has in hand.

Glancing sideways at me, he slides the knife in his front pocket and the brass knuckles in the shirt pocket. "You would like to know that, wouldn't you?"

I quirk a brow. "Just curious."

"Going to do a few things today. Handle business. These aren't the only weapons I'll be bringing. The rest are in the SUV."

"The rest? How many?" I inquire.

"I've lost count," he chuckles.

I laugh a little. "I remember Daddy promising to get me my own purse gun and one for the glove compartment of my car. Granted, I hardly ever drove my car because Daddy wanted me to ride with his driver—he had bulletproof windows—but whenever I did, I remember him having someone tail me. He always had someone watching me, and they always had way too many guns lying around."

"And did he ever get you one?"

"No. Mom told him she'd chop his hand off if he dared."

We both laugh out loud. It's harmonious, his boisterous and genuine. Laughing this way with him feels strange. I haven't laughed like this in a while. It feels good and wrong.

"She only wanted to protect me." I stand from the bed and walk toward him, adjusting his collar. My eyes then shift up to his. "I would feel safer here if I had one."

"Would you?"

"Yes."

"Why? So that one day, when you're angry enough, you can shoot me through the back of *mi cabeza*?" *My head.*

"Draco," I exhale. "I think if I wanted to kill you while you slept, I would have done it already." I pull away from him. "You have guys like your cousin, Thiago, walking around and I don't even want to know why, but I'm assuming it's because of something your mother has said." He shifts uncomfortably, pulling his gaze away. "I don't trust him. And some of the guards—I don't know. I know you rely on them, but I can't trust them all either. The only one who treats me like a person is Patanza and even she can't fully be trusted, because she feels indebted to you."

"So you're saying you don't feel safe enough with me in charge?" he questions.

"No—it's not that," I respond quickly.

He raises a stern, serious brow, squaring his shoulders. "Then what is it?"

I open my mouth, but clamp it shut right away. I think of those days here—before he finally pulled his shit together and decided to treat me like a human. I was tossed around. Starved. Abused. Mistreated. He was supposed to be here that day when it all happened in the cellar, but he wasn't.

"It's nothing," I murmur. "Just forget I brought it up."

His eyebrows draw together, shoulders still tense, as he steps toward me. I sit back down on the edge of the bed, and he comes closer, closer, until his thigh is pressed on my knee. Bringing a hand down, he tilts my chin and looks me straight in the eyes. His whiskey irises don't sparkle or shimmer. They are serious. Hard and dark again.

"You have to learn to trust me, Gianna," he murmurs. "Trusting me is all you have. I won't let that happen to you again."

I cringe inside, pulling my gaze away.

He takes note of my silence, probably knowing I won't speak on it anymore. "If getting you a gun will make you feel better, we will get you one. I'll even let you pick it out yourself." I pull my eyes up, and his have softened a touch.

"Seriously?"

"As long as you promise to never pull it on me, then it's my word. When I'm back, we'll discuss it."

I feel my mouth twitch. I want to smile, but something is preventing it. Perhaps it's because making that promise is one that I'm not sure I can keep. If something happens to me again because of him, I don't know if I'll be able to handle it—living with this man. I'd blame him all over again.

I would try to run, he would try to stop me, and I know the only way I would be able to get through him is over his dead body. He would have to die.

He catches me off guard, pulling me from my thoughts by placing a warm kiss on the apple of my cheek. "I have to go. Patanza will be guarding the upstairs area. If you decide you want to go to the library, just let her know. She will show you where it is."

I nod. "Okay."

He pulls his fingers away from my chin and steps back. "I mean what I say, niñita. No one but me will ever touch you again. You will get whatever you want as long as you respect me. Everything you desire can be yours, just as long as you are mine. Remember that, *mi reina*."

"Of course," I murmur. He walks to the door, glancing back once before finally disappearing. When it's shut behind him, I remain still, listening to his footsteps drift down the hallway. "How could I ever forget that?"

Draco returns when the sun is perched on the horizon.

The etching of my pen on the paper drowns out all sounds. It's the only thing I can focus on, until I hear a throat clear to my left. I glance sideways, stopping the flow of my words. The first few buttons near his collar are undone, his hair not as sleek as it was when he left. It's messy, like he's been running his fingers through it.

He looks aggravated. On edge.

I drop the pen, peering up at him as he leans against the frame of the library door. "I take it you like it in here," he says as I sit back in my seat. "Patanza says you've been in here all day."

"I have. It's peaceful." I point to the window to my left. It's arched at the top, a floor-to-ceiling window. The sunset is beautiful, its warm glow showering the oblong library. The books are all tucked away in alphabetical order. They are mostly romance novels and, like Draco said, all written in Spanish. No matter. I will still read them.

The wooden beams above give the library so much height and depth, matching the mahogany floorboards. A spiral staircase leads up to an open second floor, consisting of even more books, some of the shelves filled with antiques. A day bed with a brown headboard is set up in front of the window up there as well, decked with gold and white pillows. It looks comfortable enough to read and even sleep on, but I can tell most of this furniture hasn't been broken in.

Down here where I am, there is a large curved desk full of all the supplies I need, recliners, and a coffee station set up in the corner.

"How was it today?" I ask when he shifts on his feet. He's quiet. Somber.

He releases a heavy sigh. "Rough. Don't want to think about."

I pause, thinking of a proper response. "Do you need to talk about it?"

Walking closer, he plants his knuckles on the desk, still standing on the opposite side. His hair tumbles onto his forehead, curtaining his whiskey eyes. He focuses on me, lips mashing together.

"Draco?" I call when he pulls his hard gaze away and looks out the window.

"Tell me about your day," he commands with a gentle voice. "What are you writing about?" He drops his line of sight to my paper, but I sit forward, covering most of the words with my elbow. His mouth twitches when he meets my eyes again.

"I don't like to share what I'm working on so soon," I tell him. "It's still a work in progress."

"A love story?"

"Hmm . . . no. Not really."

"Figuring out ways to take me down?" When he says that, I can see the spark and challenge in his eyes, his mouth forming into a subtle smile.

I return a smirk. "If you don't trust me, why do you even let me sleep with you?" I ask, flipping the paper over and then folding my arms, leaning back in my seat.

"I never said I don't trust you." He pulls up, spine stacking.

"You act like you don't."

"I don't trust you *away* from me," he says, and he walks toward the door. "Which is why we'll be spending the rest of the night together in the pool, like I promised. Let's go back to the room and change clothes." He turns halfway, extending his arm, gesturing for me to join him.

"You're serious?" I smile a bit, standing from my chair and walking around it.

He bobs his head slightly when I take his hand. "I told the butlers to bring my favorite tequila out. I could use a few shots. Couldn't you?"

I grin. "I really could."

In less than fifteen minutes we've changed clothes and are heading to the pool.

"Why were you so upset when you got home?" I ask as Draco and I walk through the gates to get to the pool. He's not wearing a shirt or any shoes. He has on black swimming trunks, his gold crucifix necklace resting on the center of his toned chest.

"What makes you think I was upset?" he questions, placing his towel down on one of the chairs. I place mine on the lounge chair beside his.

"You were tense." I gather my hair up and tie it in a loose bun. "It's kind of easy to tell when you're pissed."

He looks at the pool water, taking a step forward. A butler comes out with a tray in hand and on top of it sits a bottle of Don Julio and two shot glasses with red jewels embedded in them. They look real, like rubies.

Draco bobs his head, gesturing for him to place it down on the table beside me. The butler does just so, taking off with a bob of his head. Several guards are outside the iron gate beyond the pool, their backs facing us.

Draco steps over, grabbing the bottle of tequila and the glasses and bringing them to the pool. He takes the steps down to get into the water, placing everything on the edge of the pool.

"Get in," he orders.

I step out of my flip-flops, moving forward and dipping my feet in the water. It's cold enough to make me shiver, but I jump in anyway, plunging beneath the water and swimming toward him.

When I rise, I'm only a step away from him. His chin is tilted, his warm eyes on me. Reaching over, he pours a shot into each glass then picks one up, handing it to me.

I take it with wet hands and he goes for his next.

"You like to show off," he murmurs.

I smile a little. "Only enough to grab your attention."

His eyes flash down, scanning my breasts in my white bikini top. He raises his glass in the air and I do the same. "To new beginnings," he says. With a bob of his head, he brings the rim to his lips and tosses it back without so much as a wince.

I down mine, getting a strong, fierce burn that immediately sweeps through my entire body. He pours me another and one for himself, taking it back again. I toss mine back and the burn floods my veins.

One more shot and he finally sets his glass and the bottle down.

I sigh. Tequila isn't really my thing—especially not without a chaser. What can I say? I'm a wimp, and I've never been big on drinking hard liquor.

Approaching me, he grabs my waist and picks me up. I lock my legs around his waist and wrap my arms around his neck, relaxing them on his shoulders. His mouth immediately crushes mine, his fingers running up my spine and up to the nape of my neck. He reaches for my hairband and tugs it, causing my wet hair to tumble down around my shoulders.

"This business isn't easy," he murmurs.

"How so?"

"I had to have one of my men kill someone today. Someone I thought I could trust to handle some of my cash."

"An accountant?" I tip my head back to look into his eyes.

He nods. "One of them."

"How many do you have?"

"Three."

"Why?"

"To make sure my numbers add up the same every time. Can't trust just one."

Makes sense.

"That man had a family. A daughter and a son. His wife does food-catering jobs, runs her own business. She lost a husband, and those kids lost a father, because he stole from me. If it had been less than five thousand, I would have let him off with a simple warning and slight punishment. But he took over fifty grand. His numbers weren't adding up. I got news that someone said he bought a new house. He made it so obvious that I almost felt stupid for having him ended. He probably assumed I wouldn't catch on. He was taking small chunks week by week."

I drop my gaze to his chest. "Why didn't you just lock him up or something, like you do everyone else?"

"Thought about it. I don't enjoy killing, but when it comes to my reputation, it happens. Just so everyone knows not to try to fuck me over. I don't take stealing my shit lightly—especially when it comes to my money. It's a privilege to even get the chance to work with me."

I sigh.

"I want to forget about it for now," he says, looking at my lips.

"How?"

"Distract me."

I smile and then pull away from him, my feet landing on the pool floor. Half-swimming, half-walking to the tequila, I pour another shot for us and hand him his glass.

When he takes it, I come closer, running my palm down his chest. I continue down, even when he tenses up, untying his trunks. My hand slips beneath his trunks and I cup his manhood in hand lightly, my lips landing on his jawline.

His breath streams out, tattered, hard.

"Distraction enough?" I ask, fondling, teasing.

"For now." He drinks his shot and picks up the bottle of tequila again. Man, he never quits. "How many men have you slept with, niñita?"

"How many men have *I* slept with?" I repeat, pulling my hand from his swelling cock with a light scoff. I toss my tequila back, letting it ride down my throat and glide through my veins. "I was only with Toni, before you. He took my virginity. He was my first at a lot of things."

I rest my elbows on the edge of the pool as he pours another shot for himself. I'm getting a bit of a buzz. I'm definitely tipsy. "So you've only been in bed with two men?"

"Well, if oral counts, two men *and* a woman." I don't know why I say that. I should feel embarrassed or hate the thought of when Francesca ate me out, but I don't, and when he realizes that I don't, he flashes a crooked smile.

He circles the rim of his glass, watching me with heated eyes. "You think I regret making her do that to you?"

I laugh, swimming backwards. "Not at all, actually."

"Good. Because I don't." He brings the glass up to his lips and chugs it down. After letting out a sharp gasp and putting the glass in its rightful place, he swims my way, collecting me in his arms and pinning his body to mine. "Making her do that showed me what you really are."

"And what am I?" I challenge, feeling the liquor settling in now, boosting my confidence.

His face comes closer, full lips hovering above mine. He wraps his large hands around my waist and hoists me up. I ease my legs around his torso, arms slinking over his broad, wet shoulders.

"You're a freak," he rasps on my mouth, warm breath trickling over my damp skin. "You've always wanted to try something with a woman. It was a fantasy, I could tell. That's why you didn't fight back."

"I didn't fight back because you threatened me," I laugh.

"No, niñita." His chuckle is deep, sensual. "If I'm recalling that day correctly, you spread those legs good and wide for her and you moaned even louder when I forced her deeper. You couldn't control yourself. And, fuck, seeing you like that made me so goddamn hard. Seeing how wet your pussy was—feeling it after she was finished . . . *shit*." He swallows hard, and I can feel him growing harder, his cock pressing on my leg. "I may have spoken, but I had no real words to say to you at the time. You're a naughty girl, but you play innocent. Every time we fuck, you reveal a glimpse of that naughty side. Every time my cock is buried deep inside you, I'm shedding a layer of that innocence away, exposing you for what you really are. A freak. And not just any freak. *My* freak."

My breath goes unkempt as I feel his fingers slowly rolling my bottoms down. His mouth is still hovering over mine, only a hairs breadth away. I want to move, thrust or grind, but I can't. I won't make the first move.

But I do want him to kiss me. I want him to take me—fuck me in this pool relentlessly. I don't care who hears or sees. I don't care as long as I get the pleasure I'm aching for.

I don't know why I want him so badly right now. It has to be the tequila. Only tequila gets me this way, desperate and hungry for more.

"Just say the words," he murmurs, still peeling my bottoms off. "All you have to do is say it, *mi reina*, and it's yours. Tell Jefe what you really want."

I know exactly what he wants me to say. He knows how badly I want it.

"Jefe," I pant, threading my fingers through the hair at the nape of his neck. "Fuck me. Please. Right here. *Por favor*, Jefe." *Please, Jefe.*

He lets out a low, quiet groan, my words his undoing. My bottoms are off in seconds, as well as his. We both release hard, heavy moans when our mouths finally connect, and when I feel his thickness thrust inside me, I pull my mouth away, gasping as my head falls back.

He grips the back of my neck with one hand, forcing me against the wall of the pool. His other hand is cupping my ass, his thrusts full and deep as he stares me right in the eyes—as he takes me like the boss he is.

The Jefe.

The one and only Jefe.

He doesn't pull his eyes away for a second. He holds me tight on my ass and neck, watching as I willingly welcome it all, sighing with pleasure.

Bring his face closer, his tongue pushes through my lips, claiming, owning. I swirl mine with his, gluing our bodies, holding onto him as I feel the heat between my legs, building up for one momentous explosion.

"You are *my* freak," he breathes into my mouth. "And it will be that way for a very, *very* long time, Gianna."

I nod as the water sloshes and he brings his hands down, bouncing me up and down on his thick, long cock. I hold on tight, my mouth landing on his neck, sucking, tasting hints of chlorine and warm skin.

I'm wrapped up so tight around him, feeling my clit on his pelvis, so close to climaxing. He squeezes my ass harder in his big hands, bringing me up and down. I spot people walking from a distance, the guards at the wall. I don't know if they're watching and, frankly, I don't give a shit. Neither does he.

All we care about is this.

The escape. The thrill.

Me owning him.

Him owning me.

My fingers slide through his damp hair, dragging down to his back, nails digging in. He lets out a small hiss, bringing me to the wall again, elbows planting outside my head. He's still thrusting, my head falling back over the edge of the pool.

I open my eyes, staring up at the sky. It's not completely dark. It's the perfect violet color. The sun is somewhere close, but I can't see it at this angle. And that's okay because stars begin to fill my vision, tunneling in.

I imagine a violin playing. I imagine piercing blue eyes staring into brown ones.

Toni and Draco. A demon versus the devil.

Fighting for me.

I imagine what *was* and what *is* and, carelessly, I explode.

I squeeze my eyes so tight, holding on to him again, grinding on his hardness—on him—and I don't let up, not even when I feel my body violently shaking.

Trembling.

My eyes feel damp, but I think it's the pool water.

But it's too hot to be pool water. *Too hot.*

My body feels just as heated.

Whimpers surround me. Darkness consumes me.

"Gianna," a deep voice calls. It echoes in my brain, through every hollow, empty space.

I'm still trembling, but is it from the aftermath, or something else?

I can't tell—that is until I hear water sloshing and realize Draco is carrying me out of the pool and my back has landed on a cushioned lounge chair. I look all around me, at the sky that's still a silky purple, to the chair beside me, and then in front of me, at Draco.

His face is hard, as usual, but his eyes hold a trace of gentleness. He looks me all over before inhaling, then exhaling. His fingers thread through his damp hair, body going tense.

"What were you thinking about when you came?" he asks, voice low.

"I came?" I whisper.

"Yes. I felt you. *Saw* you."

I pull my gaze away, looking out at the ocean through the thick, wrought iron gate. "I can't remember."

"Don't lie to me." He reaches forward, gripping my face in hand and forcing my eyes on his again. "Tell me."

My lips quiver, eyes sliding down to his chest. "It was . . . Toni."

He snatches his hand away and when I look up, he's glaring. Hard. "What about him?"

"Not the good part of him. The bad. I was thinking about him and you. Comparing. You're both . . . so *brutal.* So bad. And that's what I'm drawn to. Like a magnet, I'm drawn and I can't pull away, no matter how hard I try. It's so fucking hard to fight it." My head shakes swiftly. "There were many times when I saw

Toni's bad side, but I gave him the benefit of the doubt because that's how badly I wanted him. And you," I breathe, sitting forward. My head moves left to right as I become lost for words. "You are ten times worse than he was and yet . . . still . . . there is something about you I can't pull away from. Despite the bad and all I've been through here, something about you lures me in. Dominance, brutality— it's what I crave. It's something I've craved my entire life." My breath comes out shaky. "He killed both of our fathers, and if he was still here, and I knew that, I feel like I would still stay with him. I would have found a reason to forgive him, even the tiniest excuse, because I was that weak for him." I tilt my gaze. "Does that make me stupid? Being weak for men like that?"

"Gianna, I—" I can tell he is confused. And I don't blame him. Where is all of this coming from? What's happening to me? I'm confusing myself. I don't know who I am or what I'm doing anymore. Does he sense that? "No, it doesn't make you stupid," he finally responds. He hauls me over and plants me on his lap to face him. I wrap my legs around him and he grips the back of my head, bringing my forehead to his. "It makes you a Nicotera. Nicoteras are fearless and believe they can take on anything and anyone. They enjoy the challenge. *You* are fearless." He strokes his thumb over my cheek, and that's when I realize there are tears. Those were tears on my face while we were in the pool.

"You're crying out of anger. You hate that he did it, I know. You're trying to drown it out with the tequila, but it won't work. The truth will always be there. You wanted to see the good in him, but he was no good for you." I watch his eyes, how they soften for me when he speaks. "It had to happen that way. It is unfortunate, but I don't regret anything except the fact that I wasn't there to save your father myself. Had I known it was *you* he was marrying, I would have cut that shit off before you even fell for him."

"I thought it was going to be a perfect day. One I would never forget," I whisper, voice cracking.

"You will get plenty of perfect days with me, you understand?" He grips me tighter. "I will give you the world, Gianna, because you are mine, and you always have been. You just didn't know it yet."

I bob my head, silence consuming me for several seconds. "I'm sorry he did that to your dad."

"Don't stress about it."

"If I knew his plans I never would have agreed to marry him." Anger laces my voice now, just thinking of all the times he probably sat around, plotting ways to kill Daddy.

"I'm sure you wouldn't have. But it happened. It's done. All we have is us and *now*. There is a target on both of our backs, so we might as well fucking live, niñita, hmm?" His mouth touches my cheek, a soft, damp kiss as he tips my chin. "You hear me?"

I nod, locking eyes with him. "Yes, Draco. I hear you." I put on a subtle smile. "We live."

CHAPTER THIRTEEN

Whatever *this is* between Draco and me has been hard to deny. A part of me still doesn't trust him, yet another part of me—a dark, secret ounce of me—longs for every inch of him.

I want to avoid that part of me, sinking too deep and falling for him. It will be just like how I fell for Toni. A man I thought I knew, but hardly knew anything about at all.

There's a lot about Draco that I still don't know.

I want to question why Draco leaves during the middle of the day and returns a little more frustrated than when he left. When he's locked himself away in his galería, I want to know what he's painting. Is it another photo of blood? A massacre? None of his paintings are gentle on the eyes. All of them, I've noticed, are filled with colors of red, black, and other dark, ominous hues.

Four days have passed, and we've still continued to fuck and taunt and tease. He seems to enjoy that. And I know as long as I give myself to him, then I can get whatever I want. Just yesterday, he had Patanza deliver a typewriter to the library for me. To my surprise, it came in the color red. Daddy's favorite color. I can't help but wonder if he knew that small fact or if he got it in red by chance.

I started typing on it the same day it was given to me, half-watching, half-typing as the sun fell and kissed the horizon. At dinner, I thanked him with a kiss on the cheek. He wanted to smile, I could tell, but he didn't. He held on to his cold, hard look, digging right into his meal. As he chewed and Mrs. Molina started speaking, I spotted the faint smirk tugging at his lips though.

He couldn't fool me.

When I wake up today, he isn't in bed. I gaze around the bedroom, sighing as I stare at the ceiling fan whirling rapidly. It's hot today. Even with the fan on, I can feel my hair sticking to the nape of my neck.

Why the hell isn't the A/C on?

I push out of bed, walking to the window. The sun is high in the sky. It seems much closer today, blazing down on everything it can touch.

Turning toward the bathroom, I start up the shower, making sure it's colder than my average temperature. I don't know what's going on, but it's not usually this hot in here.

Once finished, I get dressed in a black tank top and khaki shorts, slip my feet into a pair of black leather flip flops, and march out the door. Patanza is standing on the other side of the door and when she spots me, she turns fully. Sweat is misting her forehead, her cleavage, and the skin she has revealed at her belly. Her hair is in a ponytail, the ends damp with sweat.

"What's going on with the air?" I ask, peering down the hallway when I hear noises.

"I don't know," she sighs. "Jefe called someone in to fix it. This house is old. Stupid thing always goes out around this time of year." She swipes her neck with the towel she normally carries in her back pocket.

"Damn." I slide my fingertips into my back pockets. "Well, are we doing breakfast today?"

"I doubt it. He's not even here."

"Where did he go?"

"To town with Thiago." When she says that her face pinches a little, as if she disapproves.

"You don't like him," I state, and she picks up her gaze.

"Can't stand him," she mutters.

"Why?"

Her upper lip spasms, almost in a near snarl. When she doesn't speak, I sense it's because of something personal. "Come on." She twists around. "We can still have the chef cook whatever you want. I'm sure Jefe will be back soon. He doesn't like to be off the property for too long."

I follow after her, but I can't help feeling that it's something deeper than she's letting off. Her body is tense, and she's purposely avoiding my gaze. I won't touch on it though. I know she isn't going to tell. She hurries down the stairs, her hand on her gun when she meets at the bottom.

To our left, I see a few men in navy work uniforms coming in and out of the front door. They are all sweaty, sunburnt, and speaking rapidly in Spanish as they march in and out with tools.

We make our way to the kitchen, where there are three butlers fanning themselves and standing in front of a round fan. A heavyset man named Eduardo stands at the counter, whipping something in a bowl. The house chef. He's glistening like a greased pig, patches of sweat seeping through his white jacket. The hat he usually wears is off, his black hair damp.

I've come to know he's a good man. Though Draco didn't want me talking to anyone, I still made my rounds. He wanted me to be comfortable here. I had to know these people, or at least speak to them as often as I could.

The maids are sweet, but none of them have families. All of them, the butlers as well, live in homes less than a mile away from here. They stay in an apartment building that was paid for years ago by Draco himself, just so they could stay close to the property, and so his guards could keep watch of them.

They don't butt in much. They also don't speak unless spoken to. Whenever they see me, they stand tall, slightly bowing their heads at me as if I'm royalty.

Like now. All three butlers spot me walking into the kitchen, and they perk up almost instantly, uneasy smiles spreading across their faces.

I return a small one, walking toward Eduardo. "Good morning, Eduardo."

He glances over at me. There is something about Eduardo that I find comforting. He's the only one around who isn't afraid to speak to me. He says what he wants, and is, indeed, a true shit talker that makes *amazing* food.

"Good morning, Patrona!" he yells cheerfully in his native tongue, placing his bowl down. "What the hell are you doing in my kitchen? You know Jefe doesn't like you in here." He plants a hand on his hip, using the back of his other to wipe the beads of sweat away from his forehead and cheek.

I laugh. "Who cares what Jefe says? What are you making?"

"Baking a cake," he sighs. "Too damn hot in this fucking house to bake, but it's for Mrs. Molina's birthday. That woman deserves ten-thousand cakes, no matter the temperature of the house."

My eyebrows rise. "It's her birthday today?"

"Yes." He bobs his head, grinning. "I will be making her favorite meal for dinner tonight. Jefe wants everything to be in order for her. We have a busy night."

I glance over at Patanza. "Why didn't he tell me it was her birthday?" I ask in English.

She presses her lips, glances between the butlers, and then flicks her fingers, gesturing for me to come her way. My eyebrows stitch and I join her in the secluded corner she stopped at. "She doesn't like to celebrate it."

"Why not?"

"Mr. Molina used to take her to Spain every year for her birthday. They would party like college students and they'd come back happier than ever, from what I've heard. Her birthdays remind her of him. She says they will never be able to compare to that again."

"Oh." *Damn.* I look back at Eduardo, watching as he pours the chocolate batter into a cake pan. "Well, then, maybe we should make the night a good one for her. Make it great. She deserves that, right?"

"Jefe usually takes care of the birthday plans."

"Well, he isn't here, is he? How is he supposed to take care of anything if he's out running around all the time?"

She fixes her mouth like she wants to say something, but clamps it shut in an instant.

"No." I smile, placing a hand on her shoulder. "What were you going to say?"

She fights a smile, glancing at the butlers who are finding little things to pick up and clean to occupy themselves. When she brings her eyes on me again, she says, "I was going to say his parties for her are kind of lame."

I snort. "He's too uptight to plan a party. I used to do it all the time for my parents and a few of their friends. Come on." I grab her wrist and start for the exit of the kitchen. "We'll figure something out for her."

"I really shouldn't, Patrona," she says, hesitant as I string her along. "He doesn't like for us to mess up his plans."

"He won't blame you for anything, Patanza. I'm sure he'd like for us to take this burden off his shoulders, though he'll probably never admit it. He seems to be dealing with a lot right now anyway."

"He always is," she scoffs.

I let go of her wrist when we're in the empty dining room. I'm hesitant to ask my next question. I haven't asked anything so daring in a long time. "Do you think he'd let me go to the city? For a gift?"

Her eyebrows shoot up like I've just asked for access to the devil's deepest, darkest secrets. Her hands lift up and she waves them rapidly. "No, no, no, no, no. *Hell* no!"

"What?" I frown. "Why not? It's just for a gift. You guys can follow me like you do here. It would only be for an hour tops."

"You're asking the wrong bitch, *Jefa*. If I even try to answer that he'll have my head. That is his number one rule."

"What is?" I ask, aggravated now.

"To not let you off the property without his permission." Her face turns cold and grim again, like she's not backing down.

I release a breath, head shaking. "This is fucking ridiculous. He can't keep me trapped here."

"He only wants you to be safe."

"No, he doesn't want me to run away. He thinks I'll bail."

"Well . . . do you blame him?" She folds her arms. "You stare out of the windows so much we all think one day you'll decide to just jump out of one of them and end it."

Her statement catches me by total surprise. "*What?* Is that what you all really think?"

"It's clear you are not happy, Patrona. Not here. Even though he is trying to do all that he can to please you, I don't think you ever will be . . . and I guess I can understand why, after all you've been through."

I swallow hard, looking toward the French doors. I don't have anything to say—at least not out loud. I thought I was doing a good job of pretending I didn't mind my life here. I guess my feelings are more transparent than I thought.

Is that what Draco thinks? That I want to die? That I want it all to end? Because he would be wrong. They are all wrong. It's not that I want it to end . . . it's something much deeper, and I have yet to discover it.

I can hardly sleep. I have nightmares, all of them filled with blood and death. I feel like I'm losing my mind sometimes.

I pull away from her, turning to leave the dining room.

"Do you want me to ask Eduardo to make you something to eat?" Patanza calls, following after me. "I can have the butlers bring it up."

"No." I stop, peering over my shoulder. "It's okay. I'll just eat later. I'm not that hungry right now." She starts to follow me when I take a few steps out, but I hold my hand up, lightly shaking my head. "Patanza, do you think that, just this once, I can walk around alone. No offense to you," I add quickly when her face falls, "but I just want some time alone."

She looks at me long and hard. It's against his rules, I know, but I can't deal with her tailing me. I want to go to the library without someone all over my back— without someone standing at the door, waiting for me to finish.

"Sure," she finally sighs. "But when you see him, tell Jefe that being alone is what you wanted."

I nod, taking off. "I will."

CHAPTER FOURTEEN

I t's around 3:00 p.m., and Patanza is helping me with decorations. They aren't bad, but not the best either. Purple and blue balloons were brought in—Mrs. Molina's favorite colors. The dishes are purple and blue as well. I blow each balloon up with the helium tank provided.

After taking my small escape and sitting on the terrace with a few glasses of white wine and one of those Spanish romances, I feel much better. I didn't mean to lash out at Patanza, which is why I have her helping me now. I want her to know that everything is okay between us, and that I don't blame her for doing her job.

The butlers stand only a few feet away, setting up small stations for finger foods and desserts. I can feel them looking at me, as if I shouldn't be doing any work at all. They look at the door often, like they expect Draco to come storming in at any second to grill them for letting me help.

"How long are they going to be like this?" I ask.

"It's their job to do this, not ours," Patanza grumbles, tying the end of one of the blue balloons. I can tell she's annoyed doing this. She didn't want to help, but had to because . . . well, because I asked. "They aren't used to the commanding people around here helping out with stuff like this. The guards, you, Mrs. Molina, Jefe—no one. They and the maids usually handle everything. It's their job to."

"I don't mind helping. I can't go into town so I might as well do something to pass the time." I finish blowing the balloon up and then pinch the end, handing it to her. She ties it, rolling her eyes at my last statement.

"Who says you can't go into town?" a familiar voice calls behind me.

I twist in my seat at the dining table and look sideways, spotting Mrs. Molina coming in. And *wow . . .* she looks amazing.

Her streaked gray hair is pinned up, not a stray piece dangles. Her dress is like a gown for a goddess, yellow and billowy with a gold belt at the waist. Her leather sandals have jewels on the gold straps. A smile sweeps across her lips as she comes closer.

"Wow, Mrs. Molina," I release a hoarse laugh. "You look great!"

She bows her head playfully.

I look over at Patanza and her eyebrows are furrowed as she sweeps her gaze over Mrs. Molina as well. She's mildly shocked, like she's never seen her dressed this way before, not even for her birthday.

"Why are you so dressed up?" Patanza asks, eyebrows bunching together.

"Because I want to be," Mrs. Molina retorts. "And because it is my 60th birthday. That's a huge milestone in the Molina family. Most don't get to live to see that age, you know."

"I had no idea you were turning sixty, Mrs. Molina. It makes your beauty even more impressive." I step around my chair.

A bigger smile graces her lips. Ever since that conversation I heard between her and Draco, I've grown to like her. She doesn't stare like a hawk. She doesn't treat me like some lost child anymore. She treats me like she's known me my whole life, having normal conversations with me during breakfast, buying me clothes whenever she goes into town. The clothes are really not needed, seeing as I have way too many to wear as it is, but I don't complain. It's appreciated, and I'm glad to know she actually thinks of me whenever she happens to go out.

"*Gracias, cariño.*" *Sweetie.* She touches my cheek with a gentle palm. "But who says you can't go to town?" she asks again.

"Jefe says so," Patanza butts in, eyes rolling.

Mrs. Molina's arms fold. "What does he think? That she will run away?"

Patanza cocks a stern brow, looking from her to me. She doesn't say anything but her know-it-all glare shouts it all.

"I am not going to run away," I groan, running my fingers through my hair.

"I'm sure you won't. My son can be so overprotective sometimes. He has to give you freedom—let you breathe! You can't stay cooped up in here or you'll go crazy. Trust me, I know."

"Exactly!"

"You should come out with me today," Mrs. Molina insists.

"Did Jefe say you could take her off the property?" Patanza asks in Spanish, but it is more of a threat than anything.

"No, and he doesn't have to because I can leave whenever I please, Patanza. My son cannot control me like he does with his guards and her." She gestures at me. "It's my birthday and she's coming with me. There is a new brand of *vino rojo* at the market that I want to try. I told them to save me a bottle just for today's special occasion. I want to make this a great night and my son has agreed that I can get whatever I want. All I have to do is call."

Patanza drops her balloon, folding her arms. "I can't let you take her."

I frown at her just as Mrs. Molina does. "Should we call him then?" she challenges in her native tongue. She draws out the clutch from beneath her arm and pulls out a burn phone. When she flips it open, Patanza exhales.

"Whatever," Patanza mumbles. "Call him."

"No need." Mrs. Molina looks over at me. "*Amor*, go change clothes. I will be waiting by the door when you're ready. I've already asked Guillermo and Diego to take me. As long as we have guards with us—his eyes and ears—it will be fine."

I beam, stepping sideways. "Are you sure?" I gasp.

She nods. "Go—but hurry. I have a few stops I want to make while I'm there."

I do my best not to squeal but I can feel it in my throat, begging to be unleashed. I look at Patanza and she's shaking her head, straightening her back with her hand on the handle of her gun.

"He's going to flip shit," she grumbles in Spanish.

But I ignore her and rush around Mrs. Molina, zooming up the stairs and into

Draco's bedroom. I change into a gray maxi dress and sandals, making my way into the bathroom to brush my hair and then toss it up into a loose bun. There are sunglasses in the closet and I grab a pair.

I noticed Draco keeps money in the top drawer of his dresser. There are five thick wads of them. I slide off the rubber band from one of them and unroll it, taking a few bills and stuffing them in the black leather satchel Mrs. Molina bought me. He never said I could use it, but also never said that I *couldn't.*

I guess there's really no point in my using it. He doesn't expect me to go anywhere to spend it on anything. But with his guards with us, I don't see the harm in going out for just a few hours.

I'm out of the bedroom in no time. As I waltz down the stairs, I spot Mrs. Molina standing at the front door with a tote bag now strapped on her shoulder.

"You ready?" She smiles broadly.

I nod when I meet up to her. "Yes."

"Good. Come." She grips the doorknob and opens it. Guillermo and Diego are already posted at the car, waiting for us. When I step out, the sun beams down on me, kissing my skin. I slide my sunglasses on as we walk to the black Mercedes. Guillermo opens my door as Diego opens hers and we slide into the back seat at the same time.

When the doors are shut behind us, I look over at her. "Are you sure he'll be okay with this?"

She gives a small smirk that almost resembles his. "No."

My eyes stretch.

"But he can't stop us right now, can he?" she adds. "I've learned that with Draco you have to *take* what you want. Waiting around for him to give you permission gets you nowhere. If he doesn't see you make a stand for yourself, he won't take you seriously. He used to try and keep me trapped in there. Let's just say we had one conversation over dinner one night, and he hasn't tried to hold me back since, though he does make sure I take my precautions."

Guillermo climbs behind the wheel as Diego gets into the passenger seat.

"Plus, I'm sure those two clowns up there have already told him." She looks between them.

Diego huffs a laugh, but his mouth doesn't move. Guillermo looks through the rearview mirror and gives a slight eye roll. Well, if they are still willing to take us, I'm guessing Draco is fine with it.

Good.

No more leashes.

I deserve freedom, and I've wanted to get out of the house for weeks now.

The ride is refreshing. Even though the air conditioner is on, I roll my window down and stare out at the road and tall palm trees. The palm trees transform into shrubs and the road turns into a dirt one as the car veers left and continues up a winding road.

I look back, watching the mansion grow farther and farther away. It's a beautiful home, but it feels so much better being outside of it than in it.

I'm surprised he isn't raising hell about this. Maybe he's beginning to trust me. Maybe he knows where my best instincts lie.

We take a long dirt road past small, various colored stucco homes. Children are playing outside but when they see our car, they stop kicking their *fútbols* and stare. Some wave. Some don't. They must know whom this car belongs to—or they suspect it's trouble.

It takes twenty minutes to get to the city of Lantía. It's a small city indeed. There are corner markets and Mexican food stands everywhere. The food smells amazing, and when I inhale, I feel a pang, remembering the ride on my wedding day.

Smelling all the food—the *tortas* and cakes—and then having it all drowned out with the scent of hot copper and being blinded by a black hood.

A chill shoots up my spine just thinking about it.

"Are you okay?" Mrs. Molina asks, and I shoot my gaze over to hers.

"Yeah." I nod when she places a kind hand on top of mine. "I'm great. Just glad to be out of the house."

She scans me, and I can see the worry in her eyes, but I force a small smile, then turn to look out of the window again.

The car finally slows down and I look ahead, spotting tall cream-colored and red tents. The area is busy, with men, women, and children milling around. It's a market. A large one.

Guillermo parks the car and then kills the engine, he and Diego hopping out immediately. They don't come for our doors right away, and Mrs. Molina sighs, peering out.

"Ay, ay, ay," she groans.

"What are they doing?" I ask, watching them walk through the area, hands on the gun handles in their holders.

"Doing a small sweep. Making sure no one looks suspicious. Same routine every time we go somewhere." They return several minutes later and finally come for our doors. Diego opens mine, and I step out onto the red dirt, the heat wrapping me up. The air is much thicker, and it's way hotter out here than it was at the mansion; I guess that's because we were closer to the water there.

Gravel crunches from somewhere. Before I can pick my head up, I see a pair of leather shoes step up to me and without meeting his eyes, I already know who the hell it is.

I carry my gaze up his black dress pants, the cream-colored shirt tucked in to the trim waist, sleeves rolled up, revealing his strong forearms.

His shirt is open at the top, revealing the crucifix again, the large Adam's apple, and of course, the wicked smirk on his lips.

"You've got to be fucking kidding me," I gripe when Diego shuts the door behind me.

Draco stands tall before me, shoulders broad. A gun is in a holder on his belt, an impressive silver watch on his wrist. "What? You thought I'd approve of you being out here *without* me?" When he quirks that cheek, I want to punch him right in the gut.

"I only wanted to explore—get a little freedom," I tell him. "It's already enough having your guards tail my ass all day."

"You have freedom. I'm just tagging along and *they* are keeping you safe." He steps toward me, clasping my chin between his forefinger and thumb. "My woman doesn't walk these streets alone. It's not safe."

"I was wondering why they were being so lenient on letting us out," Mrs. Molina calls from the front of the car, placing a pair of sunglasses on. "I was only bluffing with Patanza."

"She is not happy, Mamá. You shouldn't mess with her emotions that way."

"Oh, please." She waves a hand. "She should be glad she has the break. Poor girl works too damn hard. She deserves to be out here, too."

He exhales and then looks down at me when Mrs. Molina walks to the nearest fruit stand. "What do you want from here?"

"I want to buy your mom a gift," I tell him, turning to walk. He catches up to me without much stride. "Why didn't you tell me it was her birthday?"

"Didn't think it mattered. She normally isn't this cheerful on this day." He gives her a sideways glance as she picks up a papaya, grinning at the woman behind the stand. "But I won't ruin it. She wanted you to come out with her, so I'll give her whatever she wants today as long as it keeps the smile on her face."

"Hmm."

As we walk, I notice people are quick to step out of our way. Not one person stands in our path. They literally make a gap for us to walk through. Some of the women smile so hard at him I think their faces will break.

Some people shush others, while some scatter to different stands to get away from the walkway.

"Jefe! Jefe!" a child shouts, rushing our way with a grin. His mother panics, trying to cling to his arm, but Draco holds up a hand at her, giving a slight reassuring smile. She eases up almost instantly, and the child, a young boy with matted hair and shorts that seem years too small for him, meets up to us, breathing hard and grinning all at once.

"I made this for you," he says in Spanish, tossing his long hair back. He opens his palm and hands Draco a carved flower made of wood. "I carry it around every day. I was hoping one day you would show up again."

Draco takes it, studying it intently. "Do you?"

"Yes! I remember you bringing my mom flowers one day when she was sad. She still has them. She made a garden with the seeds. They make her room smell good."

Draco picks his gaze up, looking at the older woman. She blushes. He huffs a laugh.

He leans forward and murmurs, "You did well on it, Mateo. I'll put this in my art room back at home. Keep this up, and it will make you a lot of money later on." He holds the flower up between his fingers.

Mateo bobs his head and steps back.

"Hold on." Draco grips his shoulder and I can see the worry in his mother's eyes. She steps forward, watching intently. Draco stands tall, pulling out a clip of money from his front pocket. He takes out six bills and then stuffs them in the boy's hand. "Tell your mother to make something good for dinner and to buy both of you some new clothes and shoes."

Mateo nods and Draco cocks his head, telling him to go on.

"Ma! Look!" the boy yells, running back to her.

The woman's eyes glisten when the boy stuffs the money in her hands. She brings her fingertips up to her lips, whispering her thanks over and over again.

Draco walks to her, capping her shoulder and saying something. She nods her head appreciatively, saying *"Gracias"* even louder now. She gives him a tight hug and then pulls away with haste.

I'm shocked that he allows it, but that's not what really catches me by surprise. It's how quiet the market has become, like the spotlight is on him. Everyone is watching. Staring. Not only at him, but at me too.

"Bonita," I hear a woman whisper as she stares at me. *Pretty.*

"Muy maravilloso," another says. *Very gorgeous.*

"Quien es ella?" Who is she?

I see a set of shoulders shrug in the crowd near the voice. Draco returns, hooking his arm through mine and leading the way through the market.

"You gave him a lot of money," I note. "How much was it?"

"Six hundred American dollars."

"You carry American money?"

"It's worth more here. Why not?" He has his head up, scanning the area himself, eyes peeled.

Makes sense.

"That was nice," I finally say when he brings me under a tent to get in the shade.

"These are my people, Gianna. It's my home. They respect me and I respect them. Some may be afraid of me, but most love me. I do for my people."

"What kind of flowers did you give that boy's mother? Chocolate cosmos?"

His smile is the answer.

"Why?"

"She used to be my tutor before my father died. She's a single mother, but she had her mother to help out with her son. Her mother grew sick, passed away a few months ago. She used up all of the money she had saved for the funeral and I heard about it. She'd always loved the flowers. She was the one who introduced me to them in my books—said she wanted to have a garden of her own one day."

A smile touches the edges of my lips.

"I gave her a bouquet to send my condolences and took care of her home. It's paid for. She has no more worries. That woman was more than patient with me, kind of like your mother was with my violin lessons. They knew I hated learning, but stuck it out with me anyway." He chuckles.

"Yeah, I can see that," I tease.

He looks around the market, watching the patrons return to their shopping. "We can't be out here for long, Gianna. Someone will call the police soon to report me, try and get the reward. I'm taking this risk for you, but I normally don't do public places like this. Not often."

"I understand. I just want to get her something—doesn't have to be big. I want to show my appreciation."

"Appreciation for what?"

"For . . . all she's done and for always having my back when it comes to you, her own son." I cock a brow at him and he raises his chin, glaring like he knows that I know something I shouldn't. He doesn't speak on it, though. Instead, he wraps an arm around my shoulders and twists me around, leading the way through the outdoor market.

"She likes books and jewelry. She collects music boxes, shells, and she loves drinking red wines and knitting. She's not too hard to please. There is a place down here where you'll most likely find something." He doesn't look at me and I'm curious as to why.

I don't speak on it, though. I walk with him and enjoy my freedom—this place. It smells good here. I can smell meat grilling, tortillas browning. It all smells so delicious and fresh.

"Thank you, Draco," I finally murmur, and he drops his eyes, focusing on me.

"Don't thank me for freedom, Gianna. Whatever you desire is yours."

My mouth twitches.

"Just don't play me for a fool," he adds on and I whip my head up, locking on his face. One of his eyebrows slides up, his face solemn.

"What happens if I do? You'll kill me?" I ask softly.

"I could never kill you."

"Why not?"

"I owe your father my life. Killing his only daughter would never settle with me and I wouldn't take pride in it."

"And also because he promised me to you." I chew on my bottom lip, stepping over large rocks. "What all did he tell you to do with me?"

"To protect you. To make you trust me. To never shed any of your blood— well, not too much of it anyway." He smirks at that. I roll my eyes.

"And you expect me to do the same for you?"

When I ask that, a smirk tugs at the corner of his lips again. "Same goes for you, *mi reina*. For this to last, it must work both ways, no?"

We meet up to a stand with trinkets, books, and other small things. It's tucked away in a corner, shelves built into the building beside it. It's a much bigger space than the other stands have, and there is so much to choose from that giddiness courses through me when we step beneath the tent.

"Have your way, niñita. I'll be waiting out here. Let me know when you finish so I can pay. I have a phone call to make." He releases me, and I step forward, smiling a little. "Go," he insists. "Before I change my mind."

I playfully roll my eyes. He hates revealing that tender side, but I won't dwell on it. If it's what makes him feel good—keeping it only between us—then so be it. I won't push or budge. Because I like him like this. On my side.

I like this mutual respect.

I like that he is willing to do whatever it takes to make the ones he cares for happy. He may not say that he cares, but I'm a firm believer in showing rather than telling. And he's shown it a lot so far.

Draco Molina is a lot deeper than I thought. He isn't the monster I assumed he was. He's hardcore, tough, brutal—but it's all for a reason.

And I'm realizing that perhaps he has every right to be the way he is.

He has every right to make everyone call him the boss. He owns who he is and he doesn't back down. Everyone looks up to him. Men want to be him, the most wanted, most powerful man in the world, whether the rest of the world knows it or not. He defies all laws but his own.

The man I thought was a monster in the dark is everything I never knew I craved. I should get to know him. I should . . . try with him, at least, because he's trying with me. Daddy saw something in him, and I think I'm seeing it now too.

He can protect me. He can help me. He is slowly but surely trying to heal me and repair the damage he caused. His effort isn't invisible to me. I notice it, and like a fool, I know I'm taking it for granted.

Because despite all he's doing, it's still not enough.

CHAPTER FIFTEEN

I have a lot of dresses to choose from, but tonight I decide to wear something a little more formal. It's a sleeveless midnight blue cocktail dress with midnight blue heels and gold jewelry to accent. I bought the jewelry from one of the market stands too, along with the gift I have for Mrs. Molina.

My hair was done by Juanita, one of the housemaids who is also the nurse around here. I didn't know she was good at doing hair, too, but when Draco brought her in and she offered, I let her.

She styles it half up, half down, so that it swims at my shoulders, braided into two French braids at the middle and leading into full, brown waves that cascade down my back.

"I love it." I smile at her through the mirror. Though I say it in English, she beams, clearly noting that I am more than happy with what she's done.

She takes off to let me finish getting dressed. Before I know it, there's a knock at the door, and Draco steps in. When he catches sight of me, his eyes grow round and he stops where he stands.

His eyes travel up and down repeatedly, as if he can't believe I'm the same woman he had tied up in the shed, or the same woman that almost killed him nearly a week ago. Or the same woman that he punished before.

He looks at me like the name he calls me—*reina*—and I can't help myself. I blush. "Is it too much?" I ask, looking down at the points of my heels.

"No." He steps forward and extends his arm, reaching for my hand. "You look fucking amazing, Gianna."

My upper lip quirks up. "Is everyone here?"

"Not yet. And that's a good thing. I want you to come with me to the terrace for a quick drink."

I nod and hold his hand tighter. He leads the way out of the bedroom and I shut off the lights, my heels clicking as we descend the hall. He keeps straight, going toward the doors that lead out to the terrace.

The sun is sitting on the horizon when we step out, the breeze gentle. It toys with the ends of my hair, ruffling the loose strands of Draco's.

There is a table covered in white linen in the corner. On top of it is a heavy-bottomed decanter filled with red wine and two wine glasses beside it. Draco lets me walk ahead of him and then he shuts the doors.

"Can't wait until tonight to drink, huh?" I laugh.

He puts on a small smirk, walking toward the table to pour wine into each one. "Just one glass. In the form of our own celebration."

"What are we celebrating?" I lean against the rails and watch as he picks up one of the glasses to bring it to me.

"Life," he murmurs. "Together."

"Together?" I accept the glass but keep my eyes on his.

"Yes." He looks me over thoroughly before picking up his wine. "I want to trust you, Gianna. I want you as my partner. The woman I come home to after a long day." I don't speak but I know he's expecting me to. Instead, he continues. "I know I did things to you—things you didn't approve of. I know you want to get past that just as much as I do, but I can't regret it."

I frown when he says that and then look away.

"I won't regret making you into a better woman. A stronger woman. I won't regret bringing the *Nicotera* out of you."

I pick my head back up, locking on his hard brown eyes again. He comes closer, using his free hand to slide it under my hair and cup the back of my neck. "Do you still hate me?"

"No," I respond.

"But you don't trust me."

"Not completely," I answer honestly.

"How can I get you to trust me?" he rasps against my lips.

I think on it for a second, my fingers tightening around my glass, glossed lips pushing together. "I need proof. Pictures of you and Daddy. Or even your father and mine. My mother. Anything that proves you aren't just making this all up—me being promised to you. I need to know he cared about you the way you say he did."

"Proof," he repeats, as if he's thinking. "Fine. I'll show you after the party. But for now," he sighs, pulling away, "let's drink to a good night."

I smile. "Sounds good."

He holds his glass in the air and I do the same. When he brings the rim to his lips and sips, I follow his lead, holding his eyes, tasting the tart wine on my tongue.

He takes a few more swigs before placing the glass back down on the table. "There is something else," I proclaim. "About Ronaldo. Where is he?"

Before he turns back around, I see his shoulders tense up, one of his fists clenching. He turns gradually, straightening his back. "I already told you his name isn't Ronaldo."

"Well, Henry—whatever." I hold the glass tighter, preparing for his wrath. "What did you do with him? When we went to the shed he wasn't there." I wince, just thinking about the shed that was full of blood when we left.

"Why do you even fucking care, Gianna?"

"Because he was my friend in there. He was the only reason I pushed forward and wanted to get out, even when it seemed all hope was lost."

His jaw clenches, nostrils flaring up. "And why do you think that is?"

I shrug. "He's a good person."

"No. He's a fucking weasel and he knows exactly what he needs to do to survive. He knows exactly who you are, Gianna. He's not a fucking idiot. He knew his only chance of getting out was through you."

"You keep saying he knew like he's not here anymore . . ."

Draco cocks a brow, not backing down.

"Did you kill him?" I whisper.

He blinks, still not responding. Instead, he turns his back to me and pours himself another glass. After guzzling it all down, he releases a loud sigh. "Don't worry about him anymore, do you understand? He isn't your problem and whatever you feel for him is out of guilt. Whatever you told him, forget it. Whatever you remember of him, fucking erase it from your memories. He is worthless and he cannot be saved. Any kin of Toni's is fucking worthless to me."

He marches for the doors, shoulders still hiked up. "You won't speak of him to me anymore, Gianna. And I mean it." He glares hard at me and as badly as I want to back down, I don't. I hold his gaze because I know he's wrong about him. I know good people when I meet them. Daddy knows good people too. He hired Ronaldo for a reason.

Instead of protesting, though, I shrug. I don't know where he is anyway. I can't save him. For all I know, the rest of him has been chopped up and he's been fed to the sharks.

If I want to move forward, I can't dwell on my past anymore. I wanted to help, I really did, but if he's not here, how can I?

"Fine, Draco." I place my glass down on the table and walk his way. "I won't speak of him anymore." His hunched shoulders relax a bit and he lifts a hand, clasping my chin between his forefinger and thumb.

"That's a good niñita."

The purple and blue color scheme didn't turn out to be so bad once the flashing gold lights I bought from the market were added. They're Christmas lights, but they work and Mrs. Molina loves the feel they give the room—a bright, cheerful atmosphere that pushes out the fear and darkness, if only for now.

Tonight is her night, and everyone should feel relaxed right now, including Draco, which is why I don't bring up Ronaldo anymore. The guilt is eating me alive though. I promised, but I was too late. I couldn't help. Now he's probably gone.

The party is just starting when we enter the room. The dining room has been cleared out. The table has been taken somewhere else for the night and the room has been filled with small, round tables. It's like a ballroom now.

Latin music spills out of the speakers, loud enough to cover up even the nearest of conversations. Even with the music, though, there is still a lot of laughing and chattering.

Laughter is good. This night should be fun and simple.

Most of the tables are surrounded by guests—people that I don't know, and not so sure I want to meet. I know Draco won't make me meet them either. I assume the people here work for him in some sort of way or he has a claim on them, but it doesn't mean he trusts them. He just knows they aren't foolish enough to betray him.

He isn't a people person. He doesn't care about crowds, but this is what Mrs. Molina wanted. A big 60th birthday bash. And she got it. It's not huge—I don't think there are more than fifty guests—but I admit, it's a great feeling to walk into a room and not feel like everyone wants to hold a gun to your head.

The guards are still around, dressed in different clothing. Black button downs and black dress pants. Their guns are still on display though, but I'm sure it was requested by Mrs. Molina to not have them so visible that people become uncomfortable.

It's hard to feel festive with a gun in your face.

Patanza is wearing a pair of black pants and a black pinstriped vest, scoping the room with a drink in her hand. Of course she has skin showing. It just wouldn't be Patanza if she didn't.

I look to my left at the table closest to us, and I'm surprised to see Morales is here. I get a kick out of that. He's the heavyset man whose expensive car I completely destroyed when I tried to escape this place.

He sees me strolling in with Draco, arm-in-arm, and turns his nose up at me, but comes in our direction anyway.

I guess he's still pissed and blaming me for having Draco draw that gun on him that day. I don't care. I still don't like him. He carries himself like he's better or smarter somehow, but I'm sure the whole room knows he's far from it.

"Jefe!" he yells when he gets closer, holding out his arms and expecting a brotherly hug.

Draco swipes a hand across the tip of his nose. "The fuck are you doing in my house, Morales?" he bites out.

"I was invited, Jefe," he says in a placating voice. "By your beautiful mother. She wanted me here."

Draco stares at him. Hard. Morales presses his lips and looks at me, knowing he can't battle his glare. "And you . . . the lovely woman who wrecked my beautiful Mercedes. You know I miss that car, don't you?" His accent is thick.

"*No me importa*," I return, shrugging. *I don't care.* His eyes stretch wide, as if he wasn't expecting me to know any Spanish. Yeah, I'm not just some stupid American bitch that wrecked his car. And he knows it. He focuses on Draco's grip on my hand and then brings his eyes back up.

"Well, I'm going to get a drink," he continues in Spanish. "You two have a good night, huh?" He claps Draco's shoulder but Draco growls at him, a deep, throaty, feral one.

Morales' eyes stretch and he backs off in an instant, spinning around and rushing to the bar set up by the window.

"What's up with him?" I ask.

"He's an ungrateful son of a bitch," he grumbles, leading the way through the crowd. "Got him a car that cost more than the worthless shit he brought here, and he complains about the color to me. If he didn't have such a large connection to my cartel, I would have spooned his fucking eyeballs out, that way he'd cherish the fucking values of life, not gripe over material shit."

"I guess I should take partial blame for that. I am the one who completely destroyed that car." I laugh and his mouth twitches, fighting a smile. "Come on. Let's go get a drink and find your mother."

CHAPTER SIXTEEN

Two *hours have* passed and Draco is much more relaxed than he was when we first entered the room. I guess I can give credit for that to Mrs. Molina. She kept bringing drinks to him, probably knowing how much more lenient her son is while under the influence.

Don't get me wrong, he's still like a hawk on me. He has me on his lap at one of the round tables, holding me close to him, a firm hand on my hip. He's laughing and joking, playing a tequila shot game with one of the guards named Simon.

I noticed Thiago came in about an hour ago. He was late, but dressed in a clean black suit. Draco saw him as well, and he's been watching him ever since. He still doesn't trust him, and I don't blame him. There's something sneaky about him.

The way he looks at me is an issue. He stares at me like he owns me—or like he *could*. I can't lie and say the sight of him doesn't make me uncomfortable. In fact, he makes my skin crawl. I see why Patanza doesn't like him. He's not easy on the eyes, and doesn't seem like a nice person either.

However, Mrs. Molina is happy to have him here, and I don't want to complain and ruin her night. I know if I say even a peep about it to Draco, he will handle it in his typical Jefe fashion. He would cause a scene in front of all the guests simply because he could. Just because there's a party going on doesn't mean he won't prove who calls the shots around here.

Mrs. Molina opens her gifts one by one, and when she comes across mine, her eyes grow as wide as discs, her smile stretching. She looks up at me, and I tip my wine glass, a small smile on display.

"I can't believe it," she sighs. She holds up the knitting needles made of gold, carved delicately with vine and leafy designs. "They are so beautiful," she coos.

"I knew she'd love it," Draco murmurs. I'm glad she does. It wasn't cheap. I was surprised they were even selling it at the market, but they had special gifts behind the counter, for the patrons looking for the more exquisite things. I'll have to remember it the next time I go out—if I ever get the chance.

After Mrs. Molina opens all her gifts, thanking each person profusely for them, the cake is cut, the music picks up again, and people go back to the bar for more drinks. They really know how to party here. Shot after shot. Bottle after bottle.

I've only had three glasses of wine. I can't do hard liquor tonight. I'm still bothered—feeling guilty about Ronaldo. I know I shouldn't, but I can't help it. I made him a promise and couldn't fulfill it. Whatever's happened to him feels like it's at least partially my fault.

"Want me to get you another drink?" I ask Draco, twisting in his lap.

He looks toward the bar, noticing it's pretty vacant. Most people are dancing or mingling. "Yeah, reina. Go. Get yourself another, too."

I press my lips and nod, standing up. Before I can get away, he grabs my hand and folds it over, bringing my knuckles up to his lips. He kisses them, warm brown gaze heavy on mine. I feel the hot swirl at the pit of my belly and smile.

"Hurry back," he says.

"I will."

I take off as Simon picks up a card from the deck and then curses through his teeth, picking up a shot glass and downing the tequila. I'm not sure what game it is, but he has to take a shot every time he plucks certain ones. Draco is winning. He's only had two shots so far, and they've been playing for over an hour.

I make my way toward the bar, feeling several eyes on me. I don't look to find out who is staring. Of course they'll stare. They don't know who I am, or why Draco has me so close to him. It must be an unusual thing to witness.

I stop at the bar, asking the butler for a whiskey for Draco. I decide to get another glass of wine for myself, hoping it will cool my nerves. It's the red wine Mrs. Molina wanted from the market, and it's delicious, not too bitter or too sweet. Just the way I like it.

"I don't think I officially introduced myself to you," a deep voice says behind me.

I turn quickly, meeting wicked, dark eyes. Thiago puts on a crooked smile, a neat whiskey clutched in his hand.

My heart thuds in my chest, but I keep my face even, remaining calm.

"You speak English well," I note, turning to him after the butler hands me the drinks.

"I know just as much as my cousin," he assures me. "Learned young, just like he did."

"I see." I glance over at Draco. He's watching already, but he hasn't made a move. *Yet.* "We haven't officially been introduced, but I sense Draco has made it that way for a reason," I continue.

"Probably," he laughs. "He's a greedy fucker. Always has been. Doesn't want what's his being talked to or touched." He peers over at Draco, who has his forearm on the table now, fists clenched tight. "He'll be making his way over here at any moment, I'm sure."

"Why is he letting you walk around freely?" I ask, frowning a bit, and he drops his head to focus on me, his dark eyes flashing from the lights. "I heard what you did—how you're stealing his things. How can he possibly be okay with that?"

"Oh, he's not okay with shit like that. But I didn't steal his stuff. It was stolen from me by that fucking cartel."

I huff. "And you expect anyone here to believe that, with the way you walk around—all high and mighty, like you own the place too?"

He shrugs, like he really doesn't give a shit. "He's never fully trusted me. If my aunt didn't have my back so much I'm sure he would have killed me a long time ago."

"Like he killed your father." I hold his gaze.

His cocky smirk fades, lips growing thin. "He's told you about that . . ."

"Much about it, yes." I smile, a sly smile that I'm sure gets under his skin. "The thing is, Thiago, if I were you, I wouldn't cross him the way your father did. I wouldn't push him. You of all people should know what's he's capable of. Right?"

His upper lips peels back to reveal a full row of straight, slightly sharp teeth. "I like you," he chuckles. "And I see why my cousin likes you, too. You're feisty. Smart. You know how to get under a man's skin, even if his skin happens to be pretty damn thick."

I quirk a brow, holding the drinks tighter in hand.

"But, Gianna Nicotera, I think what you fail to realize is that I am not the monster here. I'm not a traitor. I do what I have to do to survive, but when it comes to my family's reputation, I don't believe in tarnishing it. They assume I work with Hernandez, but he's the one who sends me on the larger shipments every time. He's looking for a reason to kill me. They fucking robbed me, killed those guards, and left me alive to deliver the message. Of course Draco doesn't buy it." He steps closer, towering over me. My eyebrows draw together, but I keep my eyes on his, unwavering. "He thinks they left me alive because I promised them something. But there isn't anything they can give me that Draco can't. He asks, why didn't they just cut my head off and send it in a box to deliver their message? I say, because I'm a smart motherfucker who knows how to talk himself out of any situation. I did it with him just the other day, and I'm still alive for it. He won't give me credit for that though—being the smart one. The one that thinks on his toes during the worst of circumstances."

He looks at Draco, who's standing now, picking up his shot glass and bringing it up to his lips. "You should go on back to him. He told me to never talk to you. I just couldn't help myself. I always end up breaking his rules." He laughs at that, and then he turns around, giving Draco a solid stare before walking out of the room.

I sigh and turn, but Draco is already coming for me. He takes the whiskey out of my hand, roughly setting it down on the bar station. "What the fuck did he say to you?"

I step sideways. "He was being a smartass. Says he would never betray you."

He scoffs. "Bullshit."

"He seemed serious, even if he's a smart ass," I tell him, handing him his drink. "Do you really think your own cousin would risk the family business like that?"

"His father did—my uncle, remember?" he seethes, eyebrows stitching. "He can't be fully trusted."

"You grew up together. Mrs. Molina still trusts him, too, even after everything she's been through. Why can't you?"

His jaw pulses. "I don't trust anyone. This world is full of fucking traitors just waiting to put a blade in my back."

When he says that, I feel my heart drop. "You don't trust anyone," I repeat.

Just hours ago he said he wanted to trust me—that he wanted to make me his partner and do this right. He doesn't trust *anyone* now? He's just drunk. Drunk and stupid, and saying whatever will feed his bloated ego.

I grip my glass and pull my eyes away from his. "I'm going to get some air," I mutter. "Don't send your guards after me."

I walk off before he can say anything. I'm surprised he doesn't stop me, but I won't give him a reason to. Instead I keep going, leaving the room and turning to get to the corridor that leads to the library.

Mrs. Molina is standing outside the door with a piece of cake on a plate. She's nearly finished eating it. When she spots me, she sucks the icing off the tip of her thumb and smiles.

"Oh, Gia." Her eyes light up. She's a bit tipsy, too. I can tell when she starts to giggle. A butler walks by and she flags him down, handing him the half-eaten cake. "How are you liking the party?"

"It's fun," I lie with a smile.

"It is. I'm so glad you are here. My son has never behaved so well."

My mouth twitches. I don't want to talk about him right now.

"Come on," she insists, grabbing my wrist. "Walk with me. I need to sober up a bit before getting to bed."

I laugh. "Almost drunk, huh?"

"Almost?" She laughs, and then sighs, our heels clicking across the marble. I look back, glad none of the guards are following us. He can at least do that for me—leave me alone. "I don't know if Draco told you, but his father would take

119

me to Spain every year for my birthday. We would drink and party so much, no matter how old I felt. We used to have such a good time together. I miss those days with Carlos."

I look over at her as we stop right where the stairs that lead to the galería are. "You miss him a lot, don't you?"

"Every single day. And so, so much," she says, rather painfully. "I wanted to drink tonight to remind myself of him. To imagine him here with me in spirit, enjoying this night with me. It may not be Spain, but it has been a good night, with great music and delicious cake."

"It has."

She looks me over twice, gripping the guardrail. It's quiet for a few seconds. I shift in my heels, looking down at the galería door. "Do you think my son can make you happy?"

That question catches me way off guard. I tilt my head to look at her, opening my mouth, but then clamping it shut in an instant, realizing that I don't know the answer to that. "I—I don't know," I finally respond.

"I hope that he can," she says in a near whisper. "And I hope that you can make him happy, too. I hope that one day he will quit all of this, because the riches and the power don't matter. It's what his father thought—that it mattered most—but it doesn't. Draco deserves to have a life. I hate that he's a wanted man. I fear for his life every single time he steps out of the door. I fear for my own life sometimes, but I don't so much mind the thought of leaving this world. It's just being in this world without him that would kill me. Losing my son—my only son . . . well, I wouldn't want to live. Every day would cause suffering. I just want him to do the right thing one day—quit this so that he can go far away and enjoy his life."

"He seems to love what he does."

"He does. And I don't blame him." She looks down at the galería door, sighing. "After all he has been through, all he has seen, I can't blame him at all. Sometimes I wonder why he isn't *angrier*." Her head picks back up and she locks eyes with me. "I hope he can make you happy one day. Maybe not now, but someday soon. I hope Lion was right. I hope you two become inseparable."

I press my lips, wanting to smile broadly, but unable to. Daddy talked about us with her, too. Of course he did.

"Well," she yawns, stepping away from the rail. "I thought I could make it to midnight but I am exhausted. I think I should go to bed." She rests a flat palm on my cheek. "Tell my Draco that I love him."

"Okay." I smile.

Her gaze is gentle when she pulls away. She walks past me, in her purple gown, and continues walking without a glance back. I look after her until I can't hear her steps anymore.

I turn and look down the steps, at Draco's galería door. I don't want to go back to the party. I really don't want to face him just yet.

He's drunk right now, but I'm hoping he'll sober up soon and return to his regular Draco self.

I place my wine glass down on the corner table and then take the steps down, going to the door. He's been going in there a lot lately, almost every other day. I'm curious what he's been painting.

He said he doesn't mind me going in there, just as long as I don't touch anything. I'll make myself useful and see what I've been missing. It's been a while since he's brought me here. He's had no reason to bring me down to this room that makes a statement, either by punishment or by pleasure. Or a mix of both.

I make it down and reach for the knob. To my dismay, it's locked.

"Damn it," I mutter, rattling the door like it will magically open. I guess he doesn't want people in it tonight. Understandable.

I step back and look to my right, but then my eyebrows pinch together, spotting another door. It's smaller, all black with a black doorknob.

I don't know how I didn't notice it before, but seeing as it's nearly tucked behind a column and blends into the shadows, I don't think I was supposed to.

I walk toward it cautiously. This is one room that I haven't been taken into. I grip the doorknob, but it too is locked.

Releasing a heavy breath, I take a step back, looking it over. I hear the guests upstairs, still boisterous, the music playing loudly, proving the party won't be ending anytime soon.

But then I hear something else.

Something that isn't the guests at all.

It's a heavy, loud groan.

It transforms into a deep, long moan, almost like a cry for help. It's coming through this locked door. *In there.*

Leaning forward, I press my ear to it again, listening harder. I don't hear anything for a few seconds, to the point that I think I've imagined the sound, but as I start to pull away, I hear it again.

It's a man.

What the hell?

I reach up, rapidly searching the top frame of the door for a key. He usually has them around. To my luck, there is one taped to the top and I snatch it down, stuffing it into the lock and stepping inside. I check over my shoulder before shutting the door behind me. When it's closed, I'm engulfed in darkness.

My heartbeat doubles in speed. I don't know what I'm walking into, but the person sounds like they're in terrible pain. I need to see who it is.

I tip toe down the wooden steps, but each one creaks, giving me away. Whoever it is, they already know I'm here. I hear chains rattling, the groaning becoming louder. When I hear the chains, I know no one is hurt by accident. This is for a reason.

Chains mean punishment here.

With each step down, a small light comes into view. It's dim, reminding me of a nightlight.

My breathing becomes chaotic as I take the last step, the click of my heels giving my presence away even more. At first I don't see anything. The light shines on small things that are stored down here. Baskets. Buckets. Towels. Boxes stacked in the corner. Garden tools and hoses. The built-in shelves carry over to a darker corner, cutting off all access of light there.

"Please," I hear the voice croak, and I gasp.

I stop where I stand, knowing this isn't a good idea. Someone's here. Someone I probably don't want to see. What Draco does to people isn't my business anymore. He handles people his own way for a reason. I don't need to interfere . . . well, that's what I tell myself, but I don't turn back.

"Please," the crackly voice calls again. "Water. Anything. Please."

That voice. It's so familiar. My eyes narrow. I walk to the shelf to pick up the LED lantern at the top. When I switch it on, it illuminates the dark corner.

I'm in a basement, but not the same one Draco killed Kevin in. This one is smaller, the air dryer.

But that's not what surprises me.

What surprises me most is seeing the man sitting against the wall, wrapped up in chains. As I remembered, he has no arms. But now, he has no clothes either. He is completely naked and even skinnier than he was before. His lips are cracked beyond anything I've ever seen, and his face is bruised, eyes blackened, hair a damp, sweaty mess.

I wince at the sight of him, my heart dropping.

"Oh my God! Ronaldo!" I whisper, rushing his way. I drop to my knees in front of him. He looks horrible. The chains are wrapped up so tight on his body that they seem to be squeezing the air from his lungs. "What are you doing down here? What happened? I thought you were dead!"

His head moves from side to side. I can tell it hurts to talk, to move his damaged lips at all. "The Jefe . . . is what happened. That fucking jackass."

I sigh. At least he still has his wits about him. "Why is he torturing you again?"

"He assumes I know something." He swallows hard, in pain. "Shit." His tongue runs over his bottom lip. "Water? Over there."

I pick up the lantern and look in the direction he's looking in. I keep looking, stretching my arm out so the light can fill the dark spaces, and that's when I see the cases of purified water against the far wall.

"He leaves it there so that I can see it. Beg for a drop," Ronaldo rasps.

I mesh my lips together, pushing up and walking to them. Taking a bottle out, I rush back for him, set the lantern down, and then twist the lid off.

"Here." I bring his body forward and he groans in agony, but doesn't resist. "Open your mouth."

When he opens it, I pour the water in. He doesn't stop drinking until the entire bottle is empty.

"Fuck, I needed that." He slouches back again and I put the cap back on the bottle. He looks me over thoroughly in my cocktail dress. "I see you did what I said. You made the king notice you." He smirks.

I shrug. "I did what I had to do to survive here."

"I hear them talk about you. *La Patrona*," he mocks. "How did you gain such a solid position here?"

I look down, studying my red toenails. "Long story."

His smirk fades and his eyes grow a few shades darker. "You have to get me out of here."

"I'm not even supposed to be down here."

"You promised," he grounds out.

"I know I did, but it's not that easy. This is the first night where none of them are on my ass. He's starting to trust me. I can't break that. I've been trying to think of ways—hoping to convince him to let you go. I thought you were in the shed but when I didn't see you that day—"

"They took me out of there when they brought that white-haired guard and his whore in. Brought me here. What are they in there for?"

I squeeze my eyes shut for a moment. "They aren't in there anymore."

He frowns a bit, and when realization hits him, he sighs. "Shit. Dead?"

"Yeah." I look him over again. "Why didn't you tell me you knew Toni? He's your cousin, and in the shed, when we first met, you acted like you didn't know him at all."

His mouth twitches. "I didn't trust you."

"Do you now?"

"Well, seeing as you're the only person that can get me the fuck out of here, I guess I have no choice, huh?"

"Why should I break you out?" I stand, picking up the lantern. "I mean, you did lie to me. I'm on good terms with the boss. You knew Toni—knew exactly how he was. What else do you know?"

"I don't know shit," he spits out. "All I know is that Toni was fucking stupid for crossing The Jefe. He shouldn't have gotten so goddamn cocky. He brought whatever happened to him on himself."

When his eyes glisten, I ease up on my temper, but not completely. "Did you

. . . did you know he killed my father?"

When I ask that, his eyebrows shoot up, as if he's really shocked to hear it. "Lion?"

"You know that name too?"

"Of course I do. He's the reason I'm even here, in Mexico. He gave me the job, to look after The Jefe. To watch him and make reports, make sure he wasn't doing anything stupid. I never understood why he had me tailing him, but I wasn't going to ask questions. He paid me too well for that."

"But you got caught."

He looks away.

"That doesn't explain why he still has you here and is doing this to you." I gesture to him. "What does he want to know?" He doesn't speak. He keeps his gaze away, focusing on the shelves above. I frown down at him, taking a step back. "I'm not even supposed to be down here, *Henry*, so you better start fucking talking or I'll leave you down here to rot."

When I take another step away, he panics, his only chance at survival slipping away. "Shit—fine! He thinks I work for someone named Hernandez."

"Why?"

"He saw some old pictures on my camera of me with that crew but I don't work with them. I don't care about that stupid fucking wannabe cartel—hell, I didn't even know they were organized for that shit. I was with them one night at a fucking bar, hung out at their penthouse because they invited me, and that's it. I got drunk, got lots of pussy that night, and went back to watching Draco Molina. I never even met anyone named Hernandez. I went back to doing my fucking job. He caught me a week later, saw the photos I took with them, and thinks I'm one of them too. I'm not with them. I don't know shit about them, all right? I don't know what plans they have or what they're trying to fucking do. I don't know anyone by the fucking name of Thiago either, so I wish he would stop asking me that shit!"

"Shh!" I hiss. "Keep your voice down. I'm not even supposed to be down here—let alone walking around freely. They'll notice I'm gone soon." I release a thick breath, lowering to a squat. The LED light causes his eyes to glisten. I can't tell if his tears are from rage, fear, or both.

"Do you swear?" I ask. "Because if I find a way to get you out, I have to be sure. He will threaten me for it, maybe even punish me, but he won't kill me. That I know for sure."

"What makes you so sure?" he grumbles.

"Because my father promised me to him a long time ago. Another reason he hates Toni."

Ronaldo scoffs, dropping the back of his head on the wall. "I just want to be free, Gia. I want to live my life. I don't care about Toni or Draco Molina. I will run to the ends of the earth if I have to. I will hide for as long as I need to. I don't care as long as I get the fuck out of here. I won't tell anyone where the hell I've been or anything. I just want to be free. I'm tired of being tortured for something I didn't even do. Can't you see what that motherfucker has done to me? He won't stop until there is nothing left of me but my head. I can't take anymore. I'm being punished for nothing, and he's so fucking paranoid that he doesn't believe me. He probably knows it too, that I don't know shit about what's going on, but he doesn't care. He wants someone to take his anger out on."

"He has every right to be paranoid," I whisper, recalling that conversation with Thiago, how sure of himself he was. And now me. Down here with a man he believes is another enemy.

I run my fingers through my hair, glancing over my shoulder at the steps behind me, and then focusing on the shelves above. There is a kettle up there, a hand shovel, and a large pair of pliers.

Holy shit. Perfect.

I stand up and hurry for the pliers, taking them down by the handles and going back for him.

"I'm risking my life by doing this," I murmur, bringing them down and squeezing one of the chains. It pops and I hear Ronaldo release a ragged breath of relief. "But no matter what Draco thinks, I believe you. Daddy trusted you to look after Draco for a reason. I'm going to stick with my gut and believe it's because he knows you wouldn't have betrayed him . . . not like Toni did. Plus Daddy obviously didn't want Draco dead. He was keeping tabs on him for a reason . . . until he died."

He scowls. "I'm *nothing* like Trigger Toni. He betrays anyone he meets. It's why I never wanted to work for him."

"You have a smart-ass mouth like him."

He chortles.

"There's a party going on tonight. Most of the guards are drinking so they'll be slacking a little. I can't help you get out of here. You're on your own with that. I will do my best to keep Draco occupied. There's a library right across the hallway. You can get out through the window. None of the guards should bother you tonight but you have to be gone by morning if you want to make it out alive."

"You're putting your head on a platter for me," he says.

"Yeah." I grunt, squeezing the handles. "A *thank you* would be nice."

His mouth twitches when I pop the last chain. "Thank you."

There is something about his gratitude that makes the heart I thought had frozen solid, fill with warmth again. I don't know why, but I believe him. I really do. I don't think he has anything to do with this Hernandez person. Toni never mentioned anyone by that name while I was with him and neither did Daddy.

Draco is just so consumed by his own paranoia that he feels he can't trust anyone that even spent time in the same room as this person. I guess I don't blame him. He didn't become who he is overnight. He worked for his title. He has to be cautious. But sometimes being too cautious and too prideful can make a person foolish and reckless. It can cause innocent people to lose their lives.

"You defy him, and he likes that," Ronaldo says when I put the pliers back. He shakes his body a little, loosening his joints and allowing the rest of the chains to fall off. There are red marks on his skin, chain patterns. "It's why you're in the position you're in now."

"He's making up for his wrongs. I'm only being myself," I tell him, picking the lantern up.

He grins. "Are you? Or is everything so normal and boring right now that you're hoping he actually does something to you when he finds out what you've done? He's spoiling you. Pampering you. He fucks you good, I'm sure. I can tell by the way you speak about him. So highly, like you owe him or something. But you want the old him back. The brutal one. The one that tossed you around and made a fool out of you. That's the kind of man you want—the kind of man you crave so that you can have a reason to fight back or even *kill* him if it comes down to it. You're just too afraid to accept that godawful truth."

My eyebrows stitch together. *What the hell is he talking about?* He doesn't know shit about me. Before I can speak on what he's just said, I hear voices growing louder. Someone's coming down the corridor. I listen harder and it's one of the guards, shouting at another

"Shit." I hurry to the steps, listening to the guards speaking rapidly in their native language. "They're about to do a perimeter check. Draco will come looking for me soon. I have to go." I shut off the lantern, putting it back in its place. "Tonight is your only chance to get out," I whisper-hiss. "Wait for about thirty minutes. You better make it count, and you better run as far and as fast as you can. I would wish you good luck, but luck doesn't seem to be on your side much right now."

He chuckles dryly. "Luck is probably the only reason I'm still breathing, Gia."

I purse my lips and rush up the steps. I grip the doorknob, the voices becoming distant. Good. They aren't coming downstairs yet. I have time to make it back and pretend I'm coming from the library.

I hurry out, pulling the key from the lock and placing it above the banister again. I purposely leave the door unlocked, my heart beating a mile a minute. I don't know what the hell I'm doing, but I hope that I'm right. I hope that Henry gets out and he gets somewhere safe.

I'm not sure if the part of me that feels guilty is the part that still cares for Toni or for Daddy. What Toni did—it was wrong. Unforgiveable. But it doesn't mean that I've stopped caring about him altogether. I remember everything I shared with him. Every moment with him felt like bliss, but that bliss has become shadowed by the troubling truth.

I don't know how Henry will escape without arms. Maybe he won't at all, but at least I tried. If he's caught, it will be his own fault. My conscious is clear and my promise to him has been fulfilled. I did my part. He is on his own now.

Giving a thorough look around the hallway, I turn around and make way for the marble staircase. I get halfway down the hall before Patanza appears ahead of me, shouting, "Where the hell have you been?"

"Bathroom," I shout back, pretending to adjust my gown.

I enter the dining room with her again. The music is still playing and Draco and Simon are still downing shots of tequila.

He spots me, head cocking. "Where is my mother?" he asks when I'm close.

"She's tired." I take the seat beside him. "She went to bed."

"Oh." He tosses his shot back, not even wincing as he slams the cup down. "Did she say if she had a good time or not?" he asks me, leaning back and planting his elbows on the arms of his chair. He runs his thumb over the skull ring on his pinky finger.

"Yeah. She said it was a good night," I respond.

He nods and then stands, grabbing my hand. "Good. Let's go." I stand with him and we leave the dining room. But as we walk out, I look down the hallway, feeling my chest tighten. As we walk up the stairs to get to Draco's bedroom, Henry's last remark really gets to my head.

It rings.

Chimes.

Echoes.

"Are you? Or is everything so normal and boring right now that you're hoping he actually does something to you when he finds out what you've done? He's spoiling you. Pampering you. He fucks you good, I'm sure. I can tell by the way you speak about him. So highly, like you owe him or something. But you want the old him back. The brutal one. The one that tossed you around and made a fool out of you. That's the kind of man you want—the kind of man you crave so that you can have a reason to fight back or even kill him if it comes down to it. You're just too afraid to accept that godawful truth."

Am I bored?

Am I stupid?

Am I both?

Perhaps it's not about the promise I made to Ronaldo. Maybe it's something much deeper than even I want to begin to understand.

But for now I can't think much about it. My back lands on the soft bed. His lips drop down to my neck and he sucks on my skin, trailing down, kissing each breast while his hands shove my dress up.

Fingers wrap around the waistband of my panties, tugging down. His mouth moves south, lower, lower, lower, until his face is centered between my thighs.

I can still hear the music—the guests partying and laughing.

Warmth coats my sacred area, swirling on my clit. His tongue plunges in and out of me, his hand resting on my belly to hold me still before I can wriggle.

I gasp, threading my fingers through his thick hair, looking down into his hot eyes. "Fucking mine," I hear him growl and he wastes no time finishing me off.

I sink into this abyss of pleasure, allowing him to do what he wants with me.

I have to enjoy this now because I've just done something I shouldn't have.

I've *betrayed* him.

And if I know Draco, betrayal is something he doesn't take lightly at all.

He will punish me for this when he finds out the truth, and the sad thing is, I'm ready for it.

I'm ready for all he has to give me.

CHAPTER SEVENTEEN

Thunder rumbles in the sky.

I roll over, looking out of the window. I believe this is the first time it's rained since I was brought here. The sky is gray, and the clouds are thick with water.

It's a dark, gloomy morning.

To my right, Draco is still sleeping. His hair is a mess, and he's not wearing any clothes. The sheet covers only his manhood, which seems to be growing harder as I rub my hand over his chest.

After what I did last night, I feel like I owe him more than just sex. He doesn't know about it yet, but I have this feeling deep in my gut that he will find out soon. Very soon.

Tugging the sheet down, I lean on my elbows and bring my lips toward the head of his cock. I lick the length of him, sliding it down to his balls and then up to his tip again.

He shudders in his sleep, eyes rolling behind his eyelids like his dream has been heightened tenfold. Gripping his thickness in hand, I apply just enough pressure with a squeeze and wrap my lips around the head. Pumping slowly, while sucking him there, he groans deep and twitches in his sleep.

I watch him, enjoying the way his skin slides through my lips and over my tongue. The saltiness lands on my tongue too, and I swallow it down, bringing my other hand up to play with his warm, taut sack.

"Shit," I hear him croak, his voice thick with sleep. When I look up, his eyes are open, lazy but heated.

I don't stop. I keep going, feeling him tense up beneath me. I continue pumping his cock with one hand, using the other to caress his balls again. His hands go behind his head and he watches me. No words are spoken. All I hear is the slurping and smacking. I circle my tongue around the head and he shudders again, his abs contracting.

I pump him a little harder. He's so hard in my mouth. I don't know why I get satisfaction out of knowing he's close. He's so close. Rock hard and ready to explode at any second.

He squeezes his eyes shut, panting now as he jerks his hips. I move my hand and lean forward, taking his entire length into my mouth, gradually pulling away. I do this repeatedly, drawing out a rise in him.

"Fuck," he groans.

I do it again and again. His hand comes to the back of my head and he forces it down, causing me to choke around his massive length. He doesn't ease up until I feel him shooting his hot release down my throat.

His entire body vibrates, a deep sigh filling the bedroom, fingers still tangled in my hair.

"Goddamn, niñita," he murmurs when I lick his tip again, making sure he's completely clean. I pick my head up and he swipes a thumb across the edge of my lips. "I love what this pretty little mouth of yours can do."

Loud footsteps sound, getting closer and closer, and then there is insistent banging on the door. Draco jerks away from me with haste, brows furrowed, and I sit up, watching as he hops up and walks to the door, completely naked.

"What have I said about interrupting me before seven, Patanza?" he snaps after yanking the door open.

"Jefe—it's important," she says, and she sounds serious. Breathless. I swallow hard, forcing my back against the upholstered headboard. "If we could handle this on our own, we would, but this is different. You need to come see for yourself."

He stands there for a moment and then he steps back, peering over his shoulder at me. I look away, toward the window, swallowing my guilt. "Fine. Give me a minute."

He shuts the door in her face and marches for the closet. He takes down some boxers, jeans, and a T-shirt, and gets dressed in a matter of seconds. He slides his feet into a pair of tan loafers that somehow match well with the outfit and then he rakes his fingers through his hair, going for the door.

"Don't leave this room. I'll be back."

He shuts it before I can speak. I rush to the door on tiptoes and put my ear to it, listening to Patanza speaking rapidly in her native tongue as they walk down the hallway. "He's not in there, and we can't find him anywhere around the property. I sent Simon and Diego on the boat to look for him, in case he took one of your canoes, and sent the newer guards out to town to look for him. The chains look like they were cut, Jefe. Like someone did it for him. I bet it was fucking Thiago. Told you not to let him stay here. Fucker can't be trusted."

Draco curses beneath his breath, and I don't hear anything else from them after that.

My eyes are wide as I pace the bedroom. I have to act normal. I don't care if he blames Thiago. It'll get him out of this house. Draco already doesn't trust him. This would be the icing on the cake—more than enough reason to get rid of him.

"Calm down, Gia," I whisper to myself, walking to the closet and pulling down a black dress. It's a spaghetti strap, loose and gauzy. I hang it on the doorknob and walk into the bathroom to freshen up.

He wouldn't suspect me to do such a thing. There is nothing that can give me away—nothing but my shaky hands and frazzled nerves, that is.

My whole body is shaking, surging with adrenaline. I grip the edge of the counter, breathing deep. Then I turn on the water, sticking my hands beneath the stream and bringing the coolness to my flushed cheeks.

But when I look up, I don't see my reflection. I see white hair and hard, dark eyes. I see a twisted smile and blood spilling down his throat.

Bain.

I gasp, jolting as I back away.

"You're still a stupid fucking bitch," he chuckles. "Stupid to think Jefe won't find out. What's done in the dark always comes to light. *Puta.*"

I drop my head again, bringing the water up, clearing my face, squeezing my eyes tighter. I look up again and this time I only see myself, face paler, eyes even bigger.

"Calm down," I tell myself, shutting off the water and walking to bedroom. But telling myself to be calm is stupid.

Even more so when I'm finally dressed and hear Draco start to shout about fifteen minutes later.

Something crashes. It sounds like glass.

Then I hear stomping. Closer and closer.

Boom! Boom! Boom!

The door is kicked open and there he stands, teeth clenched, fists balled, seething like a raging bull. He's blind with fury, ready to charge. Ready to *destroy.*

He pulls out a gun from his waistband and points it right at me, nostrils flaring as he charges forward.

I stare at the barrel of the spotless silver gun, but I'm speechless. I can't explain, as badly as I want to—as much as I need to save my own ass, I can't. My tongue feels like it weighs a thousand pounds.

He knows. I know he knows. I did this. I let Henry go. I . . . *betrayed* him.

The gun presses down on the center of my forehead, cold and hard, and through gritted teeth, he shouts, *"WHAT THE FUCK DID YOU DO?"*

CHAPTER EIGHTEEN

"*Draco—I—*"

"No!" he barks, finger wrapped around the trigger. "Shut the fuck up! You know what fuck you did, and I should kill you right where you fucking stand for it!"

"I was trying to help him!" I shout back.

His head shakes roughly, but the gun doesn't waver.

I hold my hands up, thinking that I must have been wrong about this. Us. Maybe he will kill me—if I do something stupid enough, like this. Doesn't matter who my father is. I didn't follow his rules.

"Draco, Henry isn't your enemy. I believe what he says," I say quickly. "Daddy hired him and trusted him to watch you. You say Daddy saved your life, treated you like his own son. Why would he send someone he couldn't trust to come and look after you? Henry was only doing his job and was at the wrong place with the wrong people. I've been around Toni," I breathe, "but that doesn't make me anything like him."

"I don't give a fuck about any of that," he growls through gritted teeth, grip tightening on the gun. "You let him go without my permission. You went behind my fucking back and freed him and now he's out there somewhere. He saw too much around here! Knew too fucking much! He knows *you* are here!" he spews at me. "Have you forgotten there is a warrant on my head? *Three million fucking dollars*, Gianna, and all he has to do is lead the police back here to me! To *my* fucking home!"

My heart sinks.

Shit.

That's right.

He's wanted by many.

"B-but he won't tell," I assure him, hands still in the air. "He only wanted to be free. He knows how you are. He'll run far away and won't look back."

"He has no fucking money. Nowhere to fucking go," he grumbles. "He could quite possibly be working with Hernandez. He has a secret, and I was close to fucking cracking him, but *you* decide to be stupid by letting him go! I let you do this shit right under my fucking nose," he scoffs. "And for that, you will fucking pay."

"How do you even know it was me?" I ask, feeling foolish for even bothering to ask.

"Guillermo had eyes on Thiago the entire night. He watched him and followed him up to bed. Thiago sleeps with the door open just so my men can keep watch. *I* watched him all night at the party. The only time that armless fuck could have escaped was during the party, when we were all occupied, and *you* asked for your fucking space. I should have known better than to think I could give you that."

I swallow, but it's hard to do. My throat is so dry.

He takes another step forward, gripping the back of my neck. The gun pushes down harder on my forehead, enough to leave an imprint behind. His forefinger tightens around the trigger.

"Draco, please," I beg. He's so close to pulling it. "I didn't do this to betray you! I promised I would help him!"

"I don't give a fuck about your promises, Gianna. They're fucking worthless."

"But what if you're wrong about him? What if he really only wanted to be free? Free from you and this place! It's what I wanted before, too, and I wouldn't have told. I would have just run and never looked back."

"I'm not wrong. I know a fucking con artist and liar when I see one. But that's the thing about you—you're so blind to all of it. Hell, you fell for the man who murdered your own father. Of course you'll fall for the next man's bullshit, too. Especially one related to him."

He squeezes my neck until it hurts. I wince and cry out a little, but my eyes don't move from the trigger. He continues squeezing down. More. More. More.

"Draco!" I plead. "You said you wouldn't kill me."

He fastens his jaw and squeezes the trigger all the way down. I flinch, expecting a loud noise and some bright light to follow, but there's nothing. Only a solid, hard click.

He pulled the trigger, but the safety is on.

The safety . . .

Jerking away, he shoves me down on the edge of the bed and steps forward. "You feel that? I know you do, because I can see it so fucking clearly. Fear. That fear in your eyes still brings me joy," he rasps, towering over me. "I said I wouldn't kill you—that I can't kill you—because I respected your father too much. I *won't*. But it doesn't mean that I can't hurt you." He grabs my hair and tugs on it, getting in my face, making me whimper. "I am going to hurt you so fucking much you'll hate me again, Gianna. I'm going to teach you that fucking me over and going behind my fucking back gets you nowhere! I tried with you, I really did." He pulls away, holding the gun up in the air. "But don't think you're safe with me by any means. No," he laughs, a sinister one I haven't heard since I was first brought here. "I'll be back, and you better be fucking ready, because I am done being fucking lenient with you. By the end of the night, you will worship, obey, and submit to me. You will be mine all over again. No more fucking freedom for you."

And with those words, he's walking out of the room, storming down the hallway.

Though he's gone, the atmosphere is still thick with tension. Sweat has beaded up on my forehead, my palms clammy. I look down, realizing my hands are shaking, my breath is erratic, and my legs are wobbling like mad.

I am terrified all over again.

Of him. Of what he'll do to me.

And . . . deep down . . . I'm glad to feel this way.

Glad, because I *can't* like him. I don't *want* to like him. I don't want his charm to win me over. I don't want him to ever trust me, because I don't ever want to trust him. I can't trust a man like him.

I need to *hate* him again. I need the fight. I needed a reason to kindle my fire inside, and he's going to hand it right to me.

El Jefe vs. La Patrona.

I guess the question now is, who will win?

CHAPTER NINETEEN

Anxiety has swarmed me. Though I'm on edge, I go downstairs for breakfast, on time and dressed accordingly. The dining room is back to its original setting, clear of everything, including plates and silverware, which is strange.

I walk to my seat and sit, waiting to hear Draco come strolling in at any given second. There is less than one minute left until 8:00. I pull my chair in, and as I wait, I hear footsteps coming.

I look to the right, toward the doors. But it's not Draco I see. It's Thiago. He strolls right into the dining room, with a white T-shirt and dark-blue jeans. His dark, beady eyes sparkle from the sunlight filtering in through the window, and of course they are focused on me.

I watch him come closer and closer, finally taking the seat right beside me. Swallowing thickly, I cross my legs and shift to the left, as if it will get me further away from him.

It doesn't. I still smell him. I feel him there, staring like some deranged animal.

"Stop looking at me," I snap without meeting his eyes.

His laugh is throaty and slightly obnoxious.

"He'll kill you if he sees you sitting beside me," I mutter beneath my breath.

"Not if he kills *you* first." When he says that, I pick up my head, meeting the dark orbs for eyes. "I heard what you did. He came looking for me. Fortunately, I had an alibi. I really had no clue there was even a guy without arms staying here." He laughs again. "Why'd you do it? What did you get out of it?"

I pull my gaze away, refusing to answer.

"You're smart but stupid," he mutters. "Women." Seconds later and Draco comes into the dining room, steps still heavy, shoulders tense. None of the guards are around. I've noticed they're all pretty much gone, probably out looking for Henry.

"You eat and then you get the fuck out of my sight," he growls as he takes his throne-like chair. For a second, I'm not sure if he's talking to Thiago or me.

But when Thiago laughs and relaxes in his chair, I realize his statement was directed at me. The butlers stroll in with carts, placing dishes down in front of him and Thiago. Their plates are covered with fried potatoes, scrambled eggs, and Argentinian sausage. But the plate in front of me is . . . not what I'm expecting.

It's a sandwich. Peanut butter and strawberry jelly, to be exact.

Thiago takes sight of it and laughs so fucking hard I feel it twisting my core.

I peer up at Draco, who slides his gaze from Thiago to me. He grabs the handle of his coffee mug, bringing the rim up to his lips.

"What the hell is this?" I hiss, shoving the plate away.

"Eat," he commands when he places the coffee mug down.

"No." I twist in my chair when the butler that just poured Thiago's coffee walks behind me. I grab his elbow and say in Spanish, "Bring me what they're having."

The butler looks from me to Draco, who cocks a stern brow, giving a simple threat with his eyes alone.

Nervously swallowing the lump in his throat, he gently pulls his elbow away and speeds to the kitchen. When a minute passes by, I realize he isn't coming back.

"Eat," Draco demands again. "Better this than nothing, right?"

I clench my jaw tight, focusing on his eyes.

"You will eat lightly today," he declares when he picks up a piece of sausage.

"Why?"

His upper lip quirks, just barely, but he says nothing. Just bites into the sausage, holding my stare until I pull away.

"Shit. It's fucking intense in here," Thiago says through a mouth full of food. "Gia, want some?" he offers, sliding his plate over as if he really will give me some.

I blink at him, the way he mocks me with that sneer.

"Stop fucking around, Thiago. We have shit to do soon," Draco grumbles in Spanish.

I push out of my chair. "I'll be in the room."

"*Your* room," he says when I push the chair back in. Then he picks up the plate with the sandwich. "With your sandwich." He holds it out, a silent demand that I take it with me. His eyes are hard and threatening, jaw flexing.

Enraged, I snatch the sandwich off the plate, pull the pieces of bread apart, and smash the slices face down on the table, smearing the jelly and peanut butter all over the wood.

"Fuck you *and* your fucking sandwich, Draco."

I leave before he can retaliate. When I make it up the staircase, I'm truly surprised he hasn't come hunting me down. I rush down the hallway and into the room I'd stayed in before.

The room for prisoners.

As I storm inside and look to my right, that's when I spot the flowers on the dresser. These aren't the chocolate cosmos I've grown accustomed to.

No.

These flowers are a bright, stark blue, bold and resilient. The sun dances on the large dew-dropped petals, highlighting the white streaks between each crease as well as the black dots collected in the middle.

I stare at them longer than intended.

I've never seen anything like them before.

I step forward, noticing a note folded beneath the vase. Moving it aside, I pick up the letter and read the words. *His* words. *His* handwriting.

Blue Betrayals.

Know why they're called that?

Because beneath all that beauty, there are thorns —— large, sharp, vicious thorns.

Some of them you can't see because they are just as blue, blending in with

the soft petals, which is why you have to be careful when picking them.

If you aren't cautious, they'll stab you right where it fucking hurts,

and yet you still can't help but want to keep them.

Be in my galería at 10:00 p.m. Be on time or I swear you will regret it.

The galería.

Again.

It's back to this.

The punishments. The rage. The hate.

I release a ragged breath, pushing one of the petals of the flowers aside and spotting several thorns. They are sharp. Almost deadly. But I pull one out anyway and smell it.

It is sweet and strong and beautiful, but so sharp and vicious beneath the delicate petals.

It's . . . kind of like me.

The hours go by in a flash.

I wrote during most of the day in the library, not giving a damn if I was supposed to leave that prisoner's room or not. I got hungry, so I went to the kitchen, but a snack tray was already prepared for me, courtesy of the fucking Jefe himself. Orange slices, pretzels, Brazilian nuts, and water.

Eduardo couldn't even look me in the eye. I could tell he was disappointed in me. I didn't blame him, but it did sting a little when he didn't speak to me.

I took the tray back to the library and ate it all, hating every bite as I thought of him. There are only three guards around and they are the weakest ones. Not too bright, either, and I honestly think they are afraid of me. They are newer, but just as willing to give their life for their boss as the older guards are.

As I wrote, I questioned myself. Why I didn't just sneak out of the window in here and run away? Swim away, even?

But then, as I scribbled out all of my hatred, my craze, and the hostile words my beating heart could no longer contain, I realized that I couldn't run. I *wouldn't*. He didn't scare me anymore. Even though I shook and trembled, it wasn't out of fear, I realized.

It was out of adrenaline.

That toxic, dangerous rush I could never get enough of.

A rush I used to get when Toni would go for a drug run and the cops would show up, trying to bust him. We would have to ditch the brand new car he bought under a fake name and run as fast as our feet would allow.

Our hearts would be drumming and our minds would go numb, slipping straight into survival mode, until we were in the clear. And in the clear, we would laugh in each other's faces, so hysterically that I really assumed we were insane.

It was fun.

It seemed real.

But it wasn't.

Toni betrayed me. He killed Daddy.

And I think it's because of him, and knowing that he could be the blame, that I'd rather stay here and deal with this monster instead of running away.

I'd rather face my fears.

Face the demon that dwells inside him.

Because, deep down, I know I have one of my own. Deep down, I know I'm not as innocent as I pretend to be. Deep down we have a connection—a brutal, twisted connection that is impossible to deny.

I wish I was innocent, but when you grow up the way I did, around men like Daddy and Toni and uncles who are just as crazy and bad, you know you can't be.

You're either just like them, or you don't survive. I'm tired of being the fool, the stepping stool, and the clueless little girl surrounded by kings. Mama didn't even put up with their shit. She handled it with grace and put those who stepped out of line back in their places in a heartbeat.

I remember it well. Daddy never disrespected her, and that's because she earned that right. He was her queen. She was his ride-or-die.

I was afraid before. I thought I would be taken care of for life with Toni.

But I'm ready for my big crown now.

I'm ready to be *queen.*

Draco will not strip my power away from me. I'm close—so close to being at the top. So close to knowing how it will feel if it were *my* world. What I did only brought the *real* Draco back out again. The one whose passion runs deep, his viciousness so strong it could slay any man.

He shouldn't be lenient with me.

He should teach me, just as I want to teach him.

He should show me exactly how he wants me to be.

It's sad that I crave this, but this power—this hunger for the most ruthless man in the world—has been something I've longed for my entire life.

I'm fucking sadistic, and I know it. But I can't go back now.

Not after all I've done. It's too late for that.

It's too late for me to be good.

At 9:55 I'm leaving Draco's bedroom.

He didn't come up to change, but I heard him return, making commands to the few guards and maids as he passed by the room.

I took a shower, braided my hair, put on a silk red robe, and no shoes. It's what he told me to do—in the note that was slipped beneath the door of the library.

The robe was hung on the bathroom door, waiting for me. Why he wanted me to wear it and braid my hair and wear no shoes, I had no clue. I could have ignored it, but when I saw the note and his handwriting, my skin buzzed.

It buzzed because the main thing he wanted was: **NO CLOTHES BENEATH.**

No clothes. Just a robe, loosely tied at the waist.

I walk down the stairs, noticing the house is eerily calm. None of the maids are running around, no butlers calling orders to the others. None of the guards are posted at the doors.

As I walk down the corridor, where his paintings are, I look in the empty dining room. There is one maid there, mopping the floors. She has her headphones on. I realize this is the same maid that walked in during my first few days in Draco's bedroom—how scared she was that she did, as if I would chop off her head.

She doesn't look up as she mops, probably not even noticing me.

This is the way he wanted it.

It's a ghost town in here. Dead quiet. *Eerily* calm compared to the shitstorm that happened today.

As I walk down the corridor that leads to the galería, I stop at the top of the marble staircase. Music is playing. A violin. It's a slow song, dramatic enough to make the hairs on the back of my neck stand up.

I take each step down with each chord struck, walking until I'm at the bottom and standing in front of the half-open door.

The violin stops as I pull the creaking door open. My throat thickens.

I walk in, heart racing now, steps measured.

And then I notice. The room . . .

It's changed.

His art supplies, they are nowhere in sight.

It's almost like a completely different chamber.

Darker.

Troubling.

In the middle of the room there is a thick, black rail hanging from the tall ceiling. It extends all the way down, several feet from the floor, and I realize it has always been built in there. There is a slot in the ceiling that the railing most likely goes into.

On each end are leather cuffs with silver chains connecting them to the rails. Built into the floor are chains, similar to the ones in the brown shed, but shinier. Thicker.

A red light streams down from the ceiling, right on the spot the rails and chains are. They bounce off the marble floor, and near the staircase, where I notice he stands. The light barely shines on him.

He's there with a leather paddle gripped in hand. And on the flat of it is the word **OBEY**.

My body swims with fear and adrenaline as I take note of his serious glare, the way his jaw ticks, his shoulders hiked with wrath. He looks mean and hard . . . he looks *evil*.

I swallow the hard lump in my throat as I stop only a few steps away from the rail and cuffs. I thought surely he would take me to the bed, hate-fuck me, and then be on his way.

But this? This means business.

This is serious.

He is going to teach me, whether I like it or not . . . and I'm ready.

He doesn't speak as he walks, purposely avoiding the red light, lurking in the shadows. He comes closer and closer, and soon I can smell his cologne. He's a step away. I can feel his anger radiating off of his tan skin, burning beneath the shirt that's unbuttoned at the neckline and chest, revealing his gold crucifix and the broad pecs beneath.

"You know why you're here, don't you?" he asks, standing in front of me, tall, hovering. His voice is gravelly. Deep.

"Yes," I whisper. "You made it very clear why I'm here."

"Did I?" I can hear the jeer in his voice. "No, Gianna. I don't think I have. See, I haven't even gotten started yet with how clear I need to make myself when it comes to you."

I let out a ragged, thick breath as he circles me like a lion about to pounce on its prey. Calculating. Waiting for the perfect moment to strike. When he's behind me, I feel him standing close—so close I can feel his breath on the nape of my neck. He pushes the braid aside, bringing it over my shoulder.

"What you did, Gianna, is un-fucking-acceptable," he grumbles, still close. "You would be fucking dead if it wasn't for your father—if it wasn't for how much

I owe him. But since I can't kill you out of my respect for him, I will make you pay instead." He steps around again to face me. "I won't be gentle with you," he sneers. "Oh, no." He squeezes my face tight between his fingers. "I am going to make you *cry*. I am going to make you scream and beg me for mercy. See, I tried being gentle with you, and you took advantage of it. You got a little freedom from me and turned right around and *betrayed* me. I told you I wanted to trust you, but that trust is long gone now.

"So believe me when I say this will hurt, and I will *not* stop, even when I hear you screaming. Even when I see the tears rolling down this beautiful, angelic face of yours, I will keep going. Even when I see blood, I. Will. Keep.*Going*." He finally lets go of my face, and I release a shaky breath. "I will show you just where disobedience lands you." He points at the rails. "Get over there."

I steel my jaw, staring at the cuffs on the ends of it, the chains in the floor. I gaze down at my ruined wrists; the cuts that have healed but are somehow still sensitive. Being tied up again, it terrifies me. And not in the good way.

"Draco, you should know that I—"

Before I can finish, he's gripped me by the braid of my hair and is dragging me to the cuffs and rails. I hiss through my teeth, feeling some of my hair rip at the root as my feet scuffle forward. He jerks away when I'm standing directly beneath the red light.

His jaw is pulsing now, the paddle gripped harder in hand. He places it down on the table behind him and then returns, grabbing my forearm and drawing it up.

Wrapping the leather around my wrist tight, he watches me with hard, dark eyes, buckling it in the process. He reaches for the other and does the same, still glaring me down, breathing heavily.

When he bends down, bringing the cuffs on the floor around my ankles, gooseflesh crawls on my skin. The chains run over my feet, cold like ice, his fingers hot as he buckles each one down.

And then he rises, steps back, and looks at me from head to toe.

"You didn't fight," he notes, eyes broiling with desire. He's still pinning me with those wicked eyes of his, taking steady steps back to get to the paddle again.

"You can't hurt me, Draco," I tell him, voice scratchy, almost shaky. Because he can. He can hurt me so much and I can't do a single thing about it.

He picks it up with a small smile, gripping the handle of the leather paddle, examining it. "You think so?" he laughs. "I thought you fucking learned, niñita. I thought I'd finally—*finally*—gotten through to you. I see now that I was so wrong, and that you aren't ready yet. You aren't ready for me." He tips my chin with the edge of the paddle. "If you are with me, this is how it will go. My queen will obey and trust me. She will worship me. She will side with me at all times and she will never fucking betray me. Tonight, I will make it so that you are more than ready, and so that you *never* pull something that fucking stupid behind my back, ever again."

CHAPTER TWENTY

e circles me again with deliberate steps.

When he's behind me, I'm afraid of what he'll do. My heart is still drumming against my ribcage, my wrists already sore. I try and move my feet but I can't. I'm stuck—completely open and vulnerable to him.

Sweat builds up on the nape of my neck. As he passes, I feel the breeze there, barely cooling my hot skin. My legs are spread just as wide as my arms. Soon, they'll be tired.

He finally stops walking, and I hear rustling. I glance over my shoulder, but he's in the dark so I can't tell what he's doing. I hear steps again. I feel his breath, the heat of his body. He's right behind me.

A hand grips my braid and tugs back. Hard. I gasp as my face points up to the ceiling, at the red light beaming down on me.

"I promised I wouldn't punish you again. But if you don't keep your promises, why should I?"

"I never promised you anything," I respond, breathless.

"You promised to be mine. You accepted this life."

"Yes, I did. I accepted, but that doesn't mean that I don't have a mind or a will of my own."

He pulls my braid harder, a low growl scratching at his throat. He then presses his hard body against me, knocking me off balance. Fortunately, with the chains, it only causes me to sway.

I feel something hard pressing into my back as he pushes in a little more. It's him. He's hard for me. He likes seeing me like this.

"I seriously want to rip you to shreds, little girl," he snarls, bringing his lips to my ear. "But you know what's funny?" He drags a hand around and grips my throat tight. I almost can't breathe. Almost. "We found your armless friend," he whispers, voice cold, taunting.

Horror strikes me. My eyes grow wide, legs shaking now. "Where?"

"He didn't get far. And we knew he wouldn't. He was weak. Hungry. Useless, Gianna. He was garbage, and you sacrificed your freedom for that trash."

"Was?" My voice breaks. "He's *dead*?"

When I get no response, I jerk my arms, but it only causes the chains to rattle. He pulls from me, stepping away and bringing back a cold draft. I twist my head to look for him. I can't find him.

"Draco!" I shriek. "You killed him!" Anger builds inside me, brewing. I feel it in my core, seeping through my pores. "He was innocent, and you know it! He couldn't have hurt you! He was only doing his job!"

SMACK!

A shrill gasp floods the room after that smack. My ass stings, and I wince, squeezing my eyes shut.

SMACK!

SMACK!

Two more. They sting so much. I ball my fingers into fists, jerking as much as I can, as if it will set me free.

"STOP!" I scream.

Another smack.

And another.

And one more.

Each one is harder than the last, all in the same area. I will be bruised. It feels hot there. It hurts. I know it's probably welted. Bleeding.

Several seconds later and hands reach around me from behind, untying my robe. It falls open, revealing my naked front and he finally comes around to face me, jaw steeled, nostrils flared, the obedience paddle still in his hand.

He's shirtless now. Hard and toned.

"You don't call the fucking shots around here, Gianna!" he bellows. "You do not run anything, not even me! At the end of the fucking day, I'm the one they seek approval from, not you. I'm the fucking boss, and they all know it. You know it!" He reaches forward, cupping my breasts, squeezing to the point of pain. "You put me in this fucking position, you know that? I wanted us on the same page. I wanted us to move forward. I wanted to fulfill my promise to your father—make you mine. Make you happy here, however I could. But you fucked it up by setting him free. It doesn't fucking matter if you believe him; I didn't! And you ignored that cold hard fact and did what you wanted anyway!"

He snatches his hand away, bringing the tip of the paddle up to press it down on my pebbled nipple. I cry out a little when the pressure builds, fists clenching again.

"You're a fucking monster, Draco! You will *never* make me happy," I seethe.

And for some reason, when I say that, he freezes. Just briefly. His eyebrows draw together and he studies my face. His eyes aren't as hard as they were only seconds ago. They've softened a touch, as if my remark was a blow straight through the heart with the sharpest of daggers.

He hardens again, though, straightening his back and stomping around me. I hear the paddle fall to the ground and he makes his way to a dark corner, returning with a sharp knife. He steps up behind me, bringing the edge of the blade to my throat.

"Maybe I am a monster," he murmurs in my ear, "but you're the one addicted to them." The edge of the blade presses into my throat. It's so sharp, I feel a sting and when something hot spills down to my chest, I realize I'm bleeding. He pulls the blade away, and then I hear a loud *rip* as he cuts through fabric.

My robe splits apart and he shoves each piece over so they're hanging off my arms now. My entire back and front side is exposed. The air hits me hard, and I shiver from both the fear and the chill.

One of his hands explores my ass, gripping and pawing. He circles each cheek, and I breathe harder when I feel his other hand come around after dropping the knife. He slides it around my thigh and then between, and when his thumb skims my clit, I buckle. The chains rattle, proving I liked that a little too much.

He groans, still gripping my ass. A finger slides through my slit and then sinks inside me with ease.

"Monsters like me turn you on, niñita. Monsters like me know exactly what you need to keep you in your place. You want me to treat you dirty? Fine. I will. You can be my filthy little slut in here and the queen that reigns beside me out there. You'll get what you want. Didn't I promise that?"

My core clenches when he cups my pussy, but he pulls away in an instant and the sensation fizzles. I drop my head when I hear him walking again. He opens something and then returns.

I smell coconuts, sweet and strong. His hands come to my ass again, but this time he spreads my cheeks apart, lubing the puckered hole.

My asshole.

He does so almost gently and my breathing grows tattered.

"Draco, not there," I plead.

"Yes. Here." He doesn't stop lubing me, making sure it's wet enough for him to slip right in. I start to yank and twist and he pulls away, grabbing my braid again to keep me still. I feel his warm breath on my damp skin again. He's so close. Too damn close.

His belt buckle jingles, there's rustling, and then something hot and thick lands between the crack of my ass. It slides up and down with ease. He wraps my braid in his hand, tugging my head back and using the other hand to cup my breast.

His cock keeps sliding up and down, purposely going past the back entrance. Teasing. Provoking.

"You can't," I whisper, my eyes welling up with tears.

"I believe I can," he responds, still working up and down, lubing himself up as well.

The flashbacks hit me.

Trapped in the gray cellar.

That big man with the bruised face and broken nose.

In and out. Dry strokes.

Screams and cries for help.

All I needed was help.

And the blood.

Surrounded by so much blood.

I was helpless then, and I'm helpless now. This time I really can't fight. I'm strapped down. A hostage, all over again.

"And," he whispers in my ear, "I refuse to be gentle."

After he says that, he thrusts himself inside me. The galería is filled with a sharp gasp and a loud, heavy groan. The thrust is deep. He went right in. And when he's in, he doesn't stop. My braid is still wrapped in his hand, my face forced up. He releases a feral sound and his mouth comes down on the bend of my neck, sucking, devouring, as he strokes in and out of me.

He pumps his hips with strong, full thrusts, still cupping my breast, and then slowly sliding the oily hand around my breasts and down to my pussy, one of his fingers landing on my delicate, aching nub again.

My tears have fallen. They aren't tears from distress. They are tears of something else. Something that I can't describe. This isn't as painful as the cellar. It's familiar, but it's not the same. And it's like he knows it. Punish me by doing something he knows I will hate, but do it just so that I can't resist. So that I can't fight like I tried to do down there.

Devour me. Take me. Own me.

His way.

He fills me up with each pull and drive and my fingers curl, my legs shaking when his finger slowly swirls around my clit.

"You. Are. Mine. Gianna," he says in my ear, still going. He releases the braid and uses that hand to clutch my face, his thumb purposely removing the tears. "I own you. You accepted me. And by accepting me, that means you will take me in any way that I see fit."

Eyes hot, I feel myself slowly unraveling. He's still making loops on my nub, swelling me up. I hear myself panting and moaning as he pounds hard enough for me to truly feel him.

In and out.

Swirls and loops.

My body rolls with heated desire, swimming with ecstasy and resentment. My tears come to a halt. I'm on the edge. I'm right there. So close.

And I shatter. He doesn't stop torturing me with his fingers or his cock in my ass. He's still pumping as I cry out my pleasure, causing the chains to rattle repeatedly with the powerful orgasm, and for his groans to grow louder.

And then I feel weak. So weak. My arms are tired, and I dangle, breathing in and out.

He stops almost immediately, but I know he's not done. Bending down, he undoes the chains around my ankles. When he rises, he catches my eyes, and I hold his gaze, despite how hot he looks with sweat glistening on his chest or how hard and thick he is right now between the legs.

One arm is set free and it drops like dead weight. I catch myself just as he undoes the other arm.

"Upstairs," he commands.

I look up, my feet moving before I can even process his words. I walk up the stairs with him following closely behind me. And then I crawl on the bed, on all fours, peering over my shoulder at him. His eyes spark with lust and he stalks forward, climbing on the bed and gripping the back of my neck.

He forces my face down into the comforter, grinding his cock between the crack of my ass again. "You like when I treat you like this," he says. A statement. Hardly a question. "You like it because you don't think. You just do. You don't want to think about the terrible shit you've done. But guess what, Gianna, there is no denying it. You did it. It happened. And you did it because that's *who you are*. Don't try and blame this on guilt. You're in denial."

He pulls away and climbs off the bed, hustling down the stairs. I hear the water from the sink start up. About a minute later and he's back. He flips me over and I sigh, spreading my legs for him. He's cleaned himself up, I notice.

"Just take me, Draco," I breathe when he perches himself on his knees. My eyes are still damp with tears.

His jaw clenches. He grips my hips and picks them up off the bed, balancing my ass on his upper thighs. He slides right in, slowly, deliberately, watching my eyes. My face. Watching me.

"You need me, *reina*," he says, thrusting so slowly, swelling up inside me. My legs wrap around him, my body greedy for more. The power. The ruthlessness. "With me, there is no one to fear. No one but me. You know that."

I don't speak as I look into his hot brown eyes.

"Don't. Betray. Me. Again." Between each word he plunges harder than the last time. And just as I wanted, he gives me the power. The ruthlessness. He drills into me, bringing a hand down to my throat, fucking me like the savage I know he is.

Dominating every inch of me. Taking me like I need to be taken.

He's not gentle or light. Nothing about him is. He is hard and cruel and merciless . . . and I love it. I want it. More and more, I want it, and I can't help it.

His hand is still gripped tight around my throat, allowing me just enough air to breathe through each of his rapid strokes. Our skin claps, and I hear my moans getting louder, bouncing off the walls and the ceiling. He's groaning between each breath, so hard inside me.

He's close. I can tell.

I pull myself up, sliding right down his full length, riding him fast as I kiss him. I kiss him deep and whole, the passion burning through me, returning full force. He's swelling up inside me as I circle and grind my pussy on his cock, my fingers threading through his hair.

He's groaning loudly, and I can tell he wants to rip me off and push me away. I can tell he wants to fight against this—me on top. *Me* in control. But he doesn't.

Instead, he grips my waist and brings me up and down on top of him. Rising up, slamming down. Repeating the actions over and over, as if he can't get enough. He's hitting a tender spot, one that's already been triggered, and I breathe my pleasure past his full lips, my fingers curling even tighter in his thick bed of hair.

"Shit, Gianna," I hear him say, and those are the last words I hear before I explode—no, *we* explode. He stills, so deep inside me, as I greedily swirl my hips for more, breathing raggedly, moaning and sighing. He cups my ass in his large hands, reeling me closer, as if we aren't already close enough.

Our lips part.

Hearts thumping.

I don't know what that was, but it was powerful. And strong. And . . . real.

Almost too real.

I drop my forehead on his shoulder, but he picks it right back up, forcing me to look at him. "Never again," he says, low and deep. "Never go against me again."

"You killed him," I whisper.

His jaw ticks. "He's not dead."

That surprises the hell out of me. "Then where is he?"

"In one of the cells."

I think before speaking. "What are you going to do to him?"

He studies my eyes, then he lightly pushes me off and I land on my back. He steps off the bed, standing tall, glaring down at me. "Why do you trust him?" he demands.

I look all around the room, a slight frown creasing my forehead. "I—I don't know, Draco. I just do. He . . . saved me in there, during those first days when you weren't here, and Pico and Bain said and did those things to me. In a way, he taught me how to survive and how endure it. If it wasn't for him, I never would have caught your attention."

"You already had my attention," he grumbles.

"How?"

"You were married to a man I hated. I needed to know everything I could about him, and who he worked with. At first I wanted to destroy you . . . but then I saw you."

I drop my gaze, focusing on my toes. "If Daddy promised me to you, why weren't you keeping tabs on me then? I was supposed to be your future wife, right?"

He shrugs. "He didn't want me to have you anymore. He wasn't expressing the interest either. It's almost like he lost his faith in me—sending Trigger Toni's cousin to watch after me, making sure I stayed out of the U.S. for months on end, probably so I couldn't come near him or you. I knew it was Lion, and I couldn't even retaliate because I owed him more than my life. Let's just say that after my father died, I didn't care much about being married to Lion's daughter. I wanted to be alone. All I wanted was revenge. Lion knew that. He also knew who it was that killed my father. Probably why he started seeing me less and less. He knew that I knew who the person was, and he knew I wasn't going to stop until he was dead."

My breath becomes ragged, but I draw in as much oxygen as I can, focusing on him. "Do you have proof? Pictures? Something that shows you were close to him in any way?"

"Why do you need proof? Why would I lie about this?" he asks, slightly agitated.

"Because . . . I've been lied to before. By a man just like you, Draco. He pretended to love Daddy, and if what you told me is true, and he killed him in cold blood, then I need to know. I can't just go off of what you tell me. If . . . if I'm really going to stay here, and if you really want me to trust you and do what you say, I need proof. I need to know that you aren't just saying and doing all of this to manipulate me. I still have some family out there. Friends. People still know who I am."

"I'm sure they all assume you're dead by now. They know Toni is. Sent his wedding band finger in a box to his family."

Oh my God. His mom. His brother. I can imagine their horror. The tears rolling down their sad faces. "They didn't deserve that!" I snap, rising on my knees. "They were good people. His mom was like a mother to me, too."

"Emphasis on the word *was*." His jaw ticks.

"I want proof, Draco," I demand.

"Even with proof, you won't trust me, Gianna."

"Why wouldn't I?"

"Because I can be very impulsive. You'll never know what I'll do next."

"You already said you wouldn't kill me. That's fair enough. I don't have to know what you will do next. I'm certain I can handle whatever you throw at me. You don't kill me and I won't make an attempt to kill you. I have nothing left to lose but my life, Draco, and that already feels pretty worthless. What good would it be for me to run away—go back to the life I had—just for you to destroy it again? I know if I run, you'll find me. You'll drag me right back to you and kill anyone that stands in the way of that."

His chin tilts in a superior way, and I know I'm right.

"So I won't run. I will do my part. But I want proof. I want to know that Daddy actually trusted you and your father. I need that assurance. It will give me peace."

He looks me over in my naked, vulnerable stance before pulling his eyes away. "Fine." He picks his head up, tipping my chin. "But about what you did with the Ricci cousin . . . I won't be able trust you anymore. You stay here. You'll be mine, but I can't trust you, Gianna. You cut a potential enemy loose. He could have told anyone where I was, and they could have killed me."

I drop my line of sight to his chest. "I'm . . . sorry, Draco."

He pulls his hand away. "Sorry won't cut it. It's a pathetic word with no depth. Your apology means *nothing* to me." Stepping away, he looks toward the stairs and says, "Get out and go to my room. Shower and go to bed. I have things to handle tonight."

I blink up at him, how he avoids my eyes.

Wait.

He's serious.

He won't trust me. He probably won't even try to again.

He lowered his guard just a little, and I stabbed him right in the back like a fool, and now he won't even look at me. He *can't* look at me, because if he does, he might hurt me again. Or worse, become so blind with rage that he'll have no choice but to end me.

"Draco, I—" I reach for him, but he takes another step away.

"Go, Gianna. Now. You're lucky that was all I did to you."

Wow. He can't even punish me. Not like he used to. What does that mean? That he did trust me? That he actually felt something for me? Or does he still?

Maybe I'm wrong about him. He was trying to make something work between us, and I tore that right to shreds. His humanity was trying to break through, but I just sealed the cracks, leaving him drowning in the darkness again, and all for my own selfish needs. For his power. His control. His dominance, and that terror that I love feeling deep down.

I climb off the bed and walk down the stairs, purposely taking my time— hoping he'll stop me, grab me, spank me, or do something to make him unleash the rage I've initiated.

But he doesn't. I don't get anything at all from him.

I pick up his shirt that's down by the rails and slide into it, walking toward the tall doors. I look back when I pull one of them open, but I don't see him. I can't even hear him.

He's so quiet. He's ... hurt. Because of me. He only wanted my loyalty, and I gave him my ass to kiss.

Shit.

What have I done?

CHAPTER TWENTY ONE

I *decided to sleep* in the library instead. I didn't know if Draco would come to bed soon, and, frankly, I didn't want to sleep with him. Don't get me wrong, I feel bad—guilty, because I did wrong, and he left Henry alive, for now at least.

I don't know why, or what he was planning on doing, but I can't face him. Not until I've processed my thoughts, so I write until nearly four in the morning, letting the words of remorse flow.

I can't stop. Not for a while. When I do, I read over it a hundred times and then I fold it up, taking it with me to the daybed. I don't want him—or anyone else—to walk in and see it.

Before I can get comfortable, there is a knock on the library door . . . at four in the morning. I frown as I stare at the door. Draco would walk right in. So would Patanza. Who the hell is it?

I cautiously walk down the steps and to the door. When I crack it open, Thiago is standing on the other side, looking at me beneath his eyebrows. I frown when he flashes a small smile.

"What the hell do you want?" I mutter.

"Thought you might need some company."

"And why would I need that? From *you*, of all people?" I respond with snide.

He smirks. "Okay. I lied. I actually came to get a book. I left it here a long time ago. Has some important stuff in it that I need."

"At four in the morning?"

He shrugs carelessly. "My days never end."

I look over his shoulder, down the empty corridor, and then I sigh, stepping back. "If you try anything, I'll kill you myself," I tell him when he walks past me.

He scoffs lightly, treading past and walking right up the stairs.

I watch him carefully before walking up the staircase myself. He's scanning one of the shelves by the wall, eyes narrowed, when I make it to the top. I walk to the day bed, reaching beneath my pillow for Draco's pocketknife. I took it from his weapon wall several days ago . . . just in case. He's been too preoccupied to notice its missing.

I keep my hand beneath the pillow, my fingers curling around the wide handle. I pretend to relax as Thiago finally comes across a leather-bound book.

"Ah, *aquí esta*," he sighs. *Here it is.*

He flips through the pages and, assuming whatever he's looking for is there for him, he nods graciously. "What is it?" I ask, wary.

"Coordinates."

"For what?"

"Where I bury some of my American cash." He comes closer and I grip the knife even tighter. Sensing my tension, he releases a low laugh, leaning his lower back against the guardrail. He's only about six steps away.

"Why do you need it?" I narrow my eyes.

"It's my money."

"Why would you keep the coordinates in a book in this library? Let alone, let me see which book you keep it in?" I study the front of the book, the word *Biología* written across the front in a dusty silver.

He laughs. "What the hell are you going to do with the money? I'm sure Draco will give you enough of it if you need it."

I cock a brow. "You never know when I just might need some of my own to run away with."

He looks me over. I'm still wearing Draco's button-down shirt. It reaches the middle of my thighs. I look down, noticing the red marks on my ankles. I try and cross them, but they're still visible

"I'm sure you won't be running away anywhere." He pushes off the rail and I go still when he comes closer. "Can I sit?" he asks, sitting anyway.

I tense my jaw, the handle of the knife hard in my palm now as I slowly inch my hand from beneath the pillow.

"I know you think I'm some kind of traitor or backstabber. Hell, Draco thinks I could be too. I don't know why he stopped trusting me out of nowhere. I used to be his right hand man. Now? Well, I'm more like his errand boy."

My eyebrows draw together when he places the book down.

"What I wish he would understand is that I'm not my father. To be honest, I never liked the son-of-a-bitch. He was arrogant and got what he deserved from Draco. I'm sure you know the story." He waves a hand, leaning forward with his elbows on his knees. "I would never betray Draco. He may not think so, but he's still like a brother to me. He was all I had growing up and he's saved my life more times than I can count. I don't care about being a fucking *Jefe* or the king around here. All I care about is the money. When it comes to my life, family is first. Power? That means nothing to me, but it means everything to Draco and sometimes that is his downfall. I've told him letting that power get to his head might kill him one day. He always tells me he's not afraid of death. I'm sure he's not. Fucker isn't afraid of anything."

"Why are you telling me this?" I ask, scanning him suspiciously.

He shrugs, staring down at the book. "He likes you. Too much. That's not usually something I can say about Draco to a woman."

I ease up on the pocketknife when he looks into my eyes, earnestness filling them.

"I don't know how you got under his skin, or how you got him so wrapped up around your finger, but if I were you, I wouldn't fuck that up. Do you know how hard that is to come by? Getting Draco to do whatever you want him to do? That shit is fucking hard, believe me. Unless you are his mother, it doesn't happen.

Even with my aunt, he's not always so lenient. If I would have smashed that sandwich on his expensive table he would have cut off several of my fingers for it. But not Gianna Nicotera. No," he shakes his head with a light laugh. "Not you, little rebel."

I swallow hard, unsure of what to say.

He holds my gaze for a few seconds before placing the book beside him. His eyes drop down to my lips and I frown when his chest comes forward. His eyes, they're still connected to my lips, his hands gripping the edge of the daybed as he slides in closer.

I snatch out the knife and flip it open before he can get too close. The edge of the blade lands right at the center of his throat, right below his Adam's apple, and he freezes, but that doesn't stop the deep chuckle from bubbling inside him.

I bare my teeth, leaning closer. "Back. Off. I'd hate to kill you and then have to explain that to your cousin, or worse, Mrs. Molina."

He holds his hands in the air, playing innocent. I keep my hand leveled, ready to slice at any time, if need be.

"Whoa, calm down, Nicotera. It was just a test." He draws back completely, but I keep the point of the knife aimed at him. "You like him just as much. Crave him, don't you?"

I don't have an answer for that question, so I say nothing. *Do* nothing.

"Yeah," he says, grinning. "You do. The answer is written in your eyes. You can't hide it. You like that twisted fucker, probably a little too much. Even after all the shit he did to you. I guess that's a good thing. Someone who can handle the havoc he causes. If you would have let me kiss you, I would have had to tell him. Or I would have had to kill you myself." He flashes one of his sharp, smug smiles.

I frown, wondering deep down if Draco told him to do this? But why would he? He doesn't want Thiago anywhere near me. Draco is too selfish to even think about sharing me in any way.

Thiago is just a prick. He's full of himself, for sure, and I'm certain he probably would have told Draco if I'd done something. He's just as intimidated by me as everyone else. Good.

I guess it's better to just get rid of me altogether than constantly have to face me.

"Go, Thiago," I demand, voice low.

He holds his hands in the air innocently. He stands and walks backwards, toward the winding staircase. "I'm gone. No problem." He sighs, dropping his hands. "But before I go I have to ask . . . are you going to tell him about this? My little test?"

"Should I?" I quirk a brow, folding my arms.

"Only if you want me to die." His upper lip quirks up. "You're thinking he sent me in here to do this. No, he didn't. Even if you'd done something, he would have beaten my ass for it, but he would have believed me. I always bring proof." He grins.

I roll my eyes. "For the sake of your life, no, I won't tell him. There's no point. It was a stupid test. It didn't work, and now I'm over it."

He grins again, pointing a wagging finger at me. "I like the way you think."

I stand up. "Get out."

He laughs, that annoying laugh that can get under anyone's skin, picking up his book and then taking off. I watch him from the railing upstairs as he makes his way to the door. Before he can go, I call after him.

He peers back, meeting my eyes.

"Why does Patanza hate you?" I ask.

He turns completely, this time with a full-blown, cheesy grin plastered on his face. "She hates me, huh?"

I nod subtly.

"Long story short . . . she got drunk during one of her first nights here, was all over me at a party and wasn't doing her job. Draco told me it was okay to be with her, just as long as I protected myself. He didn't want one of his best guards getting pregnant. So, of course I fucked her. Out by that dirty ass shed in the back. Shit, she was so fucking loud. She was a good fuck, too. Rode me like she was riding a fucking bull."

I grimace a little.

"The next morning she sees where we are—we passed out outside the shed— and she told me I took advantage of her. She said she never would have done anything with me. She said she was going to tell Draco that I raped her." He scoffs.

"Good thing I recorded it, huh? I wore a camera that night. I always do to parties and on my shipment runs. Sometimes just for the hell of it." My eyes stretch wide. I realize he must have been wearing one the night I freed Henry. It's how Draco knew for sure it wasn't him. He filmed it all. He had proof. He's probably wearing one now. "She saw the tape, begged me to delete it, but I said no. It was my proof, just in case Draco didn't believe me, or might have thought she changed her mind. She's hated me ever since, all because she was ashamed that I, the annoying cousin, let *her* fuck *me* like the animal she is, and all the other guards found out. I'm hoping one day she'll get over it, though. Would be nice to have some of her pussy again. She's aggressive as hell. Drained my balls good and dry that night with her mouth and her pussy." He laughs out loud, and it sounds more like a snicker. "What you should know about me is that I always, *always* have proof, Nicotera. You have to have it when it comes to working for '*The Jefe.*'" He makes air quotes with his empty hand. "Remember that."

I press my lips when he takes a step backwards. He turns, and when the door is shut, I slouch back down on the daybed again.

Thiago is an arrogant shithead, but from what I'm gathering, he's no fool. He doesn't want to feel like a traitor. He looks up to Draco, in a sense. I can tell.

For some reason, I believe him when he says family comes first, but I can tell he can be selfish if it comes down to it. I believe they left him alive on purpose—whoever this Hernandez person is.

It was a power move. Keep the closest person alive and unharmed, just to cause a fuss and make Draco paranoid. This Hernandez person knows him well. Almost too well. They knew exactly what they were doing to Draco by setting Thiago free—and unharmed at that.

I feel someone tapping my arm. I roll over with a groan and an extremely sore ass. Patanza is standing above me with clothes in hand.

"Get up. Draco wants you down for breakfast," she says, tossing the clothes beside my head.

I sit up, rubbing my eyes. "What time is it?"

"You have thirty minutes," is all she says, and then she looks me over twice before shaking her head with a scoff.

I frown. "What the hell is that for?"

Taking a step back, she scans me again, like she's wondering what could possibly be wrong with me. "He was just starting to trust you, and you fucked it up," she finally spits at me and I straighten my back, peering up at her. "You don't realize how hard it is to gain his trust. You had it, Gia, and now it's gone."

"I understand exactly how hard it is," I retort, standing. "It's not easy for him, and I get that."

"No, you don't." Her voice is a little louder. "Because if you did, you would have left that man in chains in that basement, and let Draco handle it the way he wanted to, whether you liked it or not. You think you proved something by going against him, but the only thing you really proved is that you *don't* want him to trust you. You want him to be wary of you. You want him to have a reason to watch his back while he's around you. And, Patrona, if that's what you want, then by God, keep doing shit like what you did down there. But don't expect me or anyone else around here to defend you when the day comes that he decides you're not worth it anymore, because we won't. He is *our* Jefe. He pays us well, takes care of us, and he has never lied to us or gone against his word. He takes care of the other guards' families—he pretty much gives us whatever we want, and the only thing he asks for in return is our loyalty. All he wanted was your loyalty!" Her head moves from side-to-side as she takes the first step down the staircase. "The sad thing is, I don't even know how you can make up for what you've done. We got him back, yeah, but he's still going to lose a lot of sleep over this . . . but I guess it doesn't matter because if he's losing it, you are too."

Before I can speak, she's storming down the spiral staircase and marching for the door. It doesn't close, so I know she's waiting for me outside of it, probably an order he gave.

I look down at the clothes. An orange dress with spaghetti straps and a pair of gold sandals. She also brought my toothbrush, the toothpaste, and my brush.

Walking down the staircase, I make my way out of the library, past Patanza who ignores me at her post, and enter the nearest bathroom. This bathroom doesn't have a shower, but there is a large basin and a wide mirror. It's decorated with gold and black.

I freshen up and get dressed in no time, taking note of the cut on the middle of my neck.

When I walk out, Patanza is already standing in the middle of the hallway. "Let's go," she says, turning before I can catch her eye.

She troops up the marble stairs and I follow behind her, raking my fingers through my hair. Once I'm inside the dining room, she takes a few steps aside and stands posted at the doors. I look at her for several seconds, but she merely ignores me.

Whatever.

I walk to the table and take my seat, making sure to sit carefully. I realize I'm close to the time deadline because Draco walks in right away, avoiding my eyes as he takes the seat at the head of the table. Mrs. Molina comes strolling in as well with a yawn, taking her seat across from me. The butlers approach the table with hot food and we eat in silence.

Well, Draco and I do.

Mrs. Molina perks up after her first cup of coffee. She's talking about some movie she watched late last night with some of her favorite Latino actors in it. I smile at her when she looks at me, but the smiles are forced. Since she's talking to me, I figure she doesn't know what I did, and Draco probably wants it that way for a reason.

Why?

Does he not want her opinion of me to change? Or is he holding back because if he tells her, she'll know he punished me in some way, after promising he wouldn't?

"What are your plans today, *hijo*?" she asks him, digging her spoon into her hot cereal.

He shifts in his seat. "I will be going to town today," he responds, and I pick my head up, looking at him.

"Really? To do what?"

"Run a few errands." He drops his spoon. "Thiago will be coming too. He has a lot of making up to do."

"Making up?" she asks, laughing. "So you were wrong? He is not against you?"

"I didn't say I was wrong. But he's proved himself worthy so far."

"How so?" she asks.

"Phone was checked, as well as the tapes we received. He had the cameras in the SUVs running and Guillermo and Patanza looked over the tapes. He was held at gunpoint, as it seems, and they let him go but took everything. They're trying to get under my skin now. Trying to get me out of hiding." He drums his fingers on the table. "I still don't trust him completely." His eyes swing over to me. "Can't seem to trust anyone lately though."

When he says that, I cringe inside. Mrs. Molina doesn't pick up on his snide remark. Instead, she flags the butler down, asks for more coffee, and then she says, "Well, I told you, Draco. You have to give people chances. You assumed something and he proved you wrong. Thiago is your cousin. You boys grew up together. He trusts *you*."

Draco scoffs lightly. "I wouldn't go so far as to say that, Mamá."

She shrugs. "It was worth a shot."

After we wrap up on breakfast, Draco takes off without a word said to me. I slouch back in my chair, finishing up the much-needed coffee before trudging up to the bedroom and taking a shower.

After I'm done, I look into the mirror, at the red marks still on my right butt cheek. I hiss as I run a finger over one of the welts. I could do something to help it heal, but I won't.

Somehow, I feel like I deserve the pain. I deserve to see it.

He only wanted my trust.

He only wanted me.

It's a shame.

I sleep in the bedroom, hoping he'll come up so we can mend things, but I don't get the chance to. I know he's here, most likely in his galería painting, but he's keeping his distance from me . . . and for some reason it causes an ache to build in my chest.

It's there because Patanza is right.

I can't sleep. Not with how heavy my conscious is.

As I start to doze off I swear I feel someone watching me. I feel their fingers running through my hair when they're close, a soft caress on my cheekbone. I feel them there. *Him* there, but I don't move. I curl up even more, sighing when his finger traces the scar on my throat.

I hear him let out a deep sigh when his palm runs down to my hip, squeezing lightly. I don't know if he can tell that I'm not asleep yet. But I'll pretend to be if it means he's close—If it means he feels safer with me this way.

But, before I know it, he's gone and it's cold again. The bedroom door clicks shut and I don't see him again for the rest of the night.

The next day, around noon, there is a knock on my door. Patanza is standing on the other side when I open it and she exhales, seeming agitated.

"Jefe wants you to get dressed to go out. Meet him downstairs."

"Go out where?" I ask.

She shrugs. "Don't know. Just hurry."

I get dressed and ready in less than twenty minutes and follow her down. Draco is standing by the door with tan slacks on and a light-blue button-up shirt tucked in. The pants sit low enough on his hips to look comfortable, but still formal.

He spots me and watches me walk down in my burgundy jumpsuit. It's a sleeveless V-neck with a collar around the neck. The cleavage is wide open and cuts down, just below my navel, showing off the curves of my breasts. It's revealing, and most likely makes a man wonder what's beneath the outfit. I wore it on purpose, along with strappy, open toed heels, so he can stare like he's doing now.

But, just like the typical Draco Molina, he forces his eyes away, focusing on one of the paintings on the wall.

"We're going somewhere?" I ask when I'm close.

"Out," is all he says, and he opens the door to walk outside. Guillermo and Diego are standing beside a black SUV. They open the back door for us when we get closer. Draco steps aside, letting me in first. As I slide across the bench, he puts on a pair of sunglasses before climbing in as well.

I sit by the opposite window, glancing sideways. He's dialing a number on his burn phone. He brings the phone to his ear, speaking in Spanish about someone meeting him at a certain place and someone else not answering the phone. I assume he's talking to someone about Thiago with how aggravated he's becoming. He ends the call, finally putting his attention on me without a word.

Guillermo starts the car up and Diego straps himself into the passenger seat. There is a Mercedes in front of us, black of course, but there is also a silver car in front of that one.

"Are your guards in those other cars?" I ask, still feeling him staring.

"Yes."

"Where are we going?" And why are there so many of them?

"To town."

"For what?" I inquire, treading as lightly as possible.

"Business."

I know he won't say more than that. Honestly, I don't care. It's nice to get out of the house after all the hostility.

We ride along the dirt road, passing by those familiar little houses again. Kids are playing, but this time they don't stop to watch the expensive cars go by. They carry on with their lives without a care in the world. They are younger kids. The older ones are most likely in school.

We ride for nearly an hour. I shift in my seat repeatedly, keeping my gaze out of the window. Draco has been quiet the entire ride. I keep staring out, on the verge of falling asleep, but then I see something I don't expect.

The car slows down but I keep staring.

A blue field. A field full of them. The Blue Betrayals.

Water sprinklers are running, refreshing them, keeping them hydrated and healthy. I realize this area is secluded, protected by a gray fence. It's shadier here somehow, perhaps because it's almost on a hill, slanted. There are trees, too, big and bushy, which is unusual for this kind of land.

I look back at Draco who tucks his phone into his pocket and then opens his door. "Get out."

Blinking rapidly, I pull the door handle and step out. Diego pops up beside me, his handgun gripped between his fingers. He doesn't look at me, which isn't surprising at all. Draco steps around the front of the car and looks out at the field of flowers. It's massive, way bigger than the garden of chocolate cosmos.

"It's the only place away from home with grass that doesn't get too dry," he says to no one in particular. "The hill helps. The sun can't shine directly on them. They are meant to be in cooler zones. With the sprinklers and my gardeners, they have lasted a long time." He walks through the gate and begins down a dirt path. Diego steps behind and nudges me, and I look sideways at him before following suit.

As I walk through, I can really see the thorns. Some of them stick out in the walkway, sharp like blue claws. If I fell, they would cut me—pierce right through the skin.

Draco continues walking along the path, and I notice there's an outhouse about a yard away, at the end of the path. It must be where he's going.

Diego and Guillermo are behind us, the other guards posted along the street to keep watch. I try to keep up, but Draco's strides are longer. I get the feeling he doesn't want me catching up.

So I keep walking, taking in the Blue Betrayals. I can smell them when the wind blows, hear their petals whispering. A few more steps and we are here, standing less than a foot away from the outhouse.

Draco moves over, as do I when he cocks his head at the guards and they come rushing forward. Guillermo unlocks it with a key, and when the door creaks open, I gasp.

Inside, there is a man. And not just any man. It's . . . *Henry*. He's surrounded by a cluster of the blue flowers, as well as their thorns, body propped on the dirty toilet. I have to cover my nose, the stench is so strong.

Henry isn't alone in there. There's another guest, with yellowish-white scales and beady red eyes. It's hanging off his shoulders, the head moving up around his hair, the tongue making a soft hissing noise as it flickers.

He's been bitten several times by it. An albino snake. There are marks on his arms and thighs. He's sweating like a pig. He's absolutely filthy, and there is blood crusted all around his swollen mouth like he was punched repeatedly.

Henry groans in agony, and I step forward, but Diego holds a thick arm up, keeping me back with a stern brow. Tears build at the rims of my eyes. I feel so sorry for him. This is my fault. I only made matters worse.

"What did you do to him?" I bark, turning to face Draco.

"Her name is Silvia," he announces, ignoring my tantrum.

I clench my fists as he maneuvers around me. "Draco, this is ridiculous. I'm the one who let him go. Why are you punishing him for it?"

"She lives here, in these fields. She loves these flowers. She can slither right through them and hardly get pricked. It's fascinating really. We saw her one day and I was about to behead her, but the way she moved through these flowers, like the thorns were feathers or something, well, I figured I'd keep her alive. She was fearless, and, surprisingly she hasn't left yet. She's a gorgeous snake, too. I don't think she's from here, though. Might've escaped from the zoo that's less than a mile away."

"Draco," I breathe, switching my gaze from him to Henry. "He's dying."

"Exactly. She's poisonous. And she can sense a coward and a liar just as well as I can."

Henry's head falls, hitting the wall.

"Just kill him, then. End it. Stop torturing him!"

"Why would I do that?"

Anger blinds me. I step forward, shoving past Diego and snatching the gun out of Draco's holder.

Guillermo immediately draws his gun on me, Diego following suit. But they are wary, because I'm not pointing at Draco. I'm pointing at Henry. His eyes are sealed. I'm sure he doesn't even know I'm here. He can't go out so slowly. It's better to end it.

Right now.

"Do it then," Draco murmurs, head tilting. "Go ahead. Kill your coward friend."

My hand trembles, finger barely squeezing the trigger. But I keep it aimed, right at his head, like Daddy taught me at the gun range when I was sixteen.

One eye open, level my hand, steady my arm.

I stare at Henry for a long time, my eyes burning with remorse. I try and level my hand but I can't. I can't kill anyone else. I want him to stop suffering, but not like this. *Not like this.*

A hand drops down on the gun and Draco lowers it, standing close, focused solely on me. "There is no need to kill him. I'm sending him to Brazil."

"What?" I look up, eyes damp. "Brazil? Why?"

"He'll live there. *Live*, Gianna."

My eyebrows furrow. I look from Draco to Henry, hands still shaky. He takes the gun from me, placing it back inside his holder and then holding up a hand at the guards. They lower their weapons in an instant, but they keep their eyes on me.

"Why?" I ask again.

"Because it's what you want. And if it will give you some kind of peace, fine. But he doesn't get to go back to the United States. He'll be in Brazil on his own and being watched after. Tabs will be taken. He won't be completely free. I will still have eyes on him at all times, no matter what he does."

Relief hits me, swelling in my chest like an inflated balloon.

"Draco, I——" I don't get it. I seriously don't.

"Silvia has been devenomized, but that doesn't mean she won't bite." He smirks. "He's drugged up, but he will be fine . . . unless he does something stupid." Draco snaps his fingers and Diego walks forward, picking up Silvia and returning her to the fields. And just like he said, she slithers away without a care in the world, practically invincible to the thorns.

I look up at him, speechless.

"You made your call, and now I've made mine. *Together*. King and queen." He holds my face between his fingers. "Don't say I've never done anything for you. This is a huge risk for me, but that's how much I want this to work. I thought about it. About Lion. About what he promised me long ago. He wouldn't send a threat my way. He would have told me to let Henry go, too, or made it happen himself."

"Yeah," I whisper. "He would have."

"I see so much of him inside you. How the fuck am I supposed to ignore it?" He digs into his back pocket as Diego and Guillermo drag Henry out of the shed. Handing a black and white photograph to me, he says, "Your proof."

The photograph is old. But in the picture is a man with a beige fedora. His skin is really tan, and he has a thick, black moustache. I feel like I've seen him before. He has a cigar pinched between his lips, and his arms wrapped around a young, familiar-looking boy. Beside the boy is Daddy. *My* Daddy. He has a cigar as well, but he's holding it up in the air with a wide smile on display for the camera. He looks both relaxed and elated, like he loves them. Like he cares about them. Like he *trusts* them.

"This was taken the first time ever I met Lion. I was twelve, and I trusted him right away. He came here, to Mexico, one summer. He helped my father get a visa into the country. They set up deals together. They were almost partners—Lion ran shit in the United States, and my father ran Mexico. That was the order, plain and simple, and it worked."

I look up at him slowly, but I can't read his eyes. Not behind those dark sunglasses.

"Read the back," he murmurs.

I flip it over and there are words in red ink. *Holy shit.* It's Daddy's handwriting. Sloppy and masculine. I remember it well. Mom hated it.

The words are: **Keep this with you forever, kid. And always stay strong.**

That's all it says, but I can hear Daddy saying those words, almost like a whisper in my ear, echoing.

"He gave this to you?" I muster.

He nods, just barely. "Proof enough?"

It is. This one picture alone shouts a thousand words. There is love buried in the ink. There is respect. These men were close. Draco looked up to him; I could tell. The way he's leaning toward him, but still making sure his Dad is close.

"Are there more?" I ask.

"Several, in my father's storage."

Grunting pulls me from my thoughts, and I look up to see Diego and Guillermo carrying a naked Henry to the SUV. Draco touches my cheekbone, and when I look at him again, his sunglasses are gone.

"He wanted this, Gianna. You hate me for some of the shit I do, but it's time to stop fighting it. This is what I do. It's how I live. I'm done with these games. I'm not trying to hurt you anymore."

I nod, swallowing hard. "Then don't hurt me."

He lets out a deep breath when I hand him the picture back. He tucks it into his back pocket again and then presses a hand on the small of my back, guiding me back to the SUV.

"You still don't trust me," I say when we're halfway there.

He doesn't answer, because he doesn't trust me.

"No more bullshit," he says, voice firm and deep.

I start to speak when we're closer to the SUV, but just as I open my mouth, something booms, and the ground shakes around us. Gasping, I look to the right and see that the silver Mercedes has exploded. Fire shoots up, smoke billowing in the air instantly.

Guns cock, and the guards begin to shout as they rush around the cars. Guillermo and Diego drop Henry on the dirt path in a heartbeat, rushing for the vehicles.

But in a matter of seconds, the second car explodes too, sending three of the guards flying back into the field of blue.

A scream slips out of me as I'm tackled to the ground.

CHAPTER TWENTY TWO

Draco *is on* top of me, panting hard and heavy. The thorns from the flowers prick me in the back and under my arms and I cry out from the pain, but my cry is muted when another explosion happens.

This explosion deafens me. It's closer. My ears ring and Draco's eyes are squeezed tight, his teeth gritted together as he tries to tolerate the noise. Flames build up behind him, aiming for the sky. The thorns feel much sharper now, piercing into my skin.

I think I'm crying. Screaming. I don't know. I can't tell.

It hurts. Everywhere.

Draco's eyes grow wide as he finally hops up, but crouches quickly to stroke my chin. He's shouting something but I can't hear him. He then turns in a matter of seconds, drawing his gun and rushing away.

I hear my moans now. I see the dirt path only a few steps away and I roll toward it, my legs and hands getting stabbed, my face getting nicked and sliced, until I land on the dirt, free of the thorns.

I lift my hands up in the air. They're covered in blood.

Then I look at the cars. They've all been blown to pieces. Some of the debris surrounds me. Something heavy and warm runs over my belly and I look down, spotting Silvia slithering over me, making her way through the flowers again, disappearing into the blue.

Too shocked to panic, too hurt to scream or cry, I try and sit up, pushing on my bloody hands. The dirt stings the punctures, but I make do. A shadow hovers over me as I struggle to stand, and he shoves me right back down to the ground.

He steps over me, his feet outside my head now, sneering down at me.

I don't know this person.

He's new, and he's not one of the guards. He grabs my arm and hauls me up, running through the field while tossing me over his shoulder.

All of my pain subsides, the adrenaline of terror flooding me all over again. I can hear men yelling. I can hear Draco shouting, furious, trying to figure out what the hell is going on.

Where the hell did this man come from, and how did he get past the guards? Past Draco?

I scream to the top of my lungs for Draco, like I did in the cellar that horrible day. I scream until my throat becomes scratchy, but the man keeps going, holding on tight, even as I fight and kick. He's too strong.

We pass through the shadows, and I finally see Draco rushing down the path. I scream out one more time when I realize he's searching for me. "Draco!"

He hears it, spots us, and begins running to me, pumping his legs hard, gun in hand.

But the man keeps going, breathing hard and heavy. I continue kicking, even with blood running down my arms and on my face.

Draco's figure becomes distant as he runs between houses, and I panic, screaming again. Cars honk their horns and tires squeal as the man runs through a small town.

Before it can register, something dark covers my head, and I land on a hard surface. I hear a door shut and a man shouting at someone to hurry the fuck up. I'm in a vehicle. The floors are hard, made of metal.

The car pulls off with a loud screech of the tires and I hit a wall. I snatch off the hood, breathing deep. But when I turn to look, there is a gun pointed right at my face.

"You try anything, and I will blow your fucking brains out," the man says, his English fluent. He's clearly Hispanic. His hair is spiky, and his skin is very tan. One of his eyes is gray, like he's blind in that eye, a cut above his eyebrow.

Panicked, I look out of the back window and I see Draco.

"Draco! I'm in here! Draco!" I scream, leaning on the window, banging on it with bloody hands as he searches the area. "Draco!"

He sees me in the van and starts running again, coming for me with two guards behind him. The man with the gun curses beneath his breath when the car comes to a halt. I look through the windshield and see traffic. Too much traffic to pass through.

"Go through the fucking alley! Go!" he shouts at the driver. Draco is closer. I yank at the handle on the door, but it's locked. Banging on the blood-smudged glass again, I shove my body at the door, hoping it will pop open somehow.

Gunshots are fired as the driver whips the steering wheel around, and Draco and the guards hide behind other vehicles, returning fire whenever they can. But it's too late.

The van splits and turns down a thin alley. The mirrors are knocked off, sparks flying as the body of the van tries to fit through.

And it does.

"No!" I scream. "No! Please! Draco!"

"Lost them!" the man with the gun shouts. "Keep going! He might have other people around."

I turn to look at the man with the gun. As he starts to turn in his seat to look at me, I kick him in the face with my heel and then pounce forward, gripping his throat tight, choking him.

He struggles to get out of my hold, trying to bring the gun up and hit me with it as blood gushes from below his nose, but I duck, keeping my grip tight on him.

"Shit!" the driver barks, turning down an open road.

The car comes to a dramatic stop and I fly forward, landing between both of them, my back hitting the radio. The man with the gun catches his breath, but he is furious. His eyes are like hot coals, flaming hot, blood oozing down his face.

He brings a hand down to my throat, squeezing tighter than I ever could.

I claw at his hand, unable to breathe as the squeeze shuts off my windpipe.

"Fucking kill you!" he roars.

"You know you can't, so let her go!" the driver shouts. He reaches over to pull his hand away.

The man with the gun flares his nostrils and then grabs me by the hair, yanking on it and shoving me to the back of the van again.

This time he brings the gun up and watches me. He doesn't waver. Doesn't pull his eyes away as the driver speeds up.

I breathe raggedly, glaring back.

"He'll find you and kill you," I say through gritted teeth.

"Oh, I'm sure he'll find us, but he won't be able to kill us." He sounds so sure of himself. Who the hell is this man?

"What do you want?" I demand.

"It's not what I want." He rubs his throat, mostly where it's red from my grip, and then swipes his nose. "It's our boss who wants you. You're a feisty little bitch, too. Hope I get paid extra for putting up with this shit."

The driver huffs a laugh at that, but I continue my grimace. I look out of the bloodstained window, hoping he'll show. Hoping he'll come out somewhere and save me.

But he doesn't.

I don't know why they haven't drugged me or knocked me out cold. They haven't even tied me up. I don't know why they're holding off, but something tells me that's not a good sign.

CHAPTER TWENTY THREE

The van turns right, and I bobble sideways as we pass over a bump in the road. The driver continues up a secluded road where more men stand outside, nodding their heads to let the driver know he's clear to go.

After about two more minutes, the van finally begins to slow down and soon, comes to a stop. There is a white gate ahead that he parks behind, two guards in all black standing there.

The driver hops out immediately and starts speaking to them, explaining the damage to the van. He then comes around the back as the man I attacked remains seated in the passenger seat, the gun still pointed at me. He's pissed. I can tell.

Who cares? He's already ugly anyway. One scar won't make a difference.

The back door flies open and the driver flicks his fingers, telling me to get out. With a scowl, I slide across the back, stepping out barefoot. The man with the gray eye took my shoes off during the ride here.

When my feet land on the asphalt, I hear someone let out a low whistle and I look over. One of the guards is drooling like a dog, giving me a look that I find absolutely disgusting.

"Fuck off," I hiss in Spanish.

"Shit," he says in his native tongue. "You were right, Lonso." He looks at the man that had the gun in the passenger seat. "She is a feisty little bitch."

The driver pulls out a gun and nudges me with it. I can tell he doesn't deal with their shit often. Either that, or he just doesn't care. "Let's go. To the gates."

The other guard posted there opens it for us and I walk ahead, a gun pointed at my back, studying the large stucco home. It's nothing like Draco's, but it is big. The roof is tan and there is a two-door garage, pillars built on the porch and the balcony on the second level.

The guard that was standing at the gate takes the lead and I follow him to the house. When he opens the front door, I feel my chest tighten. I don't know what's inside. I don't even want to find out. But I keep my chin held high, giving a dirty look at the guard before passing by.

The driver grabs my elbow when I'm in the foyer, leading the way now. He walks past a den, a dining room, and even a kitchen, veering left until double doors appear at the end of the hallway.

When he opens the door, I'm truly surprised by what I walk into.

It's not some kind of holding room with white walls and no furniture. It's not a room with cages and chains. No, in fact this room is fully furnished.

The floors are made of hardwood, a loveseat perched against the cheetah-print accent wall. I notice the pillows on the loveseat are cheetah print as well, along with the rug in the middle of the room, some of the vases, and even some of the glasses set up by the scotch on the tray.

I almost want to throw up it's so much.

The driver pushes me forward a little and I look back at him.

"Go. Sit. Hernandez will be here to speak with you soon."

"This is his home?" I ask.

The driver smirks. He walks to the corner table where the scotch is and pours a glass. I think it's for him, until he comes in my direction and offers it.

I look down at it before meeting his eyes, then turn my back on him and walk to the loveseat. I sit, one leg crossed over the other, and glare up at him, jaw ticking.

He simply shrugs, his long, black ponytail falling behind him as he tosses the drink back himself. The guard, Lonso, walks in, already frowning at me. I return his frown and narrow my eyes at him when he shuts the door and walks to the table.

They both sit and pull in their chairs. Lonso whips out a deck of cards and the driver sighs, planting his elbows on the table. "We're in for a long fucking day," he mutters.

"Fuck, yeah. And I'm fucking starving. I told Lorenzo to order us some fucking tamales or something." Lonso gives me a sideways glance. "Are we supposed to feed the bitch?"

"You know Hernandez will be pissed if we don't offer her something."

I roll my eyes and scoff. These men are fucking amateurs. Compared to Draco's, I'm honestly surprised they even got to me. This Hernandez person already seems like a fucking joke.

The clock on the wall tells me four hours have passed. I've paced the room, keeping a sharp eye on the guards and the door, while also searching for something I might be able to use to take them out with.

Besides the guns in their waistbands, there is nothing. I could use the vase, bash it over one of their heads, but they're large men. They probably wouldn't even bat an eye.

"How much longer?" I snap as I sit back down.

They both ignore me, now playing a game of dominos over chump change.

I keep staring at them. The driver merely ignores me. I get it. He's obviously the veteran here. He's used to this. But the other one, Lonso, lets me get under his skin so much I almost want to laugh. He's the rookie, wanting so badly to be a top dog here.

"What the hell are you looking at?" he finally snaps at me, bushy eyebrows furrowing.

I challenge him, narrowing my eyes, leaning closer, still staring.

"Just ignore her," the driver mutters, sliding a domino across the table.

Lonso clenches his fists on the table and finally snatches his eyes away. "Stupid bitch."

The door to the left clinks and then pulls open, and I look at it, my back going stiff. I watch as a feminine figure approaches. "I tell you, Alonso, that is no way to speak to a lady. Especially *Draco Molina's* lady." She comes in, swaying her hips, and I don't know who the hell she is, but her presence demands respect.

A smile sweeps across her ruby lips, her hand planting on her hip as she focuses on me.

Her hair, a fire engine red, proves that she doesn't give a damn about being traditional or society's rules. Her makeup is done to perfection, lashes long and thick, eye shadow smoky. She's wearing black leather pants and a sleeveless cheetah print blouse.

I look around at the furniture, the cheetah print pattern on the pillows and curtains, and realize this must be her space. She must be important here.

The men rise from the table, dropping their game of dominos and stepping sideways.

"You're back earlier than we thought," the infamous Alonso says, smiling at her. "We got her for you. Unharmed, as promised. Though she did put up a fight." He rubs his upper lip and then his throat, grimacing at me.

"I wouldn't expect anything less," she titters. "Draco doesn't like weak women. He's always enjoyed a fighter."

I narrow my brows, still looking at her. She talks like she knows so much about him. Like she was his best friend or something. It's too personal. I don't like it.

She comes toward me in her spiky brown heels. When she extends a hand, I glare down at it, refusing to take it. "Oh, sweet girl, please," she scoffs, her hand still out. "I have no reason to hurt you—not unless you give me a reason to. After all, it's not you I want. It's him. You're just leverage. *Safe* leverage, as long as you don't try anything stupid."

My mouth twitches. She doesn't let up on that extended arm, her cheetah print nails on display.

"Who are you?" I ask with a small snarl.

She smiles a simple, meek smile. "Yessica."

"Where is Hernandez?"

Her eyes stretch wide, and she looks at the guards, busting out laughing then.

"You two didn't tell her? Aww, how cute!" They chortle right along with her, shaking their heads and sitting down at the two-top table to start up another game of dominoes.

"Hernandez?" She finally drops her hand with a sigh, realizing that I'm not going to take it.

"Honey, *I am* Hernandez. Yessica Hernandez, to be exact." Her accent thickens when she says her name. My eyes get bigger. Hernandez is a ... *woman*? How the hell did I not know this?

"You're the threat he's dealing with right now?" I'm in utter disbelief.

She laughs again, taking the seat beside me like we're buddy-buddy. I slide away, looking her over. "I like the way that sounds. Me, a threat to Draco Molina. *The Almighty Jefe,*" she teases. "No. I wouldn't say I'm a threat." She rubs a finger over one of her diamond rings. "I'm just a woman who knows what she wants. And I know you aren't a stupid girl, otherwise you wouldn't be sitting here right now."

"What do you want from me?"

"I already told you, it's not you that I want. It was never you. Draco is a hard man to find. It seems every time we catch one of his people and try to get them to talk, they get amnesia or something." She rolls her bright gray eyes. "They can't ever seem to remember where he is or even who he is. It's interesting how far they will go and still not speak."

"And you think I'll crack and hand him over to you?"

Her laugh fills the large room. "Oh, I know you won't. If he's with you, you're just as loyal as them. You wouldn't betray him by giving him up. You'd probably rather die, I bet."

I level my gaze.

"No, see, he knows that I have you. And right about now, he's waiting for me to give him something to use—something to help him find you. If what I've heard is true—about how he's taken you out in public, and that you are, in fact, a Nicotera—he will be ready to come for you as soon as he gets whatever information he needs." She scans me with her eyes. "You look just like one, too. A Nicotera. The women always look so ... *fierce.*"

She stands up and blows a breath, as if she's bored. "We have a few hours of alone time. How about we change your clothes and have some dinner? I've had a long day, and I'm famished."

I remain seated. "Dinner? Why, so you can poison me?"

"I have no reason to poison you. Honey, I really don't even want you here. But I have to have you here to get to him. Don't be so full of yourself." She waves a hand, looking at the gold watch on her wrist. "Come. I don't like my men manhandling women, but if it comes down to that, I make them. So it's either you walk with me like a good girl, or I have them drag you around like a ragdoll." Her arms fold and I see her guards square their shoulders through the corner of my eye. "Your choice."

With a small grimace, I push up to a stand. Her eyes light up, like she's truly delighted that I will be tagging along with her. Like this is some kind of girls' night out.

"Smart choice." She points a finger at me. "And I have the perfect outfit for you!" she says in a singsong voice, twirling around and gesturing for me to follow.

I look at the guards, how they glare at me, but follow her lead. I notice there is a pistol with a cheetah print handle tucked in the back of her belt. She's no fool. She wants me to see it.

I don't know what game she's playing, but I don't like it. Is this what she did to Thiago? Played friends and let him go? Or is she just doing this so that when Draco comes, he'll question why she was so lenient with me—why she hasn't killed me yet? Make him even more paranoid. I realize that's probably what she does best. She knows him all too well, and I need to know how.

"You have great hair, you know that? So much volume." Yessica brushes it into loose waves. I remain perfectly still in front of the vanity, the gold lights shining on us. She's standing behind me, her guards at the door.

We're in a bedroom, and of course, there is cheetah print everywhere, though it's accented with red. I'm finding it unbelievably difficult not to grab the gun she placed right in front of me.

She taunts. It's her thing. She did it on purpose. She's trying to put me to the test. I was taught better than that.

She's had me change into a champagne blouse and a pair of jeans that fit pretty well. We are about the same size, though I'd say I'm a little fuller in the hips and she's more top heavy.

"You'll be with me all night, sweet girl. Playing this quiet game won't be any fun for you." She steps from behind me, sitting on an empty space at the edge of the vanity. "Don't you have any questions for me? Like how I know so much about your master?"

"He's not my master," I mutter.

"No?" She smiles. "Then what do you consider him?"

I hold her gaze. "My equal."

"Oh, your equal?" She seems fascinated by that, and a little tickled. She pushes to a stand, picking up a makeup sponge and dabbing it on my cheek. I wince, not from the move she makes, but from the sting. There are several cuts on my face from the thorns. My palms and even my arms are scraped and scratched up as well.

"The explosions really did a number on you," she sighs. "Sucks it got so out of hand."

"Why do you want him so badly?" I finally ask when she draws back.

She grabs my elbow, forcing me to a stand.

"He has things I want. Important things. Let's go." She picks up her handgun and spins around, tucking it into her waistband again and sauntering out of the bedroom.

I follow her down the hallway, the guards trailing us, and when she takes a left, we're entering a dining room. This isn't the dining room we passed when I first got here. This one is much smaller. A four-top table already set up, a bright, diamond-like chandelier hanging above it. I'm so glad there isn't any cheetah print in here. Only leather and oak.

She takes a seat and then taps the chair to the right of her. I suppress my frown, walking to the seat and sitting. The guard pushes my chair in and I freeze then, giving him a cold look.

"Ease up, sweetie," Yessica says as food is brought to the table. "They won't hurt you unless I tell them to. You're making my evening entertaining so there's no need to do anything. Unlike Draco, I treat my guests with respect."

There she goes again, acting like she knows everything about him. I don't speak and when she realizes I'm playing the silent game again, she says, "Dig in."

She picks up food for her plate as wine is poured. At first we eat in silence, but I'm sure it's only because she's eating. She wasn't kidding. She is hungry. She cuts into her steak and potatoes, eating rapidly, and then guzzles down her first cup of red wine.

"Mmm." She clutches her fork and knife in hand. When she's finished chewing, she says, "You'll have to forgive me. I haven't eaten anything but an apple today. Busy, busy day." She scans me with her bright eyes. "Go on. Eat."

I stick my fork into the green beans, bringing one up to my mouth. Since it all came from the same bowl and plates, I assume it isn't poisoned . . . unless she's just that fucking crazy and has an antidote around somewhere.

As I chew, I feel her watching me. Dropping her knife and fork, she picks up her wine glass and takes a small sip. Then she says, "The scars on your wrists? Where did they come from?"

I blink rapidly at her before focusing on the scars. Insecurity eats me whole, and I shift in my seat, grabbing my wine glass to take a small sip.

"He had you chained or roped up, didn't he?" she pushes.

Still, I don't speak.

"How long?"

I breathe unevenly, annoyed by her questions now. Something hard pushes into the back of my skull and I pause on my chewing, looking over at her. Her smile is smug now. Faint, but smug.

"How long?" she asks again.

"Six days." Anger strikes me, but I remain calm on the outside. The gun is pulled away from my head and I look over at the driver again. He doesn't look at me. He simply crosses his arms in front of him, staring out of the window across the room.

"Oh, that's horrible," she coos. "You know, I've heard about you—what happened to you." She shifts in her seat, trying to get a little more comfortable. "I heard you were here, in Mexico, for a wedding. And not just any wedding, but *yours*. You were the beautiful bride that was snatched away." She lowers her wine glass. "How can you live with that? With *him*? Knowing he's the man who killed your husband?"

I lower my gaze a little, to the scars on my wrist and then my uneaten steak.

"He ruined your life, Gia, yet you're still like some lost puppy—loyal to him because he feeds you and bathes you and claims to protect you. And yet," she murmurs, "here you are. Under my roof. Snatched away again." She waves a finger at me. "He thinks he's invincible. Like he can do whatever he wants and get away with it." Her voice is harsher now. I meet her eyes and she's frowning. "He has a terrible, selfish mind."

"Draco isn't the one who ruined my life. He *killed* the man that ruined my life," I say as evenly as possible.

Her gray eyes flash with amusement. "Oh, really?" She leans forward in her seat, picking up her glass again. "Now, that sounds like some juicy gossip. Go on," she waves an impatient hand. "Tell me."

"There's nothing to tell. It's personal."

She pauses on taking the next sip, side-eyeing me briefly before sighing as if she's bored. "Listen, sweet girl. *En mi casa*, nothing is personal. Whatever you consider a delicate matter, forget about it. Either way, I will find out, whether you willingly tell me or I have to beat the answers out of you myself. Doesn't matter as long as I get down to the truth." She gloats, like she really can take me on. Let her try me. I'm almost hoping for a one-on-one match. No guns. No weapons. Just us girls.

"I'm not sure what you want to know." I clasp my fingers in my lap, holding onto my restraint. There are knives in front of me, silver and sharp. They call to me. Whisper—telling me to just kill her and take my chances.

But I'm surrounded. I wouldn't get far. I've counted the number of guards I've seen so far. Fourteen, and I'm sure that isn't even the half. She's a woman. She requires more protection.

"About the man he killed," she continues. "How did that man—your husband, correct?—ruin your life?"

"He killed my father."

She gasps, as if she's truly shocked. "Your husband killed your father!"

I don't speak or nod or do anything. I remain perfectly still, fingers balling into fists now. She's good. I have to remember she's trying to make me tick. She wants to find a reason to hurt me—make me crack.

"That is some foul shit," she laughs, rounding her finger around the rim of her glass. She sits back in her seat, crossing one leg over the other and showing off her heels. "I didn't care about my father, so I guess it wouldn't hurt me as much if that were to happen to me. But I assume you were close to yours?"

Still nothing.

She looks down at her half-eaten food. "Yes. You were. And let me guess. Draco told you the news? That's why you're so keen to him? So loyal? He was close with the Nicoteras, if I'm recalling it correctly."

Again, I don't supply an answer.

Not that she cares. She already knows the answers to all of it.

"Sucks." Her tone is nonchalant. She finishes off her wine then sits forward, dropping her leg and shooting to a stand. She walks to the window, fluffing her hair. "I wonder what he's doing now? He's probably flipping everything upside down, searching the city for his little pet. Or maybe not. Maybe he doesn't even care."

"He cares, and he'll come."

She looks over her shoulder at me, smirking. "What makes you so sure?"

"He will."

"Aw, sweet girl." She makes a clucking noise, coming up to me, her heels clicking on the floor. "He makes you feel special? You think he'll come in here like Superman and save the day." She wags a degrading finger at me. "No, see, Draco Molina is no Superman. He's the man that Superman has to take down because he's so fucked up and vile. He makes you feel these things—like you owe him—but truthfully you don't owe him shit. Trust me, I know all too well."

"How do you know?" I demand, searching her eyes for the truth.

Her upper lip quirks up. "Draco has had plenty of women before you, Gia Nicotera. You wouldn't be the first to go through the Molina Experiment. And an experiment is just what it is. It's a test to see how long you'll last with him. To see when you will crack and fold under his pressure, until he no longer finds you useful. Until you are nothing but a piece of meat he can fuck whenever he feels the urge." Each sentence comes out angrier than the last.

And then it hits me.

"You were with him," I say in a small voice, eyes expanding.

She grins, pressing a hand down on the table and leaning on it. "Oh," she exhales. "I breathed Draco. I dreamed about him. I *worshipped* him. I wanted to be just like him . . . but then I realized something amazing. I realized," she murmurs, "that I could be so much better." She looks around, holding up her free hand. "And now I have all of this, plus more." A light shrug. "Turns out I didn't need the almighty Jefe after all. But I do miss that angry sex. God, he was so good in bed. So daunting yet so fucking satisfying. That's a hard combination to acquire these days."

I curl my fingers around my fork now, pulling my eyes away. I feel her staring down at me, and then I hear a throaty laugh come from her.

"I'm sure you think the same, no?" She stands up straight again, huffing. "Well, you should rest up. It's been a long day for all of us. David here will be staying in a bedroom with you, just to make sure you don't try to run away or anything. There are pajamas and there's even a shower. Make use of it. Be the beautiful doll you are." Her heels click as she walks toward the arched doorway in the wall that leads to the hall. "Have a good night, Gia."

When she's gone, I drop my fork, looking out the window. My heart pounds in my chest, my mouth dryer now. I'm pissed, and I need to find a way out of here right now, but it's fucking hopeless. This place is locked down. The guards are all over the place. There are people everywhere, and I've noticed cameras in each room, through each hall.

Shit.

I've never needed Draco more.

CHAPTER TWENTY FOUR

I *don't sleep a wink.*

I made use of the shower, but of course David stood in the bathroom with me with the door wide open, staring out of it. He didn't watch me undress or wash, but it still bugged me he was there at all.

Still, I was relieved she sent this trained guard up and not that clown Alonso. He would have ogled like a fucking maniac.

Before I know it, the sun has come up. I'm sitting on the window bench, looking out toward the empty desert. I had hopes, deep down, that Draco would show up sometime in between, but he hasn't. Because he has no idea where the hell I am.

David didn't sleep either. He watched me, scrolled through his cellphone occasionally, the gun on the table beside him. Some other men came in to deliver coffee. He offered a cup to me but I ignored him. Sucks that he seems so normal, but will probably wind up dead later for being on the wrong side. He seems like a decent guy just doing his job.

When the sun is higher in the sky, I assume it's around noon. There's a knock at the door. Someone says something to him in a low, deep voice when he answers the door and then he turns to look at me. "Get dressed."

Hope fills me up. Maybe he's already here. Maybe he's solved this issue, and I can go back to the mansion with him . . . *maybe*.

I pick up the same clothes I had on yesterday and get dressed in them rapidly. I toss my hair up, sliding my feet into the cheetah print sandals. David opens the door when he sees I'm finished and I walk past him, following the second guard out in the hall.

David follows behind me, and even though I can't see it, I feel the gun pointed at me. We walk through the hallways, into the kitchen, and out a back door. The guard in front of me marches across the large deck and down the polished wooden steps. He makes his way across the lawn, pushing a white gate open once he's met up to it. I glance over my shoulder. David is still behind me, gun at his side.

Pressing my lips, I continue forward, across the red dirt. There is nothing out here but land and for a moment I panic, wondering if they're leading me to my death.

I look all around, plotting ways I can take them down.

Go for the guard in front of me first.

Tackle him.

Take his gun.

Shoot David first.

Shoot the other.

Run like hell.

But it doesn't come down to that because the man in front of me comes to a halt and bends down, pulling on the round handles of a door in the ground. I pause when it slings open and stairs come into view.

He gives me a sideways glance before going down first. I watch him until I can't see anymore. It's pitch black down there. Something nudges me in the back and I look back at David.

He bobs his head, telling me to go without words. Sighing, I step down, pressing a hand to the dirt wall to keep my balance. With each step down, it becomes darker and darker. David follows closely behind. When he shuts the door above, it's pitch black.

A flashlight turns on in an instant and he shines it down on me.

"Go," he says.

I continue down, heart rattling, palms clammy.

My breath is shaky as I hold onto the dirt wall. I see the last step and relief swarms me. And then I see the tunnel to my right. An underground tunnel. There are gas lamps on the floor, providing some light.

The man that was in front of me cocks his head and then turns, walking off. I follow behind, scanning the area, looking for any chance at escape. We walk in near darkness for what feels like forever, until finally, I see an opening.

It's just as dim in here, but there is furniture. Two couches with a small flat-screen TV and a game system set up in front of it. A single chair is against the wall, but it's occupied.

I gasp, seeing exactly who occupies it. His head hangs low. He has no shirt on, just a pair of dirty jeans. He's roped to the chair, his ankles strapped too.

"Oh my God," I breathe. "Thiago?"

He picks his head up, blinking slow with those familiar dark eyes. "The fucking rebel," he laughs, voice dry.

How the hell did they get him? What the hell is going on? I look at David who simply shakes his head and holds the gun up, aiming it at me. Bobbing it toward the couch, he says, "Sit."

I put on a heavy scowl, fists clenching now, but I move, walking to the couch and sitting. I sit on the one where I can still see Thiago.

David and the other man walk back to the tunnel and start talking, looking down the dark path as if they're waiting for someone to show up. I seize the opportunity to get answers.

"Thiago," I whisper. "What the hell happened to you? How did they get you?"

"They took me this time. That's how."

"But...how? I mean, I thought you were meeting Draco. I thought you were safe."

He shakes his head. "Went for a run to another town yesterday. He had someone that he wanted me to meet and said he would be there to meet the person as well, for a new deal. Some new guys from Argentina." He swallows painfully. "When we were leaving, one of them was shot. Right through the head. I only had one other guard with me and he was in the truck. He'd already been killed too. Before I knew it, I was surrounded."

Shit.

"He hasn't heard from me since then. He probably thinks I'm plotting against him again," he laughs.

"No. He probably knows something is wrong."

He looks at me through swollen black eyes. "How did they get *you*? How the hell did you even get out of his sight?"

"There was an explosion. It happened out of nowhere, probably caused by them. We were at one of his gardens, and he was finally freeing Henry—the guy with no arms. And then everything just went haywire. One of these fucking idiots here grabbed me and ran through town. Draco tried to chase after us but he couldn't get to me in time."

"Damn," he rasps.

"Are you okay?" I ask. He looks pretty banged up. His bottom lip is cut, a gash on his cheekbone.

"I've been through worse," he chuckles. "Trust me. That *puta* doesn't scare me. She tried getting me to talk—trying to find out where he's staying so she can get to him first. Good thing he never took her to that house—the one he's staying in now. He never stays in one spot for too long. Probably already packing."

I shift in my seat, looking at the guards. David turns just as I say, "I don't know how we're going to get out of this."

"He'll come," Thiago murmurs. "Maybe not for me, but for you."

I don't know why hearing that makes me feel both hopeful and defeated all at once.

CHAPTER TWENTY FIVE

It seems hours have passed now. Thiago shifts in his seat for the hundredth time, trying to get comfortable. I feel bad for him, but he keeps telling me he's fine.

I don't believe him. I only had ropes on my wrists. I can't imagine them around my whole body.

David and a new guard are standing at the entrance. The new one is looking at us while David keeps watch of the tunnel.

Not before long and I hear heavy footsteps. A younger boy appears and I lean forward to get a better look. He's breathing hard as he says, "Hernandez wants the cousin untied before he gets here," in Spanish.

Thiago's eyes dart up, watching intently as the guard watching us comes forward, slinging out a pocketknife. He slices through the ropes one by one and with each slice, I see the relief wash over Thiago's face.

Finally, the ropes fall down. As the guard cuts through the ropes at his ankles, Thiago brings a heavy fist down and punches him across the head. The guard crumples and I gasp, but Thiago leaves no room for error. He reaches down for the gun, swiping it out of the holder and pushing to a stand. One of his legs is still strapped to the chair but he doesn't let that hold him back.

He shoots the guard he punched, one bullet penetrating the skull.

David has already turned around with his gun held in the air while the younger guard fumbles for his.

Thiago aims at David, and they stare each other down. David's gun goes off, shooting Thiago right through the shoulder. Thiago lets out a heavy roar and fires back, shooting David through the forehead.

I hop up as the younger guard starts to run, but Thiago shoots him through the back. He collapses in an instant. My breathing becomes chaotic as I look at the dead guards and then up at him.

"What?" he huffs, eyes as wide as they can get. "You wanna get the fuck out of here, don't you?"

"Draco is probably here," I tell him. "He could have gotten us out of this."

"Bullshit. She wants me untied so she can kill me." He winces as he touches the wound on his shoulder. He merely looks over it though, as if he's been shot in worse places. He picks up the knife on the ground and cuts through the rope around his other ankle. "Let's go," he pants when he's free.

I don't hesitate. When he takes off, I dash after him. We half-jog, half-walk down the tunnel, him with the gun held up, ready to fire if need be.

The tunnel is mostly clear. When we reach the steps, voices rise and Thiago curses beneath his breath, gripping my arm and pulling me away, beneath the staircase. It creaks as the person walks down. They're in a hurry.

It's a man. I see his black boots, though they're cleaner than I expected. Thiago has his gun up, ready to fire it. The person steps to the right, looking around. I try and get a better look, but I can't see him in all that black.

He takes several steps toward the tunnel, his back to us, and when Thiago realizes who he is, he lowers his gun. "Shit. *Draco?*"

The man spins around and when his familiar brown eyes flash on us, my heart swells up. *It's him!* I nearly choke when he looks from Thiago to me. He looks me over, seeing that I haven't been harmed, but then there are more steps.

They creak loudly, as if there is more than one set.

"What a lovely reunion!" Hernandez chimes when she takes the last step down. I shoot my gaze over to hers as six men follow her down, their guns aimed at us. "Like I said," she murmurs. "Unharmed. Untouched. She is perfectly safe and so is your eager cousin. Though we did have to hurt him a little." She shrugs. "We tried. He didn't crack."

Draco doesn't pull his eyes away from me. They're glued. He scans me thoroughly and then says, "Come here."

I start to rush for him, but guns cock in an instant and I freeze. Draco grimaces at each guard and Hernandez lets out a dry laugh. "Don't get so excited." She walks past him, starting down the hallway. "We have business to handle first. Then you can get your prize."

He looks over his shoulder, through the corner of his eye as he watches her descend the hallway. The guards surround us, one of them grabbing my arm. Another punches Thiago in the stomach before taking the gun and Draco's voice thunders when he shouts, "Leave him the fuck alone!"

Thiago crumples to the ground, but holds his hand up, waving it. "It's all good, Jefe." I hear the laughter in his voice, and I know it pisses Draco off even more because he's not taking it seriously.

Thiago is snatched up then, dragged back down the tunnel. The guard that's squeezing my arm starts to drag me, but Draco steps forward, nostrils flaring as he says, "You better loosen your fucking grip, or I'll chop your fucking hand off."

The guard laughs in his face, shoving past him, but I feel his grip slack a little as we pass by. Draco follows, keeping close to me. The other four guards have their guns pointed at the back of his head, but he pays them no mind. All he can see is me.

We enter the room again, where Hernandez is standing in the middle of the bloody mess. "*Ay dios*, Thiago. Look at this shit," she groans. "David was one of my best men. I thought surely he would take you down if you did something stupid." She grins over her shoulder at Thiago, who grimaces back.

The guard drags me over to Hernandez and she immediately draws out a knife, gripping me by the elbow and holding the blade to my throat.

Draco tenses, rushing forward, eyes as hard as stone and jaw ticking, but a guard catches him, holding him back. He seethes hard, raging like a bull and shoving the guard's arm away. "You hurt her and I swear I will fucking end you," he growls in his native tongue.

"Aww Draco," she coos. She places the flat end of the knife across my jawline. The blade is cold. Hard. "You look at her like . . . almost like you would never let anything happen to her. Like you'd rather *die* than be without her. And I get it. She's beautiful. My God, is she beautiful. The way you stare at her—wow, you've never looked at *me* that way. I should be envious, huh?" She chuckles, a throaty one that makes the layer beneath my skin prickle.

He tries to charge again, but the guards hold him back, guns pressing into his temple and the back of his head now.

"Draco, trust me, I don't want to kill her. I hate killing women—especially ones who are clearly strong, pretty, and smart. She is very smart. We got to know each other a little. She knows when and when not to speak. Doesn't crack under pressure. She reminds me a lot of myself. I can see why you're head over heels for her. But like I've told you so many times before, *love is useless,* and it can also get you killed. You see what happens when you let it in? You see what depths you will go just to help the ones you love? You risk your life and theirs, and if something happens, there is nothing you can do about it. You just have to live with it. And that sucks," she sighs. "Which is why I don't love anymore. And I guess I should thank you for giving up on me all those years ago. If you hadn't, well, I wouldn't be where I am now. On top of my own cartel, running these men, letting them know who the *real* boss of Mexico is."

"What the fuck do you want, Yessica?" Draco finally demands, his rage skyrocketing, fists clenching.

"Oh, I think you know exactly what I want. Hell, the signs should have been very clear. I thought you'd have come to me before this, especially after the way I killed half a dozen of your men during those shipments, even got Thiago here yesterday. I knew you wouldn't come running for him, though, so I had to work harder. Find out more about you. But I heard through one of the men we took away that you had a woman in your home. A beautiful one. A *Nicotera*. Shit, Draco," she laughs. "Do you know how much money I could make from selling her? People have wanted to make Nicotera babies for centuries. It's a very powerful name. All it takes is one raw stroke to continue the bloodline, make an heir. But, you know, I'm not going to do that." She steps away from me, wagging the knife in the air. "Because I actually like her. And I'd hate to keep her hostage any longer, so all you have to do to get her back is agree to give up half the Mexico territory. Let me run it my way. I choose which cities I want, and you can keep the rest."

"You want me to make a deal with you after the shit you've pulled?" Draco snarls, shaking his head. "You are still so fucking stupid."

"No, I don't think I'm the stupid one, honey," she says in a singsong voice. "I think if you don't take this deal, then *you* are the stupid one. You are outnumbered, Draco. I can have Rico over there draw his gun, shoot you down, and there is nothing you can do to stop me. I could bring this blade across this sweet girl's throat and you wouldn't get to me in time to save her. This is the *only* option you have."

His nostrils are flaring now, the rage sparking in his eyes.

Silence showers down and I feel my belly twist up in a large knot for him. I know how much Mexico means to him. Having the entire country, his family worked hard for that, and to just hand half of it over for me? No. He would be stupid. His father—my father—would flip in their graves.

"Don't," I mouth to him. "Not for me."

A pained expression masks his face as he stares into my eyes. I can read him like I book, and I hate that he's already made up his mind. I wouldn't be able to change it even if I tried.

"Only half of Mexico," he finally grits out. "And we will negotiate which cities you can have. You don't take my biggest suppliers. You will not kill any more of my men, and you damn sure will never touch *her* again. Agree to that, and we have a fucking deal."

Yessica laughs boastfully, her head falling back and her silky red hair shaking. "I swear you are still the same. Trying to negotiate with me while I have you here, under my thumb." She steps closer to him, so close that it makes me uneasy. Her hand runs down his chest and she lingers above his belt buckle, one finger tapping the gold buckle. "But I can't forget. You are still Draco Molina. The craziest, scariest motherfucker I know. It would be foolish of me to not agree, wouldn't it?

After all, I can't kill you. I need you to tell the suppliers I take that they will work for me now. I know they would rather die than side with a woman, so you'll be there to give them the approval. I can't kill her either, because then you really won't agree." He glares down at her. I watch as she unhooks his belt buckle and then she peers over her shoulder at me.

"You know, I miss this. The fighting. The bickering. What would that sweet girl do if I dropped to my knees right now and sucked your cock, huh? What would she do if I rode you against your will and made you come in my pussy? Forced you to give me your baby while she watched? Hmm?"

My teeth clench and grit together. I'm trying damn hard not to let my emotions sway me now. She got half of his territory. She got what she wanted. She's been fucking with my emotions ever since I met her, and I'm tired of it.

I remain perfectly still, but the fiery heat I feel in my veins is hard to ignore. Jealousy sets in, tightening in my core.

"Don't worry. I won't fuck or suck him," she laughs, darting her eyes on me. She pulls from him, and I sigh through parted lips. "His cock is a waste of my time, though it was enjoyable a long time ago."

She walks to me again, gripping my shoulder and shoving me forward. "Take her." I gasp, nearly tumbling down on my raw palms, but Draco snatches away from the guards and rushes forward, catching me before I can hit the ground. He picks me up in one fell swoop, and as he does, I hear all the guns in the room cock, ready to blast lead into us.

"Settle down, boys," Yessica says, holding her hands out. "Let's not make them any more uncomfortable than they already are. Draco, you'll bring her with you and come with me to my office? Let's look over a map, decide which places will be mine, yeah? Thiago will be waiting inside. I'll even give him some water. Keep him hydrated."

He looks from her to me. He gives a small bob of his head and nothing more.

She looks between us, a smirk tugging at the corner of her lips. "I know you don't like to feel beaten, Draco, but don't consider it a defeat. Consider it a victory! I get what I want, and you still get to have a share of Mexico and keep her too. You'll have a little less money coming in, but you'll be okay. We both win, really.

And all because I gave you mercy. It's just business."

Draco doesn't speak, but I can read the words in his eyes. He is pissed, wanting so badly to unleash the monster inside him. I'm certain if I weren't here, he would, but he's holding back, doing his best to remain calm and collected so that I may live.

Do I really mean that much to him?

Giving up half his country.

Coming here to this place— *alone* —with no weapons, just to get me? He could have let me die and moved on with his life and still have his country, but he came without hesitation. Without fear.

"Let's wrap this up so we can go," he grumbles. He places me down on my feet and the men with the guns lower their weapons, taking a small step away.

"Okay, then." Yessica twirls around and saunters away in her spiked heels. "Follow me back inside, *Jefe.*"

CHAPTER TWENTY SIX

I'm *on edge.* My nerves are a chaotic mess as Draco sits across from Hernandez. She points out which cities she wants, and he reluctantly obliges. All for me.

He's doing this for me.

Why? He should know better.

He shouldn't let her win.

When they've come to an agreement, Hernandez claps like a seal. "See! That wasn't so hard, was it? Let some of that pride go, and you're a reasonable man to work with!"

She pushes to a stand, walking around her desk and behind his chair. He tenses up, keeping his eyes ahead. She whispers something in his ear while she looks at me. I hold her gaze, face hard, fists balled.

Draco stands up, glaring down at Yessica for several seconds before shoving past her and coming for me. "Get my fucking cousin so we can go."

Yessica puts on a small smile. "Sure thing, *partner.*"

He narrows his cold gaze on her, gripping my hand. She snaps her fingers at one of the guards and they take off.

Another one steps forward, a large rifle in hand. "Take them back to the van. Take them to the city, back to the church he was picked up at. I know he has his guards waiting of his own there to pick him up, so keep a watchful eye. Make sure you have plenty of backup."

Draco's jaw clenches tight.

The guard nods and turns and he walks right after him, his grip tight on my hand as we walk past her. But of course she follows us out. I keep my eyes ahead as we go through various hallways to get to the front door.

When it's open, relief sinks in.

I see the guard she sent to fetch Thiago now dragging him toward the gates. A growl scratches at Draco's throat, but he keeps his head held high and his glare solid, watching his cousin get tossed and thrown around like some kind of trash.

I hate it too, and he's not even my family. But he helped me—almost saved me.

Draco can't blame him anymore. He was on our side. He fought for him. For me, and he doesn't even care for me like that. He knows how much I mean to Draco, and he was willing to protect that.

As we walk out, though, a heavy feeling sets in. It turns my gut into a block of lead, my veins running cold. I look all around me. It's too quiet.

This . . . this is too simple.

Too easy.

And as if Draco senses it too, he tightens his grasp on my hand even more, pulling me close to his side.

Yessica's heels click behind us. She's quiet. Very quiet.

The hairs on the back of my neck stand up as the gates open. We pass through them and once we reach the van, the guard that has Thiago pulls the door open.

"Well, go on," Yessica sighs, as if bored. "Get in."

Draco hesitates, focusing on her. He looks her over repeatedly and then at the guards. Several come out of the front door, jumping into the SUVs parked up front. The one that led the way steps aside, clutching the gun, daring him to try something.

Knowing he can't do anything, Draco steps forward and allows me to enter the van first. I climb in, sliding over to the farthest window, heart still pounding. I still have this uneasy feeling, like something bad is about to happen.

If she goes back on her word—if she does something . . .

Draco looks over at Thiago. Thiago's face is complacent. Even while being tossed like an abused mutt, he's still him. Still fighting.

Draco tips his chin, a silent thank you, and then climbs into the van, across the bench to sit beside me.

Thiago looks over at Yessica, spitting in her direction as he snatches himself away and takes the step up. But before he can climb in completely, Yessica snaps her fingers, a large arm hooks around Thiago's throat, and he wheezes as he's dropped to the ground.

"What the fuck, Yessica! You said we could go!" Draco barks, sliding across the bench, but the guard with the rifle holds the gun up, pointing it at me.

Draco realizes and breathes raggedly, sliding back just an inch to get in the way of the gun. My eyes are wide now as I peer over his shoulder, watching the other guard yank Thiago up and force him onto his knees.

"You said we could go!" I shout over him. "Stop this, please!"

Thiago chuckles. "Told you never to trust this bitch," he mutters to Draco.

Draco squeezes the top of the seat so hard his knuckles turn white. He's useless. I know he's never felt so powerless in his life—not since that breakfast with his uncle. Since he saw his father die. I know he's never wanted to feel like that ever again, yet here he is.

He hates this. I hate this!

"You thought you could just walk out scotch free like that, Draco? After all you put me through before. And after what you did to my fiancé, you have to pay somehow." Something rolls across the dirt and it's a person in a wheelchair.

And not just any person.

I nearly stop breathing when I see who it is.

My heart, it fails me. Thudding slow. Dangerously slow.

My blood runs so cold, my hands shaking now.

In the chair, stitched up and much cleaner than he was yesterday, is . . .

"Oh my God," I breathe. "Henry." Henry Ricci. He's rolled over by one of the guards, right beside Yessica, who now has her cheetah print gun pointed at the back of Thiago's head.

This explains the explosions.

The threats.

"Taking those cities isn't enough. My baby here," Yessica says, stroking his cheek, "needs more. Seeing as he appreciates your pet back there for risking her life to save his, he doesn't want her dead, but he thinks someone should go after what you did to him and to one of his family members. Why not your loyal, bulldog of a cousin? Take him out the same way you did Trigger Toni. Quick and easy." She puts on a snake-like grin.

"Yessica, I swear to God if you do this—"

Draco's sentence goes unfinished.

"It's her or me, Jefe," Thiago pants. "Don't even worry about it. I was starting to get bored with this shit anyway." He shrugs. "Besides. You need her more than you'll ever need me. Fuck it. Move on."

Draco starts to say something to him, but it's too late.

The gun sounds off, causing my ears to ring and my heart to sink to the pit of my belly. Blood splatters everywhere, most of it landing on Draco's face. His clothes. Some of it even gets on me. It spills across the entrance of the van.

Thiago's body crumples forward and then falls.

Yessica lets out a small *humph* and then she turns, grabbing the handles of Henry's wheelchair and pushing him aside. "How's that, baby?" She kisses his cheek.

Henry doesn't speak. He only glares at Draco. And then at me.

"You were right about one thing, Gia. It *was* Lion who hired me to watch after Draco," he finally says, eyes cold and dead. "But my cousin needed me more. Toni. You remember him, right? Lion died, but I stayed here to keep an eye on Draco for my cousin. See, Toni heard about the promise Lion made to Draco Molina— how you were promised to him—and he wanted him dead as soon as he found out. They were out for each other; Draco probably just didn't know Toni was coming yet. Not sure how Toni found out, but he wasn't happy to hear it. My lovely fiancée here wanted Draco dead too, so we all worked together." He looks up at Yessica before focusing on me again. "We tried to figure out ways to take him down, but then he caught me, *tortured* me," he spits out, "and then he killed my cousin. It set Yessica back a few steps, but I knew she'd figure out a way to get to him. I let his men find and catch me on purpose when you set me free from the basement. I did it so she could get *you*." He grins. "I'm sure you know the truth about Toni—how he killed Lion in his sleep while they were traveling. I remember him telling me that he enjoyed it." I wince, tears of fire falling down my cheeks as he sneers. "He was so glad to get rid of him and so ready to take over—so ready to get rid of Draco, just to have you all to himself. He had to marry you first and then take care of business. But you . . . you were so fucking clueless." A smirk weaves its way across his lips and I stare in horror. "You trust anyone you meet, including me, and for a Nicotera, I'd say that is pretty fucking stupid of you, Gia."

Yessica pulls his wheelchair back and the door is slammed in Draco's face. He's squeezing the seat in front of him even harder, to the point I think he might rip a piece of it off.

Draco breathes hard, finally looking back at me with glistening eyes. I can't read his expression. I can't tell what he's thinking. He doesn't know what to say— what to do. All he can do is stare at me, and I hear the same words ringing in my head over and over again.

The chime. The echo. The haunting truth.

I was wrong.

I was *wrong.*

I was so very fucking wrong.

Made in the USA
Las Vegas, NV
16 February 2023

67637115R00118